I0639354

HARMONIC PLEASURE
MYSTERIOUS ARTS
BOOK SIX

CELIA LAKE

Formatted with Vellum

CHAPTER I
JANUARY 18TH, 1928 AT THE CRYSTAL CAVE, LONDON

"Five minutes to prep, Miss Vega." The call came from just outside her dressing room. "Be right out, Bob." Vega stretched, reaching out one hand for a dressing gown to go over her frock. She'd be fine once the evening got started, with the warmth of bodies crowded in to have a good time, but right now, she'd take a chill without it. Vega and her voice had no time for that. She heard Bob continue down the hall, the particular rhythm of steps, knock, and call. Perhaps sometime she'd make up a dance and song of it, for fun.

It felt good to be back in the routine from before the holidays. She'd just had two glorious nights off— and also the days, of course— and she'd spent almost all of them asleep. Or having a good meal before going back to sleep. Mama referred to it as her cat phase. Vega had sung her voice to threads. She'd gone through six pairs of dancing shoes between the middle of December and Sunday night.

Certainly, she'd earned every bit of a rest. Now, she didn't rush, but she didn't dally either.

Within a minute, she was out on the main dance floor, glancing around. "That chair from Saturday?" Vega gestured with her entire hand, never just her finger. Old habits stuck, and with good reason. Then she caught who was standing up from checking on one of the charmlights on the stage. "Oh, and how's your wife, Jack?"

"Solid as a rock now, Miss Vega." Jack was the club's handyman, among a number of other skills. "And thank you for asking. She's doing much better now, just a brief bad turn. That tea you sent along seems to have done a treat."

"Oh, I'm glad." He'd been off last Sunday, and she'd been worried that it meant his wife had been worse.

The other performers trickled in from the dressing rooms, some of them still coming alive for the evening. Most of them, honestly. None of them was a lark, most of them woke sometime in the mid-afternoon before getting ready for an evening of entertainment that would stretch to near enough dawn some nights.

She didn't yet know enough about most of them to know what they did on their days off. She'd started at the Crystal Cave in the middle of October. It took people a bit to warm up, and see what a new performer at the top of the bill was like. And then they'd gone into the flurry of the holidays, with not much time to talk about anything other than the night's performances and adjustments. Vega certainly hadn't shared her plans then. Now she was back to a more relaxed schedule, which would probably help with the social ties. She also hoped she could get a night or two to go out to Astralis, the family estate. She could see her parents and aunts and uncles and cousins. And look at stars. Stars were in very short supply in London's air and lights. They'd understood that she couldn't get back for the halcyon days and all those rituals. She knew what the life she'd chosen meant. That didn't mean she hadn't missed being there.

Now, she put on a smile— an honest one, really — and made all the polite chit-chat. Her name might be top of the bill at the moment. But she refused to be the sort who swept in, demanded the world, and stomped on everyone on her way by. For one thing, it was a way to leave a trail of enemies in her wake, and Grandmother Alcyone definitely would not approve of that. For another, it simply wasn't how Vega wanted to be in the world. It soured her music and her magic. That was something she would never tolerate.

Now, though, Ivy and Charles Hessian were coming her way. She wriggled her fingers at them. "Evening!" They did an excellent dance set, as well as a rather more demanding part: each of them would draw a partner or two from the crowd onto the dance floor to get things started. "You look pleased, Ivy?"

"Oh, I am. You remember how that young— well— had his hands all over me, Saturday?" Ivy said. It was an undeniable challenge of the profession, even if Vega mostly ducked it by being up on stage.

"And came back on Sunday," Vega agreed. "Wait, did you find out who he is?"

Charles slipped his arm around his wife. "Oh, better than that. That's just one ill-mannered boor, and there doesn't seem to be a shortage. Madam Helena introduced us to a talisman maker, the sort who doesn't charge the sun and the moon. He worked up a piece that should help. We picked it up this afternoon."

Ivy gave a little shimmy, making her frock glitter under the translucent wrap. "Makes it more and more uncomfortable, if the hands aren't where they're supposed to be. We had to do a bit of testing, but it's working a treat." She gestured at a piece that hung at the back of her neck, the necklace clasp, then a piece pinned just at the waistline at the back. "If a gentleman keeps his hand where he ought, no problem. If they wander, well." She shrugged, with a put-on wide-eyed innocence.

"Oh, I'm glad." Vega was. The Crystal Cave was far better at handling that sort of thing than a number of clubs Vega had sung in. And of course, a magical club had options that a non-magical one didn't. The staff had many more options to summon help. Madam Helena, who ran the place, did not look kindly on boors.

But everyone had a first time to misbehave, or get too drunk, or whatever else led them astray, and those were always unpleasant to deal with. And sometimes people had power or a position that meant they couldn't just be shown the door without consequences. "He might get quite a lot of other business if it works as you say."

Ivy laughed. "We pointed that out. If you need a piece, you let me know. I'll introduce you."

Vega nodded. That sort of magic wouldn't work

reliably for her, not without a number of adjustments. But perhaps she'd have a reason to do that at some point, or enough in the way of funds she could experiment. She did well for herself, these days, but not so well she could pay for talismans that were purely a curiosity, not a need. Not if she was taking the necessary long view about her career and her life. "I'll think about it. And I want to see how it works, too!"

"Did you do anything with your days off? You keep saying you mean to go to one of the museums." Charles leaned forward a little, twisting on one foot, warming up lightly.

"I slept." Vega said, given a cheerful stretch. "I mean, most of the time. There was a book. And my usual vocal practice." That was, in her life, a thing more like eating supper, so habitual she didn't write it out on a list of tasks for the day. She laughed, deliberately keeping it light. "Oh, I see Pasco. I need to ask him about that illusion in the third set."

Pasco, the club's illusionist, was a good bit older than most of the other performers. Of course, he wasn't generally on stage. And when it came to illusion work, age and experience counted for quite a bit. Vega had found him just as competent as Madam Helena had promised when she took the contract here. Now, he peered at her over his pincenez glasses, then made a slight gesture at a bow. "Good evening."

Vega tilted her head, because those were all the signs of someone who was nervous she was about to be difficult. She spread her hands. "I wanted to thank you for Sunday. And to check about that set of flowers. I thought it worked well except for my feet.

Can we just gesture at the sequence, so I can avoid stepping on them? It breaks the magic of it. Your illusions are good enough that I worry I'm going to slip on the petals." The combination of the practicality and the compliment did what Vega hoped, and won her a bit more relaxed smile.

"Ah. Yes." He took a step back, considering, and then gestured at the illusion work as she took up a position as she would be on stage. They didn't need to work around a microphone or cords, thanks to the magic in play, but she needed to avoid stumbling over one of the musicians or down the stairs. She took a couple of steps, wordlessly singing the tune, dah-da-da-dee, dah-dah-dee.

As she sang softly, Pasco did the equivalent with the illusion, just splotches of colours rather than any detail. They'd save that for when there were people to see and hear and applaud and hopefully toss a little in as a tip. When it came toward the end of the last chorus, she adjusted and watched Pasco do the same. The flowers cascaded down the side of her calf, away onto the floor beside her.

When she got to the end, and the little side to side sway before the pose that finished the song, he nodded. "Much better effect."

"Excellent. I knew it would be simple for you to figure out something that worked." Then she tilted her head. "Bad evening?"

"Some are better at joining our circle than others." Pasco didn't have to name names. They'd had a new singer start just after New Year's. She wasn't anything like Vega's competition; she had a different style of singing, for one thing. For another, Vega's skills were rather better. Camille would ruin her voice in a few years, if she kept on like she did. It was mostly lazy technique on her part. Potentially also the way she put on a French accent Vega suspected wasn't entirely honestly come by.

There was nothing wrong with being a performer, certainly not in a room of them. There was, however, a problem when someone made themselves difficult, treated the other performers like their own personal props, particularly when they didn't have the draw to back it up. Now, Vega offered a smile, glanced up to discover Camille had finally deigned to join the rest of them, and leaned to kiss Pasco on the cheek. "You let me know if you need an ally in reminding her of how we do things here, all right?"

He snorted, then stepped back as Madam Helena came down the stairs. They were, as usual, on the ground floor, which held the larger dance floor and tables. The kitchens and dressing rooms were downstairs, with the bar and stage upstairs. Madame Helena's private office and rooms were on the second floor, with a lift tucked into the back of the building for her use, and occasionally also for a few special guests.

The club owner was impeccably dressed. Of course, she always was, with a good two dozen gowns she rotated, depending on season, mood, and day of the week. Tonight's, for Wednesday, was a shockingly bright blue, with a deeper blue sapphire at her neck and wrists. Vega had never had a chance to look closely enough to figure out if they were truly gems or excellent paste. Honestly it didn't matter. The effect did everything needed.

"Good evening, good evening. Usual order

tonight. Please be ready. We've two birthday celebrations, one arriving around half-ten, the other
expected around midnight. It's a Wednesday, so
likely not the young men. But I gather we might get
a party in the first half of the evening after a supper
out, some sort of minor diplomatic gathering.
Wilkes, at the Ministry, let me know, of course."

The Crystal Cave was the best of London's
magical night clubs. There were two others that had
far less in the way of entertainment, only one or two
performers on any given night. As such, if there
were meetings in London that included both magical
and non-magical sorts, the magical ones often ended
up here. It worked well whether they needed a cele-
bration or to drown their sorrows.

The Ministry folks, both the men and women,
tended to be easy to deal with. If they drank too
much, they were morose rather than combative. It
was far simpler to stick a napkin over her shoulder to
protect her frock and let someone cry on her
shoulder than to let Madam Helena's doormen deal
with the problem.

No one in the loose circle spoke up with any
concerns. It was a quiet night, or at least looked to
be. A good way to ease back into the swing of things.
And of course, the joy of a nightclub was never
knowing who might walk in the door. Madam
Helena glanced around, then nodded. "Excellent.
Off you go. We open the doors in thirty minutes."

Just enough time for everyone to finish their
cosmetics and charms, and to do whatever warmup
they required. Vega went promptly off to her
dressing room, drank half a glass of water, and then
went through her own preparations. When the

chime sounded to let her know the club had opened, she was ready to begin, settled on the sofa with her feet up until time for her first set. She could hear the jazz band start up above her, a comfortable warm sound that set the tone for the night.

CHAPTER 2
THAT EVENING

T he first set went well. Vega was pleased with how her voice was tonight. Just a bit of a pleasant burr on the low notes, the sultry tones that kept young men— and a number of others— coming back. Madame Helena appreciated that a great deal. Vega retreated to her dressing room for some sparkling water and a chance to put her feet up, but at eleven, she was back out on stage.

The room was near enough full, a pleasant surprise on a Wednesday. As Vega made her way through the tables, the charmlight illuminating her, she glimpsed entirely familiar faces at one table. They were with a group of women, friends who came in regularly, but that was absolutely Aunt Ancha and Uncle Thuban. She didn't do more than nod as she went past. First things first.

The second set was better than the first in every way. The band was glorious, especially the improvisations. Benjy, the trumpeter, had a gift for not having the trumpet shout over the other instruments, which meant she'd been able to hear Kevin Stafford, the guitarist, clearly. Always the last name, with the Kevins, there being two working at the Cave right now. He'd been a relatively recent addition, a few months before Vega had started. But he'd fit right in, and the band took his suggestions seriously.

Vega herself was in full voice, her entire range, sliding from pitch to pitch with perfection. And the illusions were absolutely exquisite. Vega heard the oohs from the crowd, and the way the conversation went quiet. That was the highest compliment in a club like this, when people paid attention to the performance out of all the other options in the room.

This set was drawing from a tradition of magical ballads and gesturing at a dozen pieces of folklore and myth. She brought the last note to the end, then wriggled her fingers. "I'll be out again around midnight for the last time tonight. Do have a delightful time, darlings, but stay to see me, do!" There was an art to being direct without being uncomfortable.

She half-danced her way back, pausing behind the curtain from the staff stairs to see what happened next. One of the dance mistresses— her name was Holly, Vega didn't know her well yet— stopped by the table her aunt and uncle were at. Uncle Thuban passed her something, and Holly came straight back toward the stairs.

Vega took another step or two down to make some room, only for Holly to squeak when she ducked through the curtain, "Pardon, Miss Vega. Erm. That gentleman, did you see? Is this the sort of thing I ought to take to Ed?"

Ed was one of the doormen. Vega laughed and shook her head. "That's one of my uncles. I've no idea what he's doing here. Was that a note? Thanks for checking, though. You can never tell just from how someone looks, if one of us wants to talk to them. Or you, too, I'm guessing, the way the boys looked last Sunday."

Holly ducked her chin. "Ed had to shoo two of them out. Oh, and that Fred called by, said he'd be by at the usual. I know Jack took the note back to your dressing room. He and I were just chatting when it came in."

"Oh, excellent. He's a reliable cabbie, if you need one. Keeps his hands to himself, likes having a fare who won't be difficult. He goes to visit his mum, some seaside town, so he's been away for a week or so."

"Coo, you do know them all. Oh. They're starting up. Beg pardon!" Holly ducked her head, then disappeared out the curtain again. Her heel kicked up behind her as she stepped out and picked up the steps of the dance for some of the partnered dancing. Her job was to draw young men up into a dance without leading them on to expect more than they ought. At a place like this, with people keeping an eye out, it was a good job if one could keep people happy enough to tip a bit.

The note said more or less what Vega suspected. They'd like a word, when she was done for the evening, if convenient. Or tomorrow during the day, if tonight was impossible. Staying in town, apparently, though neither of them mentioned which hotel. Vega went and rummaged for paper and a fountain pen, writing a note to ask them to come back after her last set. The late hour wouldn't be a bother for them, at least. They were used to being up into the wee hours. The next waiter to come by took the note for her, and she saw Uncle Thuban glance at it, nod, and sign briefly that they'd do so.

The prospect of having someone back meant that she went and asked for a tray with something to drink and something to nibble on, to be brought once she went out for the last set. And she had a good tidy of her dressing table, so everything would be ready for tomorrow. Her family approved of having one's tools in order. It meant Vega only had ten minutes to sit down at the end, but no matter. It was the end of the night and early in the week, she'd manage.

The third set went swimmingly, people swaying a little at two faster songs, then leaning back and listening at the intense one. She finished with something cheerful and hopeful, putting a little edge of magic into it so people would leave in a good mood. It seemed a small thing, but a bit of hope and sunny good will went a long way some nights. Nothing false, that was the trick. Just following a thread of possibility where it might lead.

Once she got back into the staff hall, she waited, and just as she expected, her aunt and uncle were shown along promptly. "Aunt Ancha, Uncle Thuban. Do come down to my dressing room? No problem with the stairs?" Vega wanted to make it clear there would be no discussion in the public spaces, by sheer force of will. Other than the pleasantries, her aunt and uncle followed her lead.

She led them into the dressing room, then turned, pulling up the warding and the privacy charms. "We've an hour comfortably, a bit more if I let them know. Will that be agreeable?" Vega turned to pull on a dressing gown, then to step from the heels into slippers, and she couldn't quite repress the sound of pleasure. The heels were as comfortable as magic could make them, which was to say, very. But she also loved the moment where her feet could bend and arch on their own.

"That should be more than enough for a moment. We don't wish to put you out." There was a tiny hesitation before he added, and she thought honestly enough, but as if he were a bit surprised, "We've not had a chance to hear you before. And the club seems well-run." Uncle Thuban was making every attempt to be pleasant, and it was succeeding, of course. Vega knew perfectly well he was even more expert in the arts of incantation than she was.

"Not that we've a wide range of experience, but one hears stories," Aunt Ancha agreed.

"The owner, Madam Helena, she handles all manner of details smoothly. And honestly, it's tremendously helpful that we're entirely magical. We've not nearly the worries about police raids or what have you that the non-magical clubs have." Those were about drugs more than anything else, and the challenges of the magical community were a bit different. "She owns the building. We've steady guests. There's a membership fee, though obviously, people can pay at the door for a night." As they would have done. "And the rare times there are problems, we've more ways to handle that. Mostly, it's someone with wandering hands or no sense of manners." Then her chin came up. "It was rather a triumph, becoming top of the bill here."

"You've obviously earned it." Her aunt's voice was warm now. "Actually, we are here because we are hoping you'll be in London for a bit, with perhaps some time for a small quest."

"Quests are never small, Aunt Ancha," Vega said as clearly as she could.

It made both her aunt and uncle laugh, which at least suggested that whatever quality the quest had, it was not imminently dire. Though with the family's sense of humour, it could be a trifle hard to tell. Uncle Thuban shook his head. "We're honestly not sure what the proper word is. Quest, certainly, but the size and scope are harder. May I just explain, and then have you ask whatever questions you might have?"

Vega considered for only a moment, then nodded. It would certainly be more efficient. She wanted to rest her voice a little before talking more. And also have one or two of the little pastries. The kitchens had a genuine gift for them.

"Oh, yes." Aunt Ancha was glancing around. Vega made a point of decorating wherever she landed, at least a little. This time, she'd chosen prints of London on the walls, generally covering the dingier spots in the paint. There was a glorious velvet sofa along the niche across from the door, her dressing room, and a couple of footstools that served well enough for seating.

Vega gestured her aunt and uncle to the sofa. And of course, there were a few charms to personalise the place. The stars, spread across the ceiling, were shining just brightly enough to be visible right now. Vega, the star she was named for, hovered over where she sat when she was at the dressing table.

"Please, sit." Uncle Thuban stood, not taking the indicated place. "You've worked hard this evening. May I take one of these?" Vega nodded. He sat and her aunt did the same, leaving Vega more comfortable but also more than a little puzzled. Aunt Ancha also took it on herself to distribute the drinks on the tray, passing around the plate with some sort of cheese and bread. Then, more confusing, they gave her time to eat and drink.

Only once she'd set down her glass did Uncle Thuban clear his throat again and start speaking. "In brief, we— the family— have become aware that there may be some artefact associated with Grandmother Alcyone come to light in London. Or if not actually to light, nearer to the surface or to people or some such thing. We are not sure of the shape of it, or the size. Other than it's likely something designed to be carried by one person, perhaps the size of an urn or chalice or plate or something of the kind. Perhaps a piece of jewellery. Larger than a ring or pendant, however."

"And you don't know the material, either?" Vega found that vagueness odd. Both Aunt Ancha and Uncle Thuban shook their heads no in unison.

"Now, as you know, most of us can't entirely tolerate the city for long. You, obviously, have found ways to manage. But we're hoping you might as well... What's the word?" Uncle Thuban at least was making the reason for asking her more clear. That was something.

"Notice if anything tugs or pulls, one way or another. If it's the object we believe it is, that should be quite noticeable when you're nearby. A hundred feet or two, in any direction. We suspect it's buried, or at least that's by far the most logical." Aunt Ancha's voice was crisp.

Vega could see a number of gaps in this information, enough to have an entire brass band march through. Massive drums and euphoniums and tubas and all. "What precisely does this thing do? And how old is it? How do you know anything about it?" She did, in fact, have a number of questions, and they would not wait.

Uncle Thuban spread his hands. "We've additional information for you to read, if you wish. Notes and references, and such. But in brief, we believe it was a gift from Grandmother Alcyone, intended to help stabilise a number of magical effects. Created in or for the Jupiter-Uranus conjunction early in Aries, in 588 or so."

Vega knew her London history well enough for that, certainly. "Around the time that the Romans had absolutely left London, and before any of the later settlements."

"Just so," Aunt Ancha agreed. "We're not sure how the effect works now. It may shift the magic around it, or make itself more attractive to get more range. We don't believe it's dangerous to handle, but it may be tricky to find."

"And," Uncle Thuban cleared his throat, "It's not the sort of thing we want in hands that won't use it well. It's the sort of magic that can be twisted, more easily than we'd like." He then spread his hands out. "There are some hints from the divinations that other people might be interested in it. Nothing direct, you know how it goes. Depending on what it actually does, it might interest a number of different parties."

Vega frowned. "Is it dangerous?"

"How do you define danger?" Aunt Acha replied, her voice fairly steady. "No item from the Grandmothers is entirely safe, certainly not tame. Would it harm you if you found it? Likely not. Besides, you know how to handle it, where to bring it."

"Better me than other people, then," Vega agreed. That set of maths was entirely obvious.

Her uncle nodded and then moved into the practicalities. "You may draw on the resources of Alcyone's line, whether that's funds, introductions, whatever else we can offer, while working on this. Though we also expect you may have connections we don't." He gestured at the club, as an example, and that was true enough. "And if you are successful, it would be, mmm. Notable for whatever you wanted to do next. Not that we expect you to stop singing anytime soon."

"Good." Vega nodded at the last. "I'm glad everyone's clear about that."

"Oh, we might see if you could take on a larger role next November, if it's at all possible to get free for the night. Or perhaps one of the summer rites. I'm sure that the other lines don't have someone with your voice at the moment." Aunt Ancha obviously had her eye on a spot of social and magical bragging, but it wasn't as if Vega minded that in the right cause. Then her aunt focused on her, intently. "Will you?"

Vega had known what her answer would likely be as soon as they asked. It was possible to turn down this sort of request, but it had consequences. And besides, she was more than a little curious. "Yes.

Unless I find something in those notes that makes it clear I'm not the right person for it."

"Ah, we'd expect nothing less. You are as well-trained as any in the family, after all." Aunt Ancha's voice had the warm approval again.

That was another compliment, the sort that Vega felt she had not entirely earned, but she would not argue with it right now. "May I walk you out and help you find a cab? The doormen know how to find an excellent driver."

"Oh, please don't dress to be seen again." Aunt Ancha stood, coming to kiss her cheek. "If you could show us back to where we can get our coats?"

"Easily done from here." Vega said, accepting a kiss on the other cheek from Uncle Thuban. He removed a rather large folder of material from somewhere and left it on the footstool for her. She slid her feet into the slippers, lowered the warding, and then walked them out to the ground floor. She showed them the door for the coat girl and where to get a cab. Once they were properly gone, she retreated to her dressing room and refused to look at the folder. It would be better to do it in her own rooms once she'd had some sleep.

CHAPTER 3
JANUARY 19TH IN TRELLECH

Farran knocked on the door frame at half one, the two knocks that Master Philemon preferred. When his apprentice master looked up from the other side of the massive oak desk, Farran said, promptly, "Amrut said you wanted to see me, sir. Is now a good time?"

As always, everything on Master Philemon's desk was in its proper place. A few papers out in front of him, a leather portfolio to one side, one photograph of his family and an intricately carved stone vase holding three silk flowers. Not real ones, of course. The chance of some pollen or dust affecting a piece of art was too high.

Farran had the usual twitch of wanting to make sure he was tidy. But he'd done that, in the mirror, before he knocked. His shirt was clean, his collar white, the suit impeccably fitted, his shoes polished. His hair was tidy, not sticking up anywhere, a hair longer than the non-magical man might wear it, but short enough to not attract too much comment outside of Trellech. He looked like any other man entering his later twenties, as he should. He looked, in a word, respectable and cultured, the sort who could be trusted with valuable art and artefacts.

Master Philemon's reply was immediate. "Yes, you're right when I expected, as always. Come in, close the door if you would." Farran did so, unsure how to take that request at the moment. The door being closed could mean some private item to be discussed, or it could be something he'd done wrong.

Not that there had been many of those in the last year, but the memory of his first apprenticeship kept lurking unreasonably fiercely. In other offices in other buildings, there might have been an offer of tea. Here, all that sort of thing was kept to the lounge down the hall, far away from any art, arte-facts, books, papers, or whatever else the auction house might be dealing with at the moment.

"Oh, don't be alarmed. This is the same conver-sation I've had recently with the others. You started a bit behind them. That is why you're last on the list, but you've more than made up enough time to make it worth talking about now." Master Philemon gestured at the chair, and Farran sank into it. "No need to take notes, just chat. If there are lists and such, we'll do that together."

"Sir." Farran sank into the chair— a remarkably comfortable one, given the formal style— and then folded his hands in his lap before looking up. "Amrut had mentioned you'd talked, and then Percy and Nathan."

"Just so." Master Philemon leaned forward, then he said more gently. "This still makes you nervous."

"Yes, sir." There was no use lying about it. For

one thing, this was Master Philemon, who had been nothing but kind to Farran, explaining all the intricacies of an auction house's many tasks. And for another, any of the senior masters were highly skilled at reading an expression as they could identify a work of art, the maker, and whatever repairs needed investigating. "Beg pardon."

"Ah, it's not your fault, is it?" Master Philemon shook his head. "Let me say, then, before anything else, that we, all the senior masters, are pleased with your work. We are considering several options for your future, but none of them are quite at fruition yet. So this, today, is both to ask what you might prefer, and to suggest an assignment that would be interesting but which has some logistical complications."

"Not a remote castle in Scotland, sir?" Farran asked. He'd done that last year, with several of the others. The castle had not been terribly well maintained. He'd kept wanting to spend all his spare time fixing the leaks and the draughts and the uneven wood railings and stairs. It had been unduly distracting.

Master Philemon laughed, wriggling his hand. "Not Scotland, no. London. The trick is that it would require some work on any given day of the week. And I know you like to get back to Thebes on Friday evening."

Thebes was his family home. His and Uncle Cadmus's, Lena's, and these days Vivian's. But technically, formally, now Farran was of age, it was all his. That meant they'd had money to repair a number of things and put in a lift and get Lena several new lovely devices for the kitchen. They still ran it as an intellectual sort of boarding house, given the proximity to Oxford. They were a modest walk to the train station, just two stops to the centre, and a little further from a portal. Farran considered what to say. He took a breath; Master Philemon had taught him that, too. "I'd be glad to hear you out, sir, about what would be involved."

"Two or three months. Four at the outside, by which I mean if more than four are needed, we'll bring someone else in to assist, and you'll get a proper leave. It would give you additional experience and connections with several of the London auction houses. There's an estate in process. Your role would be to coordinate with each of the houses taking on parts of the sale, and determining if a piece needed additional handling."

"By which we mean letting someone from the Ministry come round, and make sure it will not cause trouble, magically speaking," Farran said. He could see why they were thinking of him for this. It would get him more experience, yes, but that particular itch was something he was truly good at. He'd notice if some coin or snuffbox or hairbrush or what have you was magical.

"Exactly. They're about halfway through the initial catalogue work now, so you'd start with what they've already done, and then look at new items as they come through the processing. A fair bit of back and forth in London, visits to specialists as needed, all that. Everyone would understand that you are my eyes and hands in the matter." That, now, was a particular mark of trust. The phrase had not yet been formally applied to Farran. He couldn't quite repress a smile and looked up to see Master

Philemon beaming back. "Just so. Now, your questions."

Farran certainly had questions. "I assume it's a large estate collection, sir? Varied in period, material, source, all of that?"

"Just so. One of those widely travelled families that has brought back many things. We know there's at least one mummy and trappings. That's already been looked at. But items from China, Japan, India, Egypt, who knows where else. Or rather, the cataloguers know."

Farran snorted at that. "And my resources, sir?"

"We'll put you up, if you agree, in a serviced flat. There's a small building that caters to magical folk, just off the Bedford Square portal. The usual arrangement is that she provides breakfast, and there's a stipend for lunch and supper, though she can also provide them for a small fee. Meals taken while working are on expenses, of course, not the stipend." Master Philemon added, "I know your personal situation is more comfortable than it was, but we believe in certain standards."

"No, that's quite sensible, sir. And to have the same for everyone." Farran considered. "My working space?" He certainly couldn't take priceless artefacts back to his rooms. For one thing, many of them were delicate, and a number of the rest were far too heavy to lift.

"We've arranged an office in King Street. Convenient enough to Spink's and Christie's, and not too far from the others." Master Philemon tapped his fingers on the desk, as if reminding himself of key points. "And of course we'll cover cab fare for necessary appointments when the Tube isn't suitable."

Farran nodded at that. He had not been to London often, but all the current apprentices had spent enough time there to become comfortable with a non-magical city and how to get around. "Thank you, sir. And my time is my own outside the work? Allowing, as you said, for appointments, or museum or gallery visits, to see similar items and all that?" It could be quite a pleasant interlude, actually, especially if the weather was at all agreeable. It was January, going into February, but if he were there for three months, it would be well into spring.

"Exactly. Mind, we know all of you flock to whatever museum or library is closest. We picked you for that reason." Master Philemon shrugged. "How about you take a day to consider it, or two, if you'd like to talk to your family?" Master Philemon hesitated. "I gather there isn't anyone in Trellech, at the moment."

Farran had had an extremely civilised parting six months ago. Lucinda was lovely, but they had decidedly different ideas of how to spend their spare time. He'd tried to do what she liked best, but he'd pine for Thebes, and she hated it out there. Or not hated, but she felt stifled and isolated in a way that had baffled Farran.

His friend Tony had tried to match him up with half a dozen young women, including Lucinda. He'd likely make another go of it in the near future, Tony considered it his duty, as a more outgoing sort than Farran was by nature. All of the women had been clever and interesting, pleasant to look at and be around. He'd not felt a spark worth pursuing with any. So now, he just shook his head. "Not at the moment, sir. Perhaps I might meet someone new in London."

"As you like." Master Philemon nodded. "Right. You can take the prospectus away with you and have a good look. Obviously, we don't expect you to be an expert on all of it. A few things are entirely within your scope. Your role with the others is to figure out what needs consultation and the general idea of who, or what skills. Questions are always welcome. You'll have your journal, so we needn't wait for the post."

"Sir." Farran nodded. "I would like to go out to Thebes tonight, if that's not a bother."

"You're caught up on all your current work." It wasn't a question. Of course Master Philemon knew that. "Take tomorrow, bring your reading with you, and we'll expect your answer one way or the other on Monday. Or sooner, by journal, if you know it."

"I appreciate the time, sir." Farran didn't quite stand, but he wasn't sure how to ask the other question he had.

Master Philemon looked at him steadily. "You're wondering about what comes after this."

"Sir." Farran couldn't help looking down. He knew that this particular lack of confidence was entirely foolish, but he still felt the sting of it.

"We are discussing options for keeping you as a journeyman here. We may have additional ideas for you; there are at least two businesses who have inquired if you might seek outside employment in due course. Or if you wished to establish yourself as an independent consultant, of course, we could assist in that. You have choices, young man, or will. A bit more seasoning will help with the range of your skills. The same with building up your own connections, distinct from mine. But do not fret over having a future. The question is which future you wish to reach for."

Farran felt himself flushing. "I also appreciate your confidence in me, sir. I should, I should go read the portfolio, yes?"

"Yes. Read it, make your notes, and I will see you on Monday. Enjoy the countryside, and my best to your uncle and to Vivian if she's about."

That, at least, was an entirely easy request. "And I'll see if Lena can make some of the biscuits you liked last time. She said she's still got plenty of marmalade."

"Ah, and that is another reason to argue to keep you nearby, if you wish. The baked goods. Off you go." Master Philemon was smiling thoroughly, and that sort of smile was contagious. Farran made it back to his own, much smaller office - just enough for a desk and chair and a good light. He settled down to first double check that he'd finished all the necessary forms for his day's work. Then he opened the information and began to read through, jotting down notes in pencil as he went.

CHAPTER 4
JANUARY 20TH AT THEBES

"Now. Let's see. Vivian, you've your drink?" Uncle Cadmus glanced around, patting his pocket. Vivian lifted her glass, which had a suitable after-dinner cordial in it.

Farran smiled. "Your glasses are on your head, Uncle Cadmus." It was after supper on the Friday, and Uncle Cadmus had shooed the three of them up to his private office. It was comfortable for Farran. Here were the scent and the feel of home, of magic as it ought to be.

That was something he'd given a lot of thought to while he was living in rooms in Trellech, the way the magic of that city pressed more. Thebes was out in the countryside, on its own. It had been a magical home for a long time, centuries. But it had a settled feel to it, well-worn, with all the rough edges and splinters long gone.

He'd spent the day happily tending to various minor chores around the house and grounds. Most of it wasn't at all urgent. He'd polished the woodwork in the main stairs. Then he'd done a bit of cautious magical repair of a bit of the iron frame in the greenhouse with Uncle Cadmus doing the metalwork. That afternoon, he'd helped Lena by hanging several hooks in the kitchen so she could reach pots and such more comfortably. She was getting on in years enough that none of them liked the idea of her having to get up and down the stepstool to reach a pan.

Uncle Cadmus blinked, reached up, and then put them on his nose. "Well." He settled on the sofa next to Vivian, leaving the other chair for Farran. "You wanted both our advice, you said." He seemed exceedingly pleased by that. Both the desire for advice, and that Farran was including Vivian in it.

Not Aunt Vivian. He hadn't been sure why, but in the end, he'd asked, several years ago, if she minded, and she'd shaken her head. He'd got the sense, though he hadn't pried, that she rather enjoyed having a relationship that wasn't solidly defined by a familial term. The rest of her life, outside of her professional realm, was defined by a vast network of relationships to other Cousins. All those Cousins were descended from the Fatae before the Fatae left Albion. Or at least, left for all intents and purposes, outside of some carefully negotiated locations and activities.

Of course, the other trick was that Vivian and Uncle Cadmus both seemed delighted with their situations. But Vivian was only here at Thebes for a Friday to Sunday every fortnight or so, with longer stays a couple of times a year. She had her own room. Of course Farran knew that. But he also knew that mostly she stayed in these rooms with Uncle Cadmus.

It wasn't an ordinary sort of marriage, or even the more scandalous sort of daring new woman. Not that either Uncle Cadmus or Vivian would be inclined to the scandals of the Bright Young Things. Uncle Cadmus was in his late fifties now, and Vivian was a decade older, though she looked about his age. It didn't bother Farran, as long as Uncle Cadmus was happy. But it was terribly complicated to explain to anyone else.

The thing was, Vivian also had a long history of investigating and solving difficult problems. She was almost single-handedly responsible for Farran ending up at Ormulu under Master Philemon. Farran hadn't known that was even a possibility. He'd worked every day to live up to the chance, and most days, he thought he was doing the thing right.

Now, though, Farran took a breath. "Please. Master Philemon talked to me yesterday." He laid out the general proposal, months in London, able to come back occasionally but not frequently. But also, he'd had time to read the details. The range of the collections under consideration made him want to roll around in them, like a puppy and a small boy jumping endlessly into a pile of leaves. He found his hands moving, as he explained that part, signing the enthusiasm he felt as he said the words. Both Vivian and Cadmus followed that as easily as the speech, and it made Vivian chuckle at the end of it.

"So the question isn't are you saying yes. It's asking what you should know or think about that you haven't come up with yet." Vivian sounded delighted, and that puzzled Farran. She must have caught something in his expression, because she said, "Go on, please."

"You seem pleased at the idea?" Now Farran glanced at his uncle. "Are you all right with it, Uncle? I'll be able to help less here. And I'll miss the spring."

Uncle Cadmus spread his hands out. "I know you love the spring here. And the summer and the autumn and the winter. But things are going smoothly. We can certainly hire in someone to help if there're tasks to be done." That hadn't been true even a few years ago, but it was better now. He then peered over his glasses at Vivian. "You're pleased, though."

"I think Philemon is entirely correct, that it would be an excellent experience for you. But it might also have some— challenge is not quite the word. New experiences."

"New experiences?" Farran was not as resistant to them as Uncle Cadmus was, but Uncle Cadmus was very much a creature of habit and custom. To be fair to him, he'd gone out to Afghanistan when Farran had been tiny. He'd had a terrifying experience there, but until that, he'd enjoyed much of it. That certainly didn't qualify as nothing new. And honestly, Vivian was also something new. Farran, and what he remembered of his parents, had made it seem like Uncle Cadmus would be a bachelor all his life.

"You know how Ormulu works, of course. You young men and women are in and out of each other's offices and flats. The lot of you go to gallery shows or the museum or performances together, you get a drink, all that. You're expected to. Forming close networks is part of how that kind of business flourishes. Even as you move on, some staying at Ormulu, others going off to start their own shops or work in the museum or become private researchers or restorers."

"Or the Ministry. Amrut's still not entirely sure whether he ought to follow in his father's footsteps." Amrut's father had been the Minister of Materia for some years, and Amrut's older brothers were tending the same direction. "Or Percy's thinking about one of the London museums. And Edith's thinking about London, too."

"Are they going to be jealous of you getting this bit of work?" That was the thing about Vivian, and the reason he'd brought it to both of them. She saw that sort of problem sooner than Farran did.

But in this case, he'd had a chance to ask, and so he could shake his head. "Not for this particular work. It's a lot of small pieces all over the catalogue, and both of them would rather specialise. But it's the sort of thing where maybe I could invite them up to see something, introduce them to the right people, if things fell out that way." Farran shrugged. When it was like that, he could manage the social dynamics well enough.

"There you go." Vivian approved. That was encouraging. "But the other part is, when you're in London, people will probably want to go out. There being a number of places to go out to in a large city. How many of the people you'll be working with are magical?"

"A few. Mostly non-magical, though. It's all the big auction houses in on aspects of the sale. Quite a coup in a number of directions, enough to make everyone willing to cooperate. My role is partly to confirm all the records, independently. But of course, also to judge if anything needs to stay in the magical community, have special precautions."

"Let me know as soon as the final catalogue's going to print. I'm certain the Carillons will be interested." Vivian was pleased about that, as if it would get her points.

"Few books, I think. Or the books might be later. I can check on that." Lord Carillon was well known for his interest in incunabula, though of course he'd looked at a number of things at auctions Farran had helped with.

"I am confident you can manage the professional side. And the social aspects of the work," Vivian pressed. Uncle Cadmus did not, and he would not have, ever. It was not a thing Uncle Cadmus leaned on.

Farran sighed, and then he stood up, wanting to walk a little, pacing behind the chair he'd been sitting in. Vivian didn't discourage him. Finally, he paused, hands on the back of the chair. "How do I do that? What will they expect me to do?"

"You've some idea of that," Vivian said. "Start there, and I'll help you fill in the gaps."

Farran considered what he knew. "You know me. I like to stay home. A good book, something to mend or fix. Bringing it back to how it was best." It was how he thought about Thebes, this house, and about the greenhouses and outbuildings and the garden. It wasn't perfection or newness he was reaching for with any of that, it was something more about the thing in use, tended well, able to do its work.

His work at Ormulu had something of the same feel. Not always, of course. It was harder to identify the work of a painting of someone's long-dead dog or horse or great-aunt. Such paintings mattered, of course. They were art. But the person for whom it had mattered most wasn't there to interact with it anymore.

Objects were easier, objects that could be used, because they still potentially had a use. Some, of course, were stuck in a glass case, never properly breathing again, never out in the world in however small a form. Now, as if prompted by the thought, he took a breath, then said, "It'll involve going out. Bars, clubs, something like that." He felt awkward at those sometimes, but he could manage most of it. "And probably a range of things to drink or take on offer."

"Probably," Vivian said, her voice entirely even. "I would like to make a gift to you of a suitable case of antidotes and such. All the common non-magical things, and a fair range for potions unless someone in those circles has a particularly clever alchemist I don't know about. Yet."

That made Farran snort. "Isn't it part of your job to know about them?"

"There is always a first time someone does some-thing questionable. That's the problem with it. That first time gets people hurt or killed. And I do not wish that for you, for all sorts of reasons, not just Cadmus's sake. And I do not wish it for your friends. I do not want Philemon to have to deal with it. Such things make him cranky. Though I'm sure he'll have some cautions and stories for you. You're a sensible young man. Just keep your head. Have your own cab fare home, know how to get back to the nearest portal, whatever that means for wherever you are." She considered. "Would you do a day's training with someone I can recommend to help you avoid pickpockets and theft?"

That was an entire line of difficulties Farran had not entirely considered. It happened in Trellech from time to time, but nothing that was a serious threat. He glanced at his uncle, but again, he knew what he was going to say. "Certainly. Though Master Philemon made it clear my expenses cover cabs and such. But I'm sure he'd give me time for your recommendation. Thursdays are best right now."

"That is because he is a man with experience of the world. All right, I'll set something up and let you know." Vivian tapped her fingers. "That sorted, London is a city full of historical delights, along with the modern ones. You've been, you know it's got a different feel magically. It's not Trellech, all magical, but the London demesne is unique, in terms of the land magic." She tapped a finger on the arm of her chair. "You likely won't need an introduction to the Keeper of London, but if you do, let me know. I can arrange something with a little warning."

"I don't expect to come to that kind of attention, no." The magical keeping of London's land magic was a complex thing, from what Farran knew. But it wasn't likely to be relevant to what he was doing. "And I assume he's still quite busy, after the flooding on the seventh." That had been horrid, far too many deaths and destruction, including damage to one of the museums.

Vivian pursed her lips. "True. You've looked at those maps? Beyond what's in the papers?"

Farran nodded. "Part of Master Philemon's portfolio. It's affecting some of the conservator availability."

Vivian nodded, then shifted the subject back to gentler things. "I think you'd enjoy spending an extended period there, long enough to get to know the place, to have a favourite route or pub or library or what have you. You are young, you should have a good time, in whatever form that takes. Just perhaps not all of them at home with a book."

It made Farran laugh. Then he shook his head. "If that's the way I should go about things, I will. Uncle?"

"Vivian has far more useful experience here than I do. I'll worry a bit, but that's mine to deal with. And you'll have your journal and can write about what you get up to, yes?" Uncle Cadmus spread his hands, cheerfully resigned.

Farran nodded. That made it much easier. How Vivian had talked Uncle Cadmus into getting a journal, he wasn't sure, but it made their physically distant relationship far easier to manage. He gathered they wrote pages and pages back and forth most weeks, so Uncle Cadmus was well in the habit of checking. "I promise I'll be sensible. And I won't be going for a week or three yet. Now, though." He cleared his throat. "Can I go down and help Lena with the dishes and whatever she needs for tomorrow? I'd like to have my hands busy."

"And she'll be glad to see you. And have a chat

when your hands aren't busy with dishes." That was the trick with signing. It made chatting while working harder.

Farran smiled. "Yes, Uncle." Then he nodded once more and took himself out of the room, leaving the two of them talking quietly on the sofa.

CHAPTER 5
JANUARY 24TH IN LONDON

B y Tuesday, Vega was no further along on the task. Her aunt and uncle had helpfully sent along a package of some reference materials, along with funds to get her started on what else she might need.

It was an interesting problem, but honestly, it really needed an archaeologist, not an astronomer. Or a singer. She was trained in two of those, but the archaeology was decidedly not one of them. She didn't even know where to find an archaeologist. There had been a whole fuss with the Research Society, what, eighteen months ago now, so that was likely no use. The entire society had collapsed in a pile of scandal. Vega gathered it would be at least another year before the actual researchers were organised enough to be much help again.

Vega didn't know anyone there to talk to. Even if she did, that was the sort of connection where going back to the aunts and uncles at the family estate would make more sense. Presumably, there was a good reason no one from the family had suggested that as a starting point.

So she had to go at the problem from a different direction. Logic suggested that if it were an artefact from the sixth century, then it would most likely be in the City or perhaps a few of the outlying areas. She didn't know which, but she remembered learning, back in her tutoring, that the city had spread out in several directions. In the end, she'd acquired several more detailed street maps. Then she'd gone to the library to see if she could borrow a couple of titles about antiquarian sites of interest, such as they were.

Tuesday's weather was not terribly promising, chilly and overcast. But it meant that during the day, when other people were at work or whatever errands they might have, she might reasonably go have a look at some part of the city. Vega knew the areas she spent time in well enough, how to get from her rooms to the club or the places she ate or picked up groceries for a little light cooking. And she knew where the parks nearby were, even if the weather had not been entirely promising about spending much time in them when she was awake.

More or less at random, she'd decided on going down to Blackfriars Bridge. One of her books had commented that the place was thick with lore, including ghost stories. Those didn't seem entirely relevant to what she was looking for. It wasn't the original site of a bridge across the Thames, from what she gathered; there'd been a previous bridge on this spot from the 1760s. But that wasn't much help. Far too recent.

And the family records wouldn't be much help. Alcyone's line favoured quiet dark places, with not many others around. Stars and a bit of river or lake that might attract a kingfisher, and few distractions. Vega's love of the city, or at least of the music to be found in a city, puzzled a number of them. But to be fair to them, especially her parents, they'd supported her doing what she was doing. Some year in the future, she'd retire to the family estates, and enjoy that too, in a different way. But maybe not for a long while yet. Not until her apparent age got too out of sync with how long she'd been around. She had at least a decade yet, probably two if she moved around a little.

That music of the city, though, that made it easier to deal with the clatter and noise, on the days that she had to do that. Often, she did her shopping in the quiet bit of the middle afternoon, and then it was only getting to the club that was chaotic. Oh, there was plenty of noise and gossip at the club but that was all part of the larger song of the evening, and it didn't jar Vega nearly as much. Maybe it was that there was a purpose to it, too.

Now, she was considering what she was hearing, as much as what she was seeing, and there was a thread of something that confused her. It wasn't exactly a sour note, but it was a note that didn't fit. The sound, over the bridge, had some woodwinds in it, but not jazz. Not a formal classical piece, either.

It was something more like a drum, a whistle, a fiddle. Something like that. The music people made when they weren't professionals, when they were playing solely for their own pleasure. Or maybe to keep time while they did some task. It had the pace of a waulking song. She'd heard women up in Scotland near one of the family spaces, singing those while they fulled cloth.

Vega found her fingers tapping along with it. She turned to look out at the water, her hands on the stone of the bridge, rather than make that more obvious. Vega didn't ignore the world around her, of course. She'd been trained better than that. People were coming and going about their business. Then, there was a whistle, the sort of appreciative whistle she was used to— well, enough— at the club, and that felt intrusive here.

"What's a lovely lady like you doing on a bridge on a day like this?" The man who'd whistled came closer. He was dapper, in the sharply tailored suit of someone with money and style, both. Or rather, a particular sort of style. A dark green herringbone tweed, a golden pocket square, a tie that she suspected meant some affiliation.

More curious, at least from her perspective, was that she could not tell whether he was magical. That was a song she could almost always pick out, a line of melody or harmony. He had neither the echoes of a Cousin, nor the melodic lines she normally heard from the folk of Albion. Or rather the interactions of a person's magic with the Pact, which was both melody and an understanding of the harmonic ground. The accent, though, that, oh. American. Yankee, if she had the terminology right.

She turned, her hip against the side of the bridge, one foot poised so she could turn and get a good few steps away. Working in a club taught all those tricks and then some, even if she couldn't use some of the magical techniques to help right here, out in the open. "Do you always whistle at women you don't know, then?" Vega pitched it as she would have in the club— making a space, but also engaging with the question. There was an art to making it not quite coy.

"Oh, not very many at all. But you? You make quite a striking figure. Lit from behind, I thought you might be the ghost, the lady in black." He gestured. "But I gather she has longer skirts. Early in the century, certainly." It gave him an excuse to gesture down toward her legs, which he certainly took his time ogling. Then he let his eyes come back up. It was all the visible appreciation she'd expected of someone taking this line of introduction. "You seemed intent on the water. You must have some task to get back to, though?"

"Oh," Vega considered her options here. If she said she was a singer, he'd ask where, and she suspected the charms would keep him from the club. Though there were all manner of private clubs out there, that might do. "I'm a singer. I've been in London long enough to settle in. I thought it was time to see a bit more of the sights."

She was paying the usual sort of attention to him, of course. In her line of work, a number of men, and some women, looked at her like that. Certainly, wanted a bit of her time, for the sparkle and shine of her to rub off on them. Nothing here seemed unusual, not yet, other than the fact he'd approached her in public. In Britain, people usually kept to themselves unless there were a visible sign of mutual interest. Americans were different that way. He didn't seem a threat, but he certainly hadn't offered anything of particular interest to her.

"And you've already traipsed around the Tower

and Westminster and, oh, where else? What sort of thing would you be interested in?" He then offered his hand. "Thomas Vandermeer, at your service. In London for some extended business." He didn't say what it was. "Would I have heard you sing anywhere?"

"Oh, the current engagement's at a private club." Vega tilted her head, the gesture she'd practised in her mirror and in her Incantation training for hours. "The sort where you need to know the right people to even know it's there." She twitched her shoulder. "Quite a coup. It's also the sort that's generous with the performers."

"Ah, indeed." He made it quite a neutral comment, but then went on, "And of course you'd encourage generosity, in hopes of a bit of your time and attention. But come, you've not said where you've seen already. You must have some favourite?"

Blast. Now she was going to have to either lie— not her preference, it was so easy to get tangled in it — or to come up with some misdirection. "Oh, well. I've not got myself together for anything organised. The club was open every night through the holidays. I barely had time to catch my breath. Today's the first day I've been able to be out and about since, oh, the beginning of November."

"Well, now, that's a pity. Perhaps you might enjoy a little company, on an outing or two? I'm often at leisure in the afternoons, though it depends on business, of course." Mister Vandermeer shrugged. "A lot of my work is over drinks or supper or a bit of dancing. If you weren't likely to be occupied, I'd ask you out for that. You'd be a delight to whatever party you graced."

"And you, sir, flatter without reason." Again, the trick was all in the pitch. The way he'd made his approach had her a little on edge. Some men pressed every opening they had, but she was finding it a little obvious for her tastes. "I'm not looking for that sort of company." Then she took a slight risk. "Are all Americans so forward?"

"It's a new era, isn't it? Opportunity for all." Something in the question made him grin. "Oh, I won't press. It's no fun if you're not willing." That sentence should have made her less wary, and it instead made her more cautious. Vega filed that away for further attention. "Here, my card." He did some quick trick with his hands, producing a card holder from inside his suit with a flick of his wrist. Or probably he had. He opened it, presenting her with a card printed for the occasion, since it had his hotel on it. The Hotel Cecil, that was quite the location.

"You do well for yourself, then, I gather." Vega twisted slightly. She knew where it was. "I've been to a few nights there. Professional interest, of course, listening to the music and a dance or three."

"Ah!" Mister Vandermeer seemed honestly delighted. "Do you have a card, then, dear lady? Or even a name I might know?"

That was likely safe enough. For one thing, it wasn't remotely her full name, just her stage name. And for another, if he did turn up at the club, that would tell her something about his magic. "Vega Beaumont." She shrugged. "No card, I didn't bring them with me." She shrugged. "I'm afraid I'm not the sort to keep a regular schedule about anything except singing. Quite wedded to my work."

CHAPTER 5   **45**

"Ah, well. A man can live in hope." He shrugged once. "Perhaps we'll see each other again. I'll leave you to whatever you were doing, then." He tipped his hat, took a step back.

"A good afternoon, Mister Vandermeer. I hope your time in London is ..." She was about to say 'what you seek,' or 'good' and the words twisted in her mouth. "What's needed."

It earned her a grin. "Oh, I've my hopes." He then spun sharply on one heel— he must be a decent dancer— and strode off. He had a rolling walk, used to covering ground, not the walk of people used to slow-moving crowds, but of someone slipping through them like a salmon upstream. She watched him go before considering her options.

She certainly didn't want to go back to her flat, she was rather afraid he might attempt to follow. That meant finding somewhere public, circling through a part of the city she didn't know well. Or she could get a cab and go somewhere. As she had the thought, a cab came trundling across the bridge, and she made the flashing thought a reality, her hand up to hail it. She did not care for automobiles, but she wasn't as sensitive to iron as some, and a quick ride would be manageable. "The British Museum, please."

The cab lurched off into traffic again, and she sat with her hands on her knee, leaning back enough she couldn't be seen from the window if they stopped. She saw Mister Vandermeer down toward the corner, as if waiting, but the cab rolled past without slowing much, and before too long they were well away.

Vega kept thinking all the way through the

streets. She couldn't shake the sense that Mister
Vandermeer had approached her, in particular.
Certainly, he hadn't seemed to speak to others on the
bridge. Not while she was leaving, and she thought
not before, at least not close enough that she'd have
noticed if he had. Vega was used to reading the
room, paying attention lightly to everything in the
audience, after all.

But people did sometimes approach her like that.
She had that bit of brightness to her, magically and
otherwise, that made people spot her. That was
partly being a Cousin, partly being a performer. It
was in how she carried herself and where she aimed
what she was doing. Even when she muffled it a bit,
it still caught attention. Vandermeer might just have
been reacting to that.

Fortunately, the museum itself was relatively
uncrowded, especially once she got up toward some
of the less visibly interesting Roman collections. She
spent an hour looking at them, at least getting a
sense and taking a few notes about what the ordinary
sort of items from that period were. For all she knew,
that might even turn out to be useful.

CHAPTER 6
FEBRUARY 10TH AT THE CRYSTAL CAVE

"There you go. Drinky to get started with the night." Albie, one of the bright young men from another of the auction houses, nudged a brightly coloured cocktail in front of Farran. Charm-bright, Farran was sure, no food was naturally that shade of bright pink. "Now's the time to show you the wonders of London. None of Trellech's provincial pleasures."

Farran took it in good humour. They'd been teasing him all week - since he started work. His accent, of course, wasn't Welsh. His parents and uncle had always made a point of proper elocution, the well-respected Received Pronunciation. Of course, that was easier because most of the people in the house in the last decade had been working at Oxford, and Oxford had expectations. "So, what should I be anticipating here?"

"The music, my dear chap. And the illusions. Now, we'll have to figure out how to go round some of the better parties. Not today, of course, but in a fortnight, when people have got a look at you. Don't make plans for next Friday." Albie looked him up and down. "Or Saturday. And you must come round to my tailor."

Farran said, patiently. "I'm fond of my current one. Couldn't possibly put him out. He saw to Papa, as well as to my uncle." Not that Uncle Cadmus was considered a sharp dresser. But traditionally minded, yes. And Farran knew he was perfectly suitably dressed, for any purpose other than being out with a fast crowd on a Friday night. Or a Saturday, he supposed. Master Philemon had trained them all in that, just as much as in any matter of art or magic. In their line of work, the aspect of the thing was often just as important as the reality. "But I suppose I could spruce up with a new tie or something of the kind. A different hat."

"Mmm." Albie leaned forward, then he crowed. The sound wasn't that out of place. They'd arrived around half-ten, after drinks in Albie's flat, not terribly far away. Bedford Square was the well-off area of magical London, with the portal convenient for trips elsewhere, and townhouses tucked away that the non-magical never wondered about. The club, of course, was on the edge of Soho, long a spot for entertainment of all kinds.

Farran couldn't help taking in the details. The construction of the building seemed solid enough. Whatever magic they were using for decorations and entertainment, the bones of the place seemed solidly made. Albie was well known here. He'd sent a message on to reserve a pair of tables for the two of them, half a dozen people who'd be along in a few, and the two who were off on the dance floor. That was one of Albie's friends, Lamb by nickname, and his girlfriend Richie. Short for Richelda, she'd said, but Farran could see why she didn't use that. She was absolutely a woman chasing fashion with a grand desire.

This was, as Vivian— and Master Philemon— had pointed out, also part of the job. Thinking of it like that made it easier for Farran. He'd thought through, in advance, what sort of things he might and might not want to talk about. Farran had certainly expected Albie to suggest drinks. He had the money to cover a round or two comfortably. And he knew, more or less, how to get home.

Last night, when he suspected Albie might propose something like this, he'd checked on that. There were three, maybe four, magical clubs in London, but this was by far the best of them right now. Everyone said so. Certainly the largest and most frenetic. But he'd stopped by on a walk last night, and had a word with the doorman about the usual practice.

It was apparently quite easy to hail a cab, or one of the staff would work a particular magic if none were handy. When it came to the drinks, Vivian had indeed sent him off with a little leather case of useful things, including a ring that would shimmer peacock green if a drink had anything other than alcohol in it.

Whatever the pink was, then, it wasn't a potion. Farran took a sip, then blinked. His expression must have been funny, or perhaps Albie was in the stage of the evening where he found everything funny, because Albie started laughing.

"I didn't expect it to taste like mint. That's, er. Startling?" Mint things should not be bright pink. Green, like the mint plants themselves, that was reasonable. He'd allow as mint humbugs might be all sorts of colours, but if they were this end of the colour range, more likely red than a shade more suited to some tropical flower.

"Have a bit more. Good for you. Come on, Farran, it's Friday. Time to relax a little. No one's going to carry tales back to the office." Albie leaned both his elbows on the table.

"Well. Not about being at a magical club, I suppose." Farran had made it easier to mark himself out as magical. Master Philemon had given him a few people to keep an eye out for. But Farran had worn his Owl House tie each day he was meeting new people this week, and Albie had picked it right up. In a quiet moment, along in one of the store-rooms, he'd smoothly introduced himself. Albie had been at Dunwich, three years ahead of Farran. That meant he was comfortably established as a junior member of staff, but still young enough to enjoy a night out.

Also, it made him young enough not to have fought in the War, and that was a curious mix here. Most of the crowd were young enough they wouldn't have either, plenty here were in their twenties. But about a third, maybe more, were older, and Farran could see a mix of visible injuries or marks or what-ever one wanted to call them. On an artefact or piece of art, that might add to the value, and here, it was more complicated. People found wearing their history where everyone could see to be uncomfortable, and of course so many people could be awful about it.

"What do you think, after your first week? And where have they put you up?" Albie nudged him. "Oh, there are some new girls here. Quite good dancers, that's the standard, and you want to hear the singer. She's, mmm." There was a purr. Albie had a girlfriend, or at least a woman he was seeing, but apparently this didn't discourage him from looking. Or listening, as the case may be.

"Serviced flat, a block or two from the portal." No need to specify which one. "Not big, but I'm not likely to be doing much entertaining, am I? Sitting room, bath, bedroom, and enough to do tea and toast for myself." Honestly, he preferred his rooms in Trellech, or even better, being back at Thebes. He would trade every minute in this club for time sitting at the table in the kitchen, Lena's realm. Farran shrugged. "And the office in King Street, you saw that."

"Rather lonely, being on your own. I thought Ormulu didn't work like that." Farran had also more or less expected this, but Albie wasn't being any too subtle about it. Perhaps one advantage of a Schola education was spotting the unsubtle at ten paces. Spending five years in the vicinity of Fox House practising the arts of obscurity every chance they got helped.

Farran shrugged. This part wasn't secret. "They take on ten apprentices every five years, see us through. We're at the stage where people are deciding what's next. A couple know they want to go into related lines of work. Me, I'm still figuring things out. This is a chance to try my hand at something different, see what it's like." And if he was any good at it. A week was far too soon to tell, in a project of this scope. He'd only just got through figuring out who everyone he needed to talk to was, and where their offices or workrooms or storage rooms were. "It seems quite a lot to learn!" He kept his voice bright.

"Any particular specialty?" Albie's voice got more cautious here. Farran had picked up that Albie apparently had a particular fondness for objects, silversmithing or other metals, and the detail work on them.

Farran shrugged. "I'm an amateur when it comes to a lot of it still. Oh, competent enough to ask the right questions and work up the catalogue entry once an expert has looked at it. I picked up an interest in some of the recent painters, the last few years. The Fauvists, and that set." Especially once Vivian had pointed out something to him about the focus of some of the magical painters of that set, in the way they chose particular, more obscure, landscapes. "And there's rather a lot of interesting Arts and Crafts work. Or, well, some of the magical applications. Not so much the fine work, as the more everyday. Talismans, mementos, engagement bands, that sort of thing."

Just as Albie was about to say something, the music shifted, from dance tunes to something with a beat. From back behind where they were sitting, a woman strolled out through the space between the tables. Several years of coaching from Vivian meant

Farran now understood what she was doing with her clothing; every sleek bias-cut line was about an image of movement and fluidity.

The woman had long dark hair, coiled and pinned up in some way that meant every time she turned her head, a small faceted decoration flashed in the club lights. Once she was on stage, he could see her gown was a purple shading to green, glittering with— they must be paste, not diamonds. But excellent paste, enhanced by just the right charms.

The head of the band announced her: Vega Beaumont, the nightingale of Albion. It was a boast, but as soon as she started singing, Farran was sure she'd earned it. Her voice had the outdoors in it. That caught him first. She didn't sound like someone made for the indoors, for narrow spaces and rooms that echoed. He fancied he could hear birds calling back and forth, the way trees shaped the sound, a burble of some lake or brook.

Farran couldn't help staring, not that staring actually made it easier to listen. Then he closed his eyes, and he could focus better. He didn't know her first song, but her second, that was a choice he hadn't expected.

The singer's voice rolled through the melody. It took Farran a moment or two to realise that it was Tom O' Bedlam, a venerable folk song, full of references to magic and enchantment and lore. That was about the asylum not too far across the river in Southwark. Or, well, perhaps the older one, which had begun not too far from where they were sitting, considering.

There was a burr to her voice, on the lower notes, or perhaps more like a cat's purr, something

contented and certain. Then the upper range sang
out pure as the nightingale she'd been claimed to be.
The combination was compelling, honestly, a raw
human sound that made emotions flow.

Farran wasn't the only one near enough
entranced. Albie, next to him, had fallen quiet, and
the chatter around them from other tables had died
away. The dancers retreated to the chairs without
making much of a sound, as if they couldn't both
stand and listen. It was one of those moments that
happened far too rarely in music, where the whole
transformed everything around it, and couldn't last.
A snowflake melting on the fingertip, a soap bubble
shimmering in the sunlight, a flash of magic. There
was a moment, amid the music, where he got a
shiver of colour— copper orange and deep blue,
more blue than the green of Vega's dress.

Then, somehow, without the world ending, she
brought the song to a close. Without a pause, she
launched Mad Maudlin, the answer of a woman
who searched for ages for her beloved, and would
not turn aside. There was something noble in it, a
determination that Farran felt about his uncle and
about Thebes and Lena, but hadn't ever felt for
someone romantic. It was a curious song to pick in a
nightclub, and yet, as with the first, no one could
stand to break the moment and move.

When the second tune ended, the musicians
shifted into something else, a twining of voice and
instruments that didn't have words, but was faster
and brighter. Now Vega's voice flew over the notes,
somersaulting up the scale, then tumbling down, to
swoop around again into some new but related
patterns. He could almost imagine the strands of

ribbon being braided in some May pole dance, or an illusionist's art formed before the eye. It was as if it knit the world back together, piece by piece, whatever worries had been carried in. That, more than the rest of it, made him wonder what else might be on offer if he stayed to listen.

CHAPTER 7
THAT NIGHT

By the time the night ended, Vega was delighted with it. She was in full voice again, like she had been the night her aunt and uncle had visited. The tips had been generous, and none of the patrons had been particularly difficult. She'd been complimentary to the band, both from the stage and in private. They'd earned every bit of it. She'd added comments to Madam Helena once she was done with her last set.

Madam Helena had snorted. "You make them look good, and sound better, and they've the sense to know it. And your routine with Pasco looked entirely perfect tonight. You?"

"I thought so too. It's just a matter of getting the angles and the timing right, but going through it a couple more times got it up to our standards." Their exceptionally high standards.

Madam Helena had snorted. "You don't order him around. It helps." Then she'd tilted her head. "You willing to consider extending your stay here?"

They'd arranged for four months, with an option to extend. Vega nodded. She had reason to stay in London now, for at least a bit. And she was clear that Madam Helena was going to give her a much better arrangement than the other clubs would. "What terms did you have in mind?" It didn't do not to bargain, or at least see if a bargain was an option.

"Hah. How about we talk about it when you get in tomorrow? But I think I could see my way to some considerations." That meant it'd be up to Vega to figure out what she wanted to ask for. That was an excellent question. Now, she just nodded, and made her way off to her dressing room to change. On the way she asked Bob to see about letting Fred the cabbie know she'd be out in a few minutes if he got the chance.

Twenty minutes later, she'd changed into a far more comfortable frock, removed all the performance jewellery and locked it in the safe, and put on her cosier shoes. She took her cloak and handbag and made her way to the door to find Fred and go home. As she came back out from the stage door to the street, she found a couple of people chatting in front of the club. Three went off in one direction, the other appeared to be waiting for a cab.

It was the young man she'd noticed earlier, because he was new, and he was with people who weren't. The rest of his table were frequent enough regulars, every fortnight or so. She'd gathered, from some gossip, that they rotated through the clubs. They spent freely enough. Not with the extravagance of someone with a lot of money flowing their way, but not people who were counting every coin, either.

Middle of the range drinks, food to nibble on for the entire table, but not a full meal.

The man glanced over at her, and then took a step backward, rather than toward her, as if giving her space. That was unusual, and Vega took a step or two closer to the door. Rob, standing there, said, "Miss Vega, Fred said he'd be along in a minute or two. He got a nearby fare."

"Thank you." She could wait easily enough, and she didn't want to retreat. One of her heels had a blister, and while it didn't ache now, she didn't want to encourage it that way. Then she inclined her head at the young man. "Your first time here, I believe?"

"You've an excellent eye. I'd say even finer than your voice, but then we'd be into the hubris of the gods, and that doesn't seem wise, does it?" He had a pleasant speaking voice, and now she could see him better. He was also well-dressed. Quality suiting, in a deep blue, a tie that strongly suggested Owl House at Schola, confirmed by the tie pin.

The comment, though, was a trifle intriguing. It certainly wasn't the tongue-tied flattery she some- times got. "Guests here rarely begin with a classical reference." She offered her hand after a moment. "Vega Beaumont, of course."

"Farran Michaels. My uncle, who raised me from 1912, is a classicist. One picks up a fair bit of it by sheer proximity." He took her hand, shook it, but also made a slight bow over it, in a way that came across as charming rather than entirely too contrived.

"And are you new to London, or just to the club?" They would need to be circumspect; the club was magical, the street was not. On the other hand, it was late enough there wasn't a great deal of walking traffic.

"I work at Ormulu. I'm in the city for a project for a few months. Albie and the others thought I ought to see a bit of the town. Or hear, as the case may be. I'm certainly intending to come back. The entire evening was..." He hesitated, as if searching for a word. "It fit together. Far better than some places, where everyone's jostling for attention."

"Ah. You are clever. Not everyone spots that. Rather fewer understand why it's important." Vega thought she might have a word with Madam Helena about this one, tomorrow. A steady guest in the crowd, who understood what they were doing, that was a foundational point all the performers could benefit from. That was no bad thing. Making sure that this man got a slightly better seat, where it meant someone wouldn't be bothering the dance mistresses and waiters coming through. That didn't hurt either.

Then something else occurred to her. "Ormulu, you said." The question now was how to ask what she wanted to know. Asking if he were a clerk would be insulting. Ah, there, that was the way to do it. "Do you have a specialty?"

"I've a knack for the feel of an object. Which ones might deserve closer attention, beyond the obvious." Now, that was a deft explanation, suggesting a magical competence without coming out and saying it. It was also exactly the problem Vega had been struggling with. The question was whether he was trustworthy, or could be sworn to be. She tapped her toe once.

Ormulu had an excellent reputation. They made

a point of keeping it so, not just to the ordinary magical standard, but by her family's line. She remembered one of her aunts saying in passing that more than one line from the Grandmothers favoured Ormulu for that reason, but she couldn't recall the details just now. "And you are..."

"An apprentice still." He was frank about that. "If you have a question, I'd be glad to let you know how you could best get in touch with someone. I'm apprentice to Philemon Ettis. Working my way towards being done, but I've a year or two yet. This..." He gestured at London as a whole, "Is meant as a seasoning of experience."

Vega nodded. "Would it be possible, then, to arrange a consultation in some form? I don't know how to put it, what the options might be. From what you have said, perhaps you could direct me to what to consider."

Mister Michaels considered only briefly. "Of course. It would be my pleasure. When would be convenient for you? I've a little flexibility in my duties, but at the end of my day might work better? I assume you're not fond of mornings."

Vega snorted. No, she was not, and for several reasons. "The club is closed Mondays and Tuesdays in this season. Perhaps one of those afternoons, when you're done?" The question of where was more challenging. "Is there somewhere I could meet you, or a preference?"

"I've a small office on King Street. If you arrived at half four, there'd still be someone at the desk." He fumbled in his jacket, then pulled out a card case, offering her the card.

Vega was about to say something else, but then

Fred pulled up. She didn't want to keep him waiting;
Friday night was good for fares. She nodded once.
"Half four, Monday, this address. I beg pardon,
that's my cab."

"Of course." Michaels made another of those
small bows, stepping aside so Rob could get the door.
Once she was in the cab, she murmured to Fred.
"Home, of course."

He chatted amiably as they went about his night,
and she made a few comments about hers. Once she
was in her flat, she stripped down efficiently and
removed all the cosmetic charms. Then she had a
quick wash to remove the more physical cosmetics
and the dried sweat of the evening. Performing was
always like that, between the lights and the dancing
and the heat of the bodies in the room. At least for
her. Tomorrow, she'd have to look at the maps and
figure out how much she did and didn't want to say
to that polite and possibly helpful young man.

CHAPTER 8

FEBRUARY 13TH IN LONDON

Monday afternoon, Farran tidied the office for the third time. It wasn't as if it actually needed it. He was naturally in favour of having things in order, and Master Philemon had trained him beyond those tendencies. One didn't want to risk some piece of art or sculpture to a pile of papers. One didn't want to risk a spill, and one certainly didn't want a client's private details out. So his desk was clear, barring some blank notepaper and his second-best fountain pen. He didn't bring his favourite to an office like this. That was just asking for trouble. And the photos of his parents and Uncle Cadmus, but those were in the corner.

The rest of the day had gone well enough. He'd gone round to Sotheby's, and looked at a handful of items of interest. Two had been magical, four had not been. But he'd been able to add some commentary on the details of one of the nutmeg graters. He'd also offered to do some research on a cameo no one else had felt entirely confident about. That was his task for tomorrow. He'd need to work on it there, and also consult a number of reference texts.

The odds were two to one that it was a fake, but proving it was always the trick. Farran was almost certain it was. It didn't feel right in his hand. But of course, while he could gesture at that, it wasn't enough for the auction to remove it. They needed actual proof.

Precisely at half-four, there was the sound of the door in the outer office, the sound of the secretary greeting someone. Miss Beaumont was expected, so shortly he heard the click of heels on the wood floor and a knock at his door. "A Miss Beaumont for your four-thirty." The secretary, a widow in her fifties, had seemed unsure what to make of Farran from the beginning, and this certainly wasn't helping. Mrs Malden was magical, but not strongly so. She kept a strict order in the offices, used by a range of magical businesses who needed a suitable space in London for short periods of time.

Farran stood. "Thank you, Mrs Malden. We might need to speak past five. I'm glad to lock up."

It earned him a slight sniff, but that was part of the arrangement, and there was a caretaker who'd come round and clean and lock up beyond that. "Well. Have a good evening, then." He didn't think the disapproval was about Miss Beaumont, who was dressed in an entirely ordinary sort of day dress, a cloche hat, and a coat.

"And you." Farran gestured Miss Beaumont into the room, then moved to get the door behind her, closing it and bringing up the warding. That was solid enough for Farran's professional purposes, both

for protecting items in the office and ensuring
privacy. "Miss Beaumont, please, have a seat. I'm
afraid I can't offer you tea. We don't do that in our
working spaces. May I take your coat?"

It took her an instant to consider, but she was
quick to figure out why. "Too much risk to whatever
you're working on?" She shrugged out of it, letting
him take it and hang it up on the hook by the door.

"Yes. There's quite a pleasant cafe across the
street, if you'd like something when we're done."
Not with him, he assumed, but a person might want
something before tackling finding a cab or the Tube
or whatever they were doing next. He waited for her
to sit, then crossed to behind the desk. "Before we
begin, could you let me know the degree of confidentiality you'd prefer for the moment?"

She tilted her head. "What are the usual options,
please? I'm afraid I've not done this sort of consultation before. And is there a fee? I am glad to pay."

"For half an hour of my time, no. If we decide
on something beyond that, then I will lay out a
proposal." Farran spread his hands slightly. "In this
line of work, it is often to everyone's benefit to have a
conversation before making commitments. For a
consultation, there is a standard oath to keep the
matter private, but permitting me to consult with my
seniors at Ormulu if relevant. For example, if they
have particular expertise or connections that would
be of some benefit. Another option would require
your permission before any further consultation."

"The second, please, for the moment." She
looked at him steadily. Farran liked that while she
wasn't certain how this normally went, she was
comfortable asking questions about it. He reached

under his notepad and passed her the card with the standard oath in the second form. She read it carefully, twice, before nodding.

Once she passed it back, he made it, glancing at the card once or twice for the precise wording. Farran felt the magic coil around him, and the sharp stab of his greatest fear. As always, it involved something precious crumbling into dust in his hands, while Uncle Cadmus looked on, absolutely disappointed and disapproving. Once he finished, Farran took a breath to steady himself, and then looked up. "Now, where would you care to begin?"

"This may be a situation where you do need to consult, but I —" She stopped. "Where would it be helpful to begin?"

"I presume you have some sort of object or piece of art or manuscript?" Farran tried to figure out how to ask the questions the best way. "I can talk about the process of having a formal assessment. Help you find a suitable specialist."

"May I ask what your role is currently?" Mistress Beaumont asked, instead. "Before I, well. It's an unusual situation."

"I'm in the final year or two of my apprenticeship at Ormulu, under Master Philemon Ettis." Farran said. This part was easy enough. He'd said it dozens of times. Maybe hundreds now, with slight adjustments for the timing. "Our role is to take an item and ensure first that it has been properly evaluated. That it is as stated, it is not a fake or fraud or has been altered. We examine it to see if it has any particular other qualities of note." He looked down at his hands. "We work with the non-magical auction houses, including the principal ones here in London.

But of course, Ormulu has a specialty in magical items. A significant part of my training is in identifying those items which have some magical property, as Albion would define it, and ensuring they're handled safely. That is much of what I'm here for. Though the cover story is assisting with the catalogue for an upcoming auction, ensuring everything is described properly."

"Which gives you a good excuse to look at each item. And, I presume, alert the appropriate person— people?— to items that need additional care?" Something in the explanation seemed to have pleased or satisfied her. She favoured him with a slight smile. Farran was not entirely sure how to read it. Of course, she was a performer by profession. She must be highly skilled in showing that connection to someone, as she chose. Getting them to lean forward, in hopes of a bit more of a smile or a laugh or a moment of her attention.

"Yes, Mistress Beaumont." He used her name deliberately now, partly to see what she did with it. "And of course, I've a wide range of experience with items to draw on now. My personal interests include classical art and jewellery— my uncle is a classicist, as I said— as well as art of the last century or so. I'm particularly interested in what are sometimes referred to as crypto-talismans, and decorative art with embedded charms or enchantments."

Something in that made her eyes widen for just a moment. "That seems quite a range. Crypto-talismans? I don't think I've heard that term before." Then she hesitated. "You may as well call me Vega, if you prefer. I'm used to it on stage."

"I am Farran, then." It suggested that she would

not disappear as soon as this conversation was over. "A term for an item that has enchantments similar to a talisman, but is designed not to look like it. No visible inscription that might be seen through a loup. They're often designed so that deconstructing the item would obscure the magical work entirely. Safer, in the era following the Pact, and a number of times since. But of course, there are limitations on the enchantment, they are tricky to spot, and so on."

"If you have experience with that, though, you must have a knack for it? Identifying which items that might apply to?" Farran nodded once at her question, and she went on. "That may be a help with my question, then." She hesitated in the way people did when they'd rehearsed how to say something, and now they were in the conversation, they couldn't put it quite that way. "I have been asked by my family to explore whether an item of interest to us, known to last be in London, might have surfaced in some form. I know approximately when it was last known to be here or anywhere, but I do not have a description of the item that's reliable."

"Bigger or smaller than a breadbox?" It was a somewhat flippant form of the question, but honestly it was a useful one.

"Smaller, almost certainly. It might be jewellery, it might be a, what did you say, decorative object. Bigger than a ring or a pendant, though." Now Vega was leaning forward slightly. "Is that something that someone with your skills could help with?"

It was an interesting question. Farran took his time to consider, as he'd been taught. Rushing at this stage could spoil everything later. "I would need more information in order to be able to say. Do you

have a means of identifying it if you find it?
Knowing that it is the object you're seeking, rather
than one of the many objects to be found in
London?"

"Yes." Vega said that with confidence. "Last
known to be active sometime around 558 CE, but
possibly older, most likely in the Roman era. I've
heard the stories of mudlarkers and such, but I— it's
more likely it's underground somewhere, possibly?
Or presumably it would have appeared by now."

"Which means it might turn up because of
building works or something of the kind. Is there a
reason your family thinks it might be found now?" It
was a highly pertinent question.

"Yes." This time, she was slower to answer.
"That's not something I can get into, but yes, they
think it has become more active. Or, just possibly,
that someone else might look for it."

What Farran wanted to do was ask who her
family was, the family that was relevant here. And he
couldn't. Not with the agreements they had in place.
Besides, she'd likely not tell him the truth if it wasn't
her true name. Beaumont was a common enough
name that it wasn't informative, and besides, it might
be a stage name. "And you don't know enough about
London yourself, a place to start?"

"No." She admitted it rather more quietly. "May
I ask if you have a suggestion?"

"To provide specific advice, I would need more
details." Farran considered the options. "And I
understand if you are not sure about that."

Vega nodded. "Quite. I am not certain how to
begin such a search, in a particular area."

"But for an item you might have some, what's the

word, resonance for?" Farran asked it rhetorically, not expecting her to answer. She didn't, not directly, but her eyes widened just slightly. That was enough to give him the direction to go next. "Perhaps we might arrange for a walk in an area of London, and I could talk through some examples. Along with, if you wished, my perception of the area in a magical sense. An hour or two's time, that would be a consultation. The fee card, here, if you wish to consider the options and let me know."

Those were kept in the holder at the edge of his desk. Farran passed one over. She took it, and then he waited. She read it twice, then nodded just the once. "Two hours of your time for a walk should give me an idea of how to proceed. And if you might help. When would be convenient? And where would you suggest?"

"I'd want to consider the specifics and propose a route, but perhaps from the Guildhall down to the Thames, then along toward the Tower of London. Several key locations in the city, each with their own history." Farran thought through his diary. "You have obligations in the evenings every day but Monday and Tuesday. Would next Monday suit at two?" It would give them time to do their walking before the crowds of people finishing work thronged the streets in larger numbers.

"Certainly. I should meet you there?" Vega shifted in her seat.

"May I send along a letter to the Crystal Cave, addressed to you, with a map and some details? But yes, meet there. It's about a mile and a half. I walked it last week, so whatever shoes you prefer for that. We won't go mudlarking, of course, ourselves."

Her mouth twitched slightly at the right corner. "No. I gather that's a specialist skill." Then she heard the bells tolling outside, five. "I've taken up plenty of your time. I'll look forward to your note with the specifics and see you next Monday."

Farran rose, offering his hand, shaking hers. He helped her on with her coat, then showed her out of the offices. He waited until he heard the lift descend before he went back to his office, closed the door, and settled down to make his own notes.

There was something about the entire situation that felt, well, much like an unknown artefact that needed exploring. It had that tremolo of magic inherent in it, the kind that had a subtle vibration to it, and that Farran was especially attentive to. And perhaps he'd ask Vivian by letter if she knew more details about Vega Beaumont.

CHAPTER 9
FEBRUARY 20TH IN LONDON

Vega had had little time or desire to think about Monday's appointment all week. She'd looked at the map and notes that Farran had sent along, but most of her attention had gone to the demands of her art and magic. She and Madam Helena had come to good terms— good for both of them— with a contract for a further six months, open to negotiations after that. Better yet, the agreement included the option for her to arrange a night here or there to guest at other clubs or do an independent performance, if she wanted. Not this month but perhaps coming into the spring.

It wasn't the agreement itself that pleased her, though it pleased her. It was the degree of trust and mutual appreciation that the agreement showed. Madam Helena ran the Crystal Cave deliberately and well, but she also trusted that this was good for everyone.

People who heard Vega elsewhere would come to

the club to hear more. And it gave Vega a chance to
try out some different sorts of music. Room to
spread her wings and experiment without the weight
and assumptions of the regulars who knew what they
wanted to hear. That would be excellent for everyone. They'd also agreed she might expand her reper-
toire at the Cave for a set every couple of nights and
see how people reacted.

The week's singing had gone well, though one
night she'd had an odd feeling. Nothing she could
pin down, certainly nothing she'd mention to
Madam Helena. But there had been a sense of being
watched by someone in the crowd on Saturday
night. They'd been terribly busy, the sort of audience
that kept moving from table to dance floor, upstairs
to downstairs. That alone had kept her on her toes,
even before one of the older men had wanted to
flatter her and praise her singing. He'd been a
delight to deal with, he knew how the game was
played, and he'd been pleased when she added a
favourite song of his as the encore to her last set.

But after, in her dressing room, Vega had come
back to the odd feeling. Being seen was one thing,
being a performer was about being seen. But this
had been somehow different, and she had not been
able to figure out who had been doing it. That was
the most disturbing part, given all her skills at
observing a crowd. Even with such a busy crowd, she
should not have felt this uncertain about it.

She had not seen Farran again as a guest, but
he'd mentioned in his note he might not be back this
week. No matter. The man had other things to do
with his time, obviously, even if most of that wasn't

obvious to her. A lot of talking to people, as well as whatever notes or research he might be doing. That was, mind, something that intrigued her about the walk this afternoon.

Vega was, of course, used to men wanting to chat her up. Women, too, not that she took offence at that. Some just wanted a bit of the glamour and the show and the beauty to rub off on them, and that was fine. Others wanted a bit more, but she knew how to fend that off. Farran had done none of that, other than having a quite sincere appreciation of her art form. In others, she'd have been suspicious that he was simply on his best behaviour.

Here, she wasn't as certain. Certainly, the man had good manners. But he was quiet, rather than flashy. He was confident. No, wait, that wasn't it. He was secure in himself and his skills, measured against others. And he'd been willing to extend himself a little, for the asking, but while asking for the usual consulting fee.

Doing it gratis would have suggested one kind of imbalance, charging more than usual would have been another. He had treated it as a straightforward agreement. The more Vega thought about it as she was getting dressed for the day, the more she thought that might be entirely disarming to the sorts of people who spent vast sums at auction.

Once she got out of the cab, she found Farran waiting out in front of the Guildhall. He was dressed as he had been the previous week. Today, he wore a suit that was impeccably neutral for the circumstances. Though this time, he wore a more vibrantly blue tie and pocket square that stood out against the grey, almost a kingfisher blue. She wondered if he'd guessed about her background, but there was no reason to think that.

As she joined him, he offered her his hand. "Vega. I'm glad the weather's not too unpleasant. Brisk." It was in the mid-forties, but that was what a good wool coat and charms were for. "Did you have questions before we set out?"

Vega stepped to one side, letting people go by. "You wanted to start here for a reason? And then the rest of the route?"

"Well. It makes an efficient enough chain of several parts of London. The Guildhall has been here and thriving for hundreds of years, and more than that, a centre of activity. The Thames in a number of ways. And then there's the Tower. And the Roman wall, just beside it. It's actually the wall I'm interested in particularly at the moment."

She tilted her head. "You have something beyond a walking tour in mind?"

Farran glanced away. She was fairly sure he was weighing how much to say and also how to say it. When he looked back, he said, "You asked about the process of perception. Listening, looking. For you, your ears are well-trained, obviously, it may come more easily."

That made her snort with amusement. "My eyes are also trained, though not in the sense of looking at the details of art." Stars were, after all, a rather different sort of thing. "But I get the idea. So you want to see what I sense, where we go. Without, mmm. Prejudging so much."

"Exactly. I checked. We can go into the Great

Hall if we're quick about it. Shall we?" He offered his arm, and she took it. Farran led her into the Guildhall building, turning from the entrance down a hall, then left into a massive hall. Vega knew, in a general sense, that the space existed, but it was much larger than she was used to, with great statue figures towering from pedestals, and livery badges hung on what seemed like every possible part of the upper walls.

"That is Gog - he has the flail. Magog has the shield and spear. You know the legend, I'm sure." Farran's voice was soft, respectful. Vega looked up, taking in the details of the carved wood, an eagle on Magog's shield, with all its heraldic implications.

"That they were the giants Brutus fought when he came to found Albion." It was not her family's origin tale, but of course she knew it. It was one of the foundational myths of Albion. There were dozens of songs about it within the magical community, some of which she was quite willing to sing. "Why did you want me to see these?"

As she stood there, she could get a sense of them, though, something in the underlying harmony of the room. It was tricky, though. There were so many things going on here, it was a constant buzz. Rather like being out on the street in the middle of the day, with dozens of noises all wanting attention.

"There are versions all over London. But there have been statues here since the Tudors. They'd be taken out for processions, nothing wrong with a good procession," Farran considered. "How old do you think these are? Or did you look?"

"I didn't." She said that first, then thought about

it, trying to get a sense of it from the sounds she
heard underneath all the clutter of the everyday
noise. Not Tudor, certainly. That was newer. There
was harpsichord in there, and definitely a hint of a
fugue played on a great pipe organ. Not her usual
run of instruments, but certainly one she knew and
knew about. "The first—" She hesitated, almost
saying the first half. "First decade or two of the 18th
century?"

"Oh, grand." Farran seemed honestly delighted
by it. "1709. May I ask why you said that?"

"Organ. An organ fugue. A bit of Bach, maybe,
or someone of the kind." She said it without
guarding it. Something in this conversation was
rather like the conversations she had had all her life
with aunts and uncles and her parents and cousins.
Somehow, this man she didn't know made a space
for her to learn and inquire, rather than be certain.

He nodded once. "Carved of wood. The
previous round had been eaten away. All right, that's
very promising. Shall we go? I think they need to let
people in for whatever's happening in here next."
There were, in fact, several people lurking near the
door, staff wanting to bring in refreshments. As they
slipped out the door, Farran gestured down toward
the south and the river.

They talked little on the way, and Vega appreciated that. The river was an entirely different
cacophony. There was noise and clamour in the
magic, in her ears, and in her nose, the stink of the
river. Farran didn't ask her to stop and focus on
anything. But when they got a bit of the way east,
where they had more space around them, he said,
"It's a bit much for me, too. But the Thames is the

heart of the city. Rivers know things different from what the land knows. And the Thames gives up her treasures, regularly. Do you think there's a chance that what you're looking for might be like that?"

Vega had to stop walking to think about that, wrinkling her nose. "I can't make out anything individual there at all. I'm fairly sure trying will give me a headache."

"Not something to try without suitable supplies, then." Farran said it, making it seem like a reasonable and practical objection. "With your permission, I could put a note out that I'd be interested in hearing about anything unusual that comes up, that looks like an item. Neither of us needs to sort through a list of, oh, rather a lot of awful stuff that ends up in the Thames."

"You'd do that?" Vega cleared her throat. "Yes, if you don't mind. And if the fee's not out of keeping with things so far."

Farran spread his hands. "If, when we're done here, you'd like to engage me for other work, I'm sure we can come to a sensible agreement. It's not a lot of time or energy, probably, it slips in with what I'm already doing." Then he shrugged, not pressing the point. "Here, we don't have time to go all through the Tower today. I'm more interested in the walls and then the Roman wall. There's only a bit of it still visible."

The Tower's music was unyielding, even when they circled up along the north wall. There was terror there, and something that was about strict order, and she couldn't make sense of it. The wall, though, that made slightly more sense. There was a definite split. "Some of that is older, yes?"

"The bottom - see the lines of red tile, running horizontal? That, I gather, is the Roman section. The upper portion is mediaeval. Can you hear the distinction?"

Given that cue, yes, she could. The upper portion, if she stood on her toes, had what she'd expect from the period. Reeds vibrating, a drum, crumhorns and whatever other instruments fit. The older section, though, that had echoes in it. It wasn't the sound of the music, exactly, though the music was less well formed here, like her mind couldn't produce an equivalent near as smoothly. Couldn't translate it, perhaps that was the framework to use. But she could hear the shift and also feel it. "Yes." Then she let out a little sound. "Pardon. That's a bit much."

"We've done a lot today." Farran considered. "I'd ask if you wanted to go to tea, but I'm thinking I should hail a cab and let you do whatever you find suitable after this sort of thing."

"Perhaps later this week? If you're free in the afternoon on the Saturday or Sunday?" Vega rubbed her temple; she did have a headache coming on after all.

Farran looked a little bemused. "I promised I'd see my uncle on Saturday. Well, Friday to Sunday. Monday next?"

"Monday next." Vega cleared her throat. "I think I would like to see if you would consult further, and to tell you a little more of what I know. If you'd plan for that."

"Oh!" Farran sounded more comfortable with that. "I'll send a note around with the options, then, so you have time to think through whatever you'd like to do. And if you'd like to suggest somewhere else to meet, glad to consider it."

Three minutes later, he'd tucked her into a cab. She looked back to find him waiting and watching until the cab turned the corner, still unsure what to make of the entire experience.

CHAPTER 10
FEBRUARY 25TH AT THEBES

It had been a quiet morning. Farran had turned up at Thebes Friday night, after a later train than usual. He'd caught the tail end of supper, and of course Lena had set a plate aside for him. He'd wanted to catch up more with Uncle Cadmus, and to have a look at some references in the library. But he'd been yawning repeatedly by nine, and he'd been asleep by half past.

Saturday morning was quiet— Uncle Cadmus liked time to read on his own— and Farran had gone for a walk through the grounds. February was never the most appealing time on the estate, but there was something about the quiet resting of the woods and the plants that Farran found extremely satisfying. It was like looking at an item that had been on some remote estate, barely handled or noticed. Then someone paid attention to it, and there was a moment where it became vivid again, at least in the mind's eye.

February was like that, the instant before the
vividness came back. Or at least it could be. The
walk was also reassuring in other ways; that things
were going well. He'd checked last night, and despite
some wind, none of the old leaks had caused problems. The doors hadn't rattled in a storm. Everything was tidy and tended to, the way Farran wanted
it to be.

The walk had also given him time to think. That
was both good and bad. The work with the auction
houses was going well. Master Philemon had come
out on the Thursday, to check, and had passed along
a good report from nearly everyone. The exception
was someone who was notorious for not noticing
someone until they'd been around for twenty years,
and there was nothing for it but time. Assuming
Farran didn't make some terrible error of judgement, at least.

After lunch, however, Uncle Cadmus and Vivian
made it clear they'd be chatting with Farran for a bit,
and there was the small procession up to Uncle
Cadmus's rooms. As always, Uncle Cadmus let
Farran come to his actual question in his own time.
That was something Farran loved, not being hurried.
He could count on the fingers of one hand the times
Uncle Cadmus had pushed or prodded, and he'd
always had good reason.

To be fair, the thing about being a classicist was
that it was easier to take the long view about almost
everything. It was an approach that had served
Farran well too. To be honest, short of the actual
auction or imminent damage to a piece, there were
very few actual crises in art. So there was the

pouring of the tea, and the asking about the current gossip of the house and the residents, and a couple of Vivian's latest projects. The ones she could talk about, of course. Vivian ran a private inquiry agency of sorts, working on particularly knotty problems. Even with Uncle Cadmus, there were plenty of things she didn't talk about. But she'd had a few interesting queries recently.

Of course, there was the other side of her life. The thing about Vivian was that she was not entirely human, and that meant she had both a different perspective on some problems and different tools. Also, it had obligations, and that was part of what Farran was wondering about in the way Vega was committed to this project of her family's. On an entirely practical level, it meant that Vivian spent about one week in four dealing with many familial matters, magical and practical. By this point, now he'd had five or six years to observe, it involved a lot of meetings with people, a certain amount of dancing as a magical and ritual form, stunningly good food for the occasional feast, and a lot of resigned patience. Cousins, he gathered, did not make decisions quickly.

If you'd asked Farran when he was twenty, he'd have said Uncle Cadmus wouldn't deal with that sort of thing well. But Uncle Cadmus seemed pleased for whatever time with Vivian he got, whatever they did in private. And it let him keep his own schedule much of the time. Farran rather envied that.

Auction work had more flexibility than a standard office job, or working in a shop, or anything like that. But it came in feast and famine. Long hours, longer the closer things got to a major sale or purchase. And then lighter ones, at other times, but with the perpetual sense that there was something he ought to be doing.

Once they'd caught up a little, Uncle Cadmus peered over his glasses at Farran. "We hadn't entirely expected you this month. Not that you're not always welcome."

Farran shrugged slightly. "I wanted a break from London. It's very— well. That's the other part I wanted to talk about with you." He'd been thinking about it all week, since that walk with Vega, the way the city had its own sounds and vibrations, and not just in the obvious sense. "Vivian, I had a consultation with someone, and I haven't been able to stop thinking about it."

"Oh, well, consultations. I might know a thing or two about that, yes." She leaned back, not quite touching Uncle Cadmus, but more relaxed. "Begin at the beginning, please."

The thing about Vivian was that she could be exceedingly intimidating when she chose to be. Farran had seen her do it once or twice, though never aimed directly at him. But somewhere along the line, he'd come to be more confident that she largely trusted his instincts. It wasn't anything she'd ever actually said. But he knew it as solidly as he knew something in his hand was an eighteenth century snuff box or a turn of the century pipe.

"Albie— Dunwich, a bit older— took me out to the Crystal Cave. One of the singers, she ended up talking to me, later. She was about to get in her cab. When she found out I worked at Ormulu, she wondered about a consultation. I know how to do those, though honestly, I'd expected it would be something more like a piece of jewellery she wanted appraised. Or silver, or whatever."

"The name?" Vivian asked it evenly, the way she had that made it hard to tell exactly how much weight she was putting on the answer.

"Vega Beaumont. She's been singing there for a few months." Farran considered. "Her note this week said she's extending the run. She didn't say how long. I made oath on the details, the second standard consultation oath. The part I can talk about is that she's curious about something in London, and where the feel of it matters."

"Ah." Vivian considered, the sort of silence that meant she was probably wishing for her file cabinets and extensive notes. "What does she look like, please, before you get into the rest of it? And what does she sound like?"

Farran wrinkled his nose up, because he wasn't sure how this was relevant. But this was Vivian, and she liked her questions answered. "Dark hair, long, not bobbed, striking against rather pale skin. Dramatic, not an English rose or peaches and cream. Pale blue eyes." He thought about the rest of it. "Wiltshire, probably?" Then he added, "Though who knows how much vocal training she's had? Plenty. Mezzo voice, with a gorgeous range, a lot of harmonics in it." That was something Master Philemon had trained him in, listening to that degree of detail.

Vivian snorted. "Such a help you've been trained to listen for it. Of Albion, though."

"Mmhmm. And English, not Welsh or Scottish." Both had their own underlying echo. He'd learned that, even if the lilt or the flow of the speech wasn't as obvious. "Anyway, I was curious about what she'd pick up. We went to the Guildhall, and then walked down along the Thames, the Tower, and the Roman wall, near there. She found the Thames far too complicated."

"Well." Vivian sniffed. "But not the rest of it?"

"No, though the Guildhall wasn't terribly busy. Well, with people. There's so much art in there." That was the sort of thing Farran loved, or a museum, until it got to be too much and he got a headache at the base of his skull. "She'd like me to consult further."

"Do you want to?" Uncle Cadmus got a comment in before Vivian, and that made Farran blink at him.

"Yes. I think I do? It's an interesting problem, but I'm not sure I can actually help," Farran said. "I'm not sure I can't yet, and I can't figure out who I'd suggest who could."

"Ah." Vivian tutted, amused. "One of my sorts of problems, then." She glanced at Uncle Cadmus. "What made you want to bring it to us, then?"

"Both of you." Farran said. "Because I don't know what I'm missing, I guess? It's an unusual question. Erm." He felt around the edges of the oath with his mind, testing each word as he said it. "Seeking an object."

"Huh." Uncle Cadmus cleared his throat. "I can see why you might like the challenge. What does Philemon say about it?"

"I've not talked to him directly, but by journal, he said that I'm quite able to take on this kind of side consultation if I wish. And that I have also been trained in how to decline or refer if I wanted. But I don't want." If he'd said this to most people, even most of the other apprentices, they'd have immediately jumped to Vega herself being the reason.

And she was, but not in the way any of them would have teased. She was certainly an attractive woman, but Farran had actually seen a number of attractive and stunningly dressed women in his line of work. Absolutely, she was talented, far beyond his own ability to appreciate. It wasn't just that she was brilliantly trained— he knew more than enough about music to know that— but it was her confidence, her presentation. Not that any of that mattered. She had asked him for his time as a professional, nothing more and nothing less.

But he'd also been able to show her something new, in the listening to the stone and the buildings and the river. Farran was curious about that, more than anything else. Most people, he thought, would either have ignored the idea, or would have backed away when it was first uncomfortable. Vega had done neither. She'd taken it seriously, and she'd been willing to explore the variation of it. Besides, the challenge of finding an unknown object was rather compelling. If he could actually make it work, there could be some significant professional possibilities down the road.

Vivian let the silence draw out. Then, she said, "What would you normally do about a potential client? The profile you'd want on them, that sort of thing. ."

"Normally, it's someone who's known. A financial overview, to make sure they can follow through on purchases. Legitimate provenance, if they're selling. In this case it would just be the fee. That's a different sort of risk. I'm out the time, if I'm wrong, but the fee should be well within her capacity." Farran hesitated. "You think I should?"

"It is a good habit. And some additional background here might be a help with the actual question." Vivian glanced at Uncle Cadmus. "Though it is a good bit easier to investigate something if people don't expect it." That was, after all, how she'd come into their lives, investigating something. That had been Farran's doing, and at the time he hadn't known what he was doing. He had just known that there was a problem at Thebes, and it was worrying Uncle Cadmus, and it needed fixing. And his friend's older sister worked for Vivian, and asking her was a thing he could do.

Now he flushed slightly. "Point. Where would you recommend I start?"

"Oh, there will be some profiles of her, I'm sure, if you check the Trellech Moon. Or the Trellech Library." Not that he'd have time to do that this week, almost certainly. "I've copies of a few things downstairs. You can look at those. Eleanor can do the searches of the Moon, if you like, and you're willing to cover her expenses. Not her time. We're less busy with that sort of task right now."

That was more than fair as an offer. Farran nodded. "I'll write to her on Monday morning, if you'd let her know?" Then he stood. "I suppose I ought to go look at things, then. And Uncle, you wanted me to look at the greenhouses again?"

"Since you're here, yes. Tomorrow morning, perhaps, when the light's better? Go look at books, why don't you? Or give Lena a hand with supper. You know she likes your company."

"I like hers even more." Farran stood and nodded. "Thank you, Vivian. And Uncle Cadmus." He left them to it. He could hear Uncle Cadmus asking something too quietly for Farran to hear, as he closed the door behind him and went off down the hallway.

CHAPTER 11
FEBRUARY 25TH AT THE CRYSTAL CAVE

Saturday was their busiest night, reliably. Not everyone who came to the Crystal Cave had to be up and about at a particular time in the morning. It was even less true on a Saturday. Magical folk were also less likely than the average Londoner to need to turn up at church. Now, she was peering out through the curtain from the back stairs, getting a feel of the crowd. Three sets, and Madam Helena had held Vega's place in the rotation until a little later in the evening.

Vega honestly preferred other nights much more. Saturdays, people were often more interested in being seen than in enjoying the music. Their dancing had a frenetic quality that didn't give any gifts. And it was definitely a night that more of the questionable potions and little packets of powders came out.

Not that Vega was a prude about that sort of thing. She didn't indulge herself, at least not anything made for general use. It wouldn't agree with her. She also couldn't deny that people sometimes needed an escape or a few hours with a lot less pain. But they did not need to do that at a table, taking up space other people might have enjoyed. Or, what seemed like half the time, making a scene that made things complicated.

Potions and powders might also have been a contributing factor in at least two-thirds of the times she'd had someone awkwardly declaiming his love, or occasionally her love. The variation was in where; outside the dressing room, the stage door, or flinging themselves on the ground by her feet. There wasn't a great deal of actual risk from any of that sort. But at best, it was uncomfortable for everyone. At worst, it meant it took her forever to get home. Not her idea of a good time.

As Saturday evenings went, this one seemed on the better side, at least to start out. She spotted several people in the crowd she'd not seen for a bit. She nodded at— what was his name? He was one of Celaeno's kin, name began with an R. He had his wife next to him, and he was someone she never thought would settle down. He knew who and what she was, just like she knew that about him. But he also made a point of tipping generously and being decent to the staff.

They had a table for two tucked against the wall. Vega had gathered from the front of the house that his wife— Beatrice, that was the name— didn't like a crowd. But what was his name? Robin. Of course it was. He'd go around chatting with half a dozen tables between performances and come back to his wife. Vega found it charming, in a sea of men who'd glance away at someone new as soon as take a breath.

There'd been some fuss about him a few years ago, but she'd been entirely busy with her own life. And besides, the Celaeno line, that happened more often than they'd admit to when they were older. Flighty, the lot of them, in a way that would be much easier to be around if they'd admit it.

That, though, got her considering the rest of the room. Most of the people there, she didn't know, but she'd seen them before. It was a good range of ages, mostly twenties up to fifties, a sprinkling older. More than a few being generous about it, bottles for the table, or a round of cocktails. That'd be excellent all round. Money spent on food and drink kept the whole place going.

As she parted the curtains and strolled out, she felt the flow of the room around her. Each of the charms was like a bead, its own unique weight and heft against skin and cloth. There were the lights, there were the acoustic charms, there were the enchantments that made the band sound even better than they did normally. The illusions, of course, for the second and third set tonight.

Vega had settled on jazz standards to lead off. She'd save the more complicated stories for a little later in the evening. Second set, rather than the third, probably, but as always, she'd play that by ear a bit. The joy of doing this here and now was that she and the band knew each other, and they were prepared for whichever order she called the music in. Being trusted to read the room, that was something she'd not been sure she'd manage when she started singing. And of course, if Vega could keep it up consistently, it would make her a singer in high demand.

Talent was one thing. Trained skill was another. Being easy to work with, and good at everything that came with being a singer? That was a great deal more rare a commodity. It was also the part she had the hardest time explaining to her family, who did not entirely understand that process.

Alcyone's line understood the dance, the procession of stars and planets through the sky and the seasons. They understood that no one person could be everything in the world. Each had skills and talents and an individual gift. But they were not made, on the whole, for the more intimate interplay of a performer shaping magic with her voice or her sheer force of presence.

The first set, everything clicked. The band was in grand form. Her voice was smooth, just the right amount of smoky purr for the club. People listened, or danced slowly, rather than chattering. When she was done with the set, she wriggled her fingers. "Back in a bit, darlings. Do give the band every attention. Weren't they fabulous?" Vega heard the conversation— and the drink orders— pick up as she strolled back through between the tables, letting the dance mistresses pull men out onto the floor. Including that Robin, apparently.

The second set began much the same, though this time she was changing up the music. A quick conference with Ernest, the bandleader, they'd agreed to spend a little time in some ballads and lore. Someone who'd learned some of the border ballads from an old Scottish granny might have blinked, but she found they made grand songs for a nightclub.

They began with "King Orfeo". There were
varieties of this, going back centuries, seven hundred
years or more. The one she sang was very much
about a love lost and found again. It had the shiver
of the Fatae magic, seeing as it was all about a king
losing his wife to the king of Faerie, and waiting for
her. Then he had to be brave and skilled enough to
claim her back.

Vega most loved the verses about Orfeo. He was
a talented singer and musician, a bard in the truest
sense. And he sang, first a song of joy, then a song of
healing, and then he's asked what boon he'll take.
His wife, of course, whether the song names her
Isabel or Heurodis, or some other form. It gave Vega
such a broad canvas to use. Her voice rolling through
the ornamentation, leaning into the magic and
charm of it. Oh, she sang entirely within the bounds
of both Albion's law and the Pact. But she could give
everyone a frisson of older times, when the Fatae
walked and danced and whispered through the land.

From there, she slid into "Thomas the Rhymer",
which had more scope to it in some ways, a variety
of speaking parts to distinguish from each other. The
band helped there, instruments sliding in and out
depending on who was speaking. The illusions began
here, too, gesturing at a tree beside her, or the roads
spreading out. High, low, and the narrow one
between. It wasn't until she was most of the way
through that she looked out into the crowd and her
eyes landed, as if drawn there, on that American.
Thomas Vandermeer.

His attention was focused on her, uncomfortably
so, for all she was up in the front of the room
wanting that, asking for that. It took her a second to

realise that she'd felt this before. The previous week, the way she'd felt someone had been looking at her. This had the same echo to it, faint elfin horns she could hear only as a whisper against the other music. Same person, same magic. Different from the first meeting, somehow, but the same as that sense of being stalked by a curious hunter.

Vega was far too much of a professional to slip, but it was a nearer thing than she wanted. She kept going, then as she drew the song to the end, she said, "Slight change of plan, do you mind? You'd all like to hear me do Tam Lin, wouldn't you?" She turned, mouthing to the band that after that. "Lady Isabel and Twa Corbies to finish the set." The trumpet player slipped off the dais to go tell Pasco about the change of plans. They didn't need him until later in the song. It would take a few minutes to get to the part with the faerie queen's trumpets announcing her procession.

Ernest raised an eyebrow, gesturing in the house code for 'problem'. Vega shrugged slightly, hoping he'd understand. He nodded once, and then the bass picked up a travelling line of notes, steady and stable. Vega came in perfectly. "I forbid you maidens all…" She let her voice curl through the early part of the piece before they got to the complexities. A rose plucked, a consequence. Vega had always rather liked Janet. The woman had the courage of her choices. There was a lot that was good in that.

It was a song that ended in love and in making a choice. Or, perhaps, the other way round. She leaned into that, though she could feel the shivers of fear as the illusions began to build. There were bare trees, reaching out across the space, along the walls, looming— Pasco was extending himself— then the glimpse at horses through them. And then, of course, the transformation sequence. The last of it brought Vega down to the ground, hands pressed flat, using every trick she'd ever learned of charm and voice to project. Finally, the triumphant conclusion brought her standing again.

The applause was overwhelming for a minute or two; the band stomping. She gestured at them, bowing, unable to get her voice to work for a moment. Then she nodded, and it was on to something more pointed. "Lady Isabel" was a curious song. Also, one that made Cousins nervous, since it involved a maiden killing an elf-knight. To be fair, he'd been trying to kill her, the same way he'd killed six others. Ballads were a terrifying business. This was far easier to sing, if also less of a showpiece.

The last song, well, that was an elegy. Ravens, watching the corpse of a fallen knight, abandoned by all he'd loved and valued. It was not a merry song, not in any sense, but it was a poignant one. And in this world, where people were not yet as far from the memory of the War as they wanted, she'd found it brought strong men to tears. But they were tears in a way that did something that mattered.

When the music faded out, the last line of it, there was silence for a good count of ten. Then someone began slow applause, then more, the swelling wave of it. Vega curtsied this time, Ernest coming up beside her to take her hand, kiss it, and then escort her back to the dressing rooms.

She'd not been there for three minutes where there was one of the waiters. "Beg pardon, Miss

Vega. A drink? Madam Helena's pleased. And there's a gentleman, sent a note."

"Something fizzy, please, and would someone ask Madam Helena what she wants for the last set?" Then she glanced at the note, and her eyes widened.

Thomas Vandermeer had been brief, but there was a sharp blade there. In plain block capitals, he wrote, "A private club indeed! I'm delighted to have had a chance to hear you sing. Do permit me to call. I believe we have interests in common." Just his initials, as if he were entirely confident she'd know who he was. She did. That was the problem. And it was a problem she did not know how to handle. There were far too many unknowns. It was like diving into a piece of music from so far back that measures and time signatures were gestures rather than anything predictable.

She didn't know quite why it made her so wary, save that she was convinced he had been there the previous Saturday, lying in wait. He'd been brash, certainly, but it was a known form of brashness. Vega was a singer in nightclubs. People wanting to presume and get a bit of her time and attention were common enough. Few of them worried her like this did. And there were, in truth, only four magical clubs with a focus on the performance of music, beyond the band for dancing. It made sense that someone inclined to a night out would come to the Crystal Cave sooner than later.

When the waiter came back— Roger, that was his name— he knocked. "Drink, Miss Vega. Madam Helena says, if you don't mind, leave it there for the night. And she asked if you want a hand getting out without whoever it was with the note spotting you."

"Caught her attention, too? Was he difficult?" Vega swallowed, feeling a rush of relief. "Yes, please. Give me twenty minutes to change."

"Yes'm." Roger promptly disappeared. Madam Helena's staff were all skilled as could be. Getting out without being spotted was a thing most of the performers needed now and again. That meant that Vega made it from the stage door to Fred's cab without a worry, back to her rooms.

She kept feeling like someone was watching her, or at least aware of her, in a way that felt entirely uncomfortable and worrisome. The sort of way that meant that she ought to talk to her aunts and uncles, and yet, where could she possibly start? Once she was home, she brought up all the warding, checked it twice, then again for good measure, before burying herself in blankets and pillows.

CHAPTER 12
FEBRUARY 27TH IN LONDON

"Your noon, Mister Michaels." Mrs Malden knocked briefly, and Farran looked up.

"Thank you. Feel free to go off to lunch. I'll lock up if I leave." She turned away with a sharp nod, and then Vega was standing there. And while she was feigning everything ordinary, Farran was certain something wasn't right. Her asking to reschedule from half-four to as early in the day as he could manage had certainly been a clue. She'd telephoned the office at ten, while Farran had been down the street. Fortunately, he'd planned to spend the afternoon working on notes for the catalogue, and that could be rearranged without too much trouble.

Now Farran stood. "Please, come in. I've nothing out on the desk. I could fetch some tea?"

Her mouth curled up slightly. "I could use a cup." Vega permitted him to take her coat, and he hung it up as she sat down. Getting the tea took a few minutes, and he brought the tray back. As he set it down, he realised she was far more plainly dressed. Her hair was up in an entirely ordinary sort of braid coiled low at the nape. Farran went back to close the door, then bring up the warding. As he sat down, he cleared his throat quietly. "You've had a problem."

"It's that visible?" She looked over his shoulder, out the window— an undistinguished view, just the wall of the next building. Farran was certainly not senior enough to have a good view.

He shrugged. "Perhaps not to most people. But that's some of how I do my work, sensing the state of things. Also, I grew up mostly in a house with a number of lodgers. Getting a sense for who's in a mood, for whatever reason, makes things easier."

She blinked at him once. "Oh?"

"Family home, a little outside Oxford. Big place, and when my uncle was raising me, money was scant. We took in lodgers, mostly people working at the university, a few widows. People who preferred a bit of company at meals, ideally intelligent, but their own space and less noise. These days, we don't need to do that as much, but we still enjoy it." Farran considered his antecedents and added, "We being me, my uncle, and our housekeeper."

There was a silence. "Not something you usually explain?"

"It's not usually terribly relevant," Farran pointed out. "But yes, I noticed you seem uncomfortable. Though asking to see me sooner was also a tip-off. May I help with something, then?"

She rocked forward in the chair for a moment, as if she were about to stand, then took a breath. "I'm sure you can't."

"But you're here." Farran took a breath and kept

himself steady. Master Philemon had actually talked about this a fair bit in their training. Items, especially enchanted ones, that had been in a family for many years could raise potent emotions. People needed to sell, to raise funds, or they knew it was a good idea. That didn't make it easy. Plenty of his training had been about how to handle the people in all stages of the process. It was as much part of his work as every bit of the art history and materia knowledge that had been poured into his brain.

There was a long silence, then she hummed something under her breath before speaking again. "It sounds like something out of a pulp novel. I met an American man on a bridge, Blackfriars, and he turned up at the club Saturday night."

"And you had an odd feeling about him." Farran could see that. "You're a performer. You've learned how to read someone's mood, at the least, if not their magic. What did he do?"

"Send a note to my dressing room saying he'd like to call. And I—" Her shoulder twitched. "I sang some of my best, Saturday night. I didn't last night, I stayed home. I don't know what to do now, who to talk to."

"Why not the Guard?" Farran said, first. It was the sensible thing to say.

"There's nothing solid there. He approached me while I was on the bridge, the way many men have approached me over the years. Or not quite the same, but there's no single thing that's obviously different. He was a trifle forward, but he kept his hands to himself." She glanced up, meeting Farran's eyes now. "Do you know how that goes?"

"Oh, yes. Not something I do myself, but I have

colleagues who make that sort of thing work for them. And I've had it done to me a few times, by women, hoping for an edge." Farran did his best to keep his voice even.

"Not something you cared for?" Vega's voice was lighter now, less of a sharp edge to it. "No, that's too personal a question, isn't it? Now I'm being forward."

Farran shrugged once. "Whatever my personal situation, that's not the way I'd choose to begin something. You either, I gather."

"No." The comment put her in slightly better humour, perhaps. "I wasn't sure he was magical. Not out there, with the noise of the Thames and the traffic and such."

"And while one can ask, circuitously, asking has consequences. And Americans have a different set of cues, and they're not anchored in the Pact the same way." Farran nodded. "So you made your excuses and left. I assume he doesn't know where you live, or you would think about the Guard."

Vega shook her head. "I've rooms in a lodging house, I don't do my own cooking. I take a cab to and from the club, though I could walk it."

"But not late at night, in your dress shoes." Farran said. "Quite." He picked up his tea, adding a sugar cube. That gave her the cue to add a bit of cream and sugar to her own, the spoon clinking as she stirred a few times. "What do you think I can help with?"

"Do you think he's—" Vega sighed, breathing out over her cup. "I can't help wondering if he's trying to find the same thing. It's a ridiculous idea. It's a venerable city, with thousands of things someone might find interesting." She gestured toward the window. "There are thousands of other shiny objects, beautiful women, even singers out there. Why me?"

"Did he say anything else about what he was doing? Or anything about his background?" Farran tried to think of the questions Vivian would ask. Or Eleanor, her assistant. That was easier to get his head around. Vivian was superlative at what she did, and that made it difficult to use her as a model, like a painter beginning by copying an epic work of the Renaissance.

Her chin came up. "Why are you asking?"

"My uncle's..." This was the trick. Generally, Farran didn't have to explain Vivian. People at Ormulu knew. She'd been the one to arrange his apprenticeship there. "My uncle's friend handles inquiries. She doesn't talk about the specific cases, but we've talked about how to think through a new set of information."

Vega's mouth twitched once, then her shoulder, before she took a breath and a sip of tea. Once she had, she said, "American. His name's Thomas Vandermeer, or at least that's the card he gave me. Thirties, maybe forty, sharply dressed, but not to stand out in a crowd. The details of the suit and the fit, you understand?"

"He gave you a card?" Farran said, but he nodded at the rest of it.

"Staying at the Hotel Cecil, or that's what the card said. On some kind of extended business, he didn't say what. But he'd had the cards printed, so not just a week or two." Vega hesitated. Farran could see she wasn't sure about something. "I gave him my

name, but I thought if he turned up at the club, I'd
— well."

"What's your sense of him, then, besides wary?"
Farran asked.

"Well, the last two songs of the set I sang on
Saturday were Lady Isabel and Twa Corbies. Do you
know them?"

"Several versions. Though most people will say
the Child Ballads, won't they? I rather prefer the
Donning versions." They had been collected by
someone in the magical community. Wenna Newton
had turned Farran onto them a few years ago. "Do
you know Wenna Newton? She does research on folk
songs."

Interestingly, Vega leaned forward a little at
that. "She's not foolish about it. I do like those. But
if I sing them, people— well, at least in London,
maybe Trellech would be different, I haven't tried—
get upset I'm not doing the versions they know
better."

"Oh, that's an interesting comparison of the art
form, isn't it? And it's not as if you could do a proper
study. Each performance is an island entire of itself,
while also being a chain of connections." Farran
considered. "Anyway. The songs?"

"I thought it was pointed." Vega shrugged. "I
don't know what he thought of it, except that the
note to the dressing room was after my set." She
looked away. "I'm used to people wanting to take me
out, get a bit of my time, hoping for more than that.
His note didn't feel like that."

Farran nodded. "So. I suppose the question is, do
you still want me to consult on whatever your question is? And is there anything else that makes sense,

given the, what's the word? Nebulous nature of the man?"

Vega let out a sigh and leaned back in the chair. "That."

"What can you tell me, then? On the consultation." Farran felt he was perhaps in over his head with the problem, though he'd write Vivian for her advice later, but he could possibly be of help.

"My family's aware of an object that may have been disturbed, enough it is potentially awake again. If you'll take that as a term here?" Vega offered.

"I've got a bibliography about the variants, but yes. More active, at least in potential." They were a particularly challenging sort of bit of material culture, because they came in many sizes, shapes, and most of all, effects. "What does it do?"

Here, Vega blushed, ducking her chin. For all her performance skills, she wasn't actually adept at dissembling. "We're not entirely sure, beyond amplifying magic around it. It might draw things to it or shift magic around it. Not if it's buried, truly inaccessible, but if it has some space to breathe."

"And we had established that it is smaller than a breadbox?" It was the classic question in a game of twenty questions.

"Yes, smaller. Portable. Maybe as small as a bracelet or torc or something like that. But I think it would need to have a fairly solid metal core if it does what we think it does. I have some notes from my family, but obviously not entirely reliable."

"Give the time scale, no." Farran frowned. "Is it safe for anyone to touch? Would it be interested in attention from anyone? Do you know the flavour of what it feels like, magically?"

Vega took a deep breath. "No. Not really. I'll likely know it when I feel it. That's not much to go on, is it?"

Farran shook his head. "Not enough. London's a big city. And I'm not an archaeologist, though I've been around a few digs. I can read a site report well enough, probably, or, well. I know someone I could ask, maybe. But that's a later step, likely. We might narrow it down based on resonances, materials, that sort of thing. Or the time it's from, there's a technique I saw for testing that, um. Two things are enough like each other they can resonate? It's a little tricky, but I've done it several times in controlled conditions."

"This is anything but controlled," Vega pointed out. "Aren't you scared of what it might be?" Then she shook her head. "Not scared, I mean."

"Respectful," Farran said. "I will not be foolish." He hesitated, then pressed a particular point. "Why is your family so concerned about it now? Other than thinking it might be more active again?"

"Mostly that." Vega admitted it, glanced at Farran and then back at the tea. "Wanting to know where it is. To get it back, ideally, though if it ended up in a museum in a managed state, that wouldn't be horrible."

"I might need to check on the laws that apply," Farran said, suddenly. "Giving no details away."

CHAPTER 13
THAT AFTERNOON

"Laws?" Vega pursed her lips. Not that she hadn't considered that possibility. But the Cousins wandered sideways around such things. Not because they didn't have their own customs and obligations. Those bound tighter than civil law. Rather, because the things they cared about weren't the same things that the rest of the world did.

That had been the point of the Pact, as her foremothers and forefathers put it, to make the distinction a great deal more clear for everyone. What her grandmother had said, when Vega had had this lesson in her schooling, was that back in 1484, having the patterns sorted better had been good for everyone.

The Cousins, those descended from the Fatae, could tend to their magics and their gifts and their obligations, without humans tromping through and messing things up. Humans could get on with their lives without someone being a trickster or worse.

The Cousin estates got much better protections in several dimensions, with people who'd agreed to do some of the more tedious bits of the work keeping them safe. Magical society had got a number of techniques out of it. As her grandmother had put it, everyone thought they'd got the best of the arrangement, which was ideal for a treaty.

The problems tended to come when a matter of the Cousins brushed up against human law. And especially non-magical law. Albion at least had an understanding that there were things covered by the Pact. Vega thought this qualified, but she wasn't sure. She certainly wasn't confident she could explain that to anyone in any kind of authority.

Farran took a breath. He was obviously gathering his thoughts. "So, there are laws about what happens when someone finds something in the ground. Who has the rights to it. Some of it depends on what kind of object it is. There's a difference between a hoard and a burial, for example. Or something found mudlarking. And that's before anyone gets into what the archaeologists want, which is to know where something came from, without anyone moving it."

Vega's chin came up. She couldn't help it, she could feel herself hardening. "And where do you stand on all of that?"

"Well, I'm not agreeing to break the law. On the other hand…" Farran held his hands up, a gesture of a pause. "Look, I need to figure out what the options are. Legally and otherwise. Can you tell me anything more about this? Why your people know about it, why it's been wherever it is, who it ought to go to."

"It ought to come back to us. To be handled

safely. You understand familial magics, surely. Does the law?"

"Albion's law does. Britain's? Not so much." Farran parried it back, promptly. "And it's been a while since I read it. It doesn't come up that often in my usual line of work. But I'm fairly sure there are clauses for familial pieces, specific lines of magic. But there may be some steps about proving that, in the Courts or such."

That wouldn't do. Or at least it would involve a great deal of fuss, multiple great-aunts and great-uncles who rarely left the family estate, and a lot of delicate dancing around explanations. Vega let out a puff of frustration. "I'll have to talk to my family about some of it." Then a thought occurred to her. They must be aware of that possibility. "Let me think about what I can say now."

Farran nodded once, then settled back in his chair and cupped his hands around his cup of tea.

Vega took a minute or two. Perhaps more like three. Then she began to speak, choosing her words carefully. "The object is something my family's been aware of for a long time. From the notes I have, it's possible one of our ancestors made it. Certainly the sort of thing that's been in the family keeping for a long time. The last time we're certain of its location was a little after 588. After the Romans had left Britain. During the time of the Saxon incursion." There were a number of ways to put that— invasion, attack, whatever one chose. Her family liked incursion, because of course, they'd been there all along, just as the early Britons had been. Before the Romans, too.

Farran nodded. "Made using the sort of materials you'd guess?"

"My family thinks it's most likely metal. Both because it's still active, and that, isn't that more likely with metal than with ceramic or stone?"

"Stone might last," Farran said. "But you're right. Silver or gold, especially, they survive better. Iron might have rusted away."

Vega hesitated. It wouldn't have been ordinary iron, she knew that. She'd have known that without having to see the notes. There was a chance it was meteoric iron, but saying that might give rather a lot about the family away. Instead, she shrugged and reiterated, trying to get her thoughts back on track, "Metal, they thought, more likely. Possibly stone. Not terribly large, smaller than a breadbox, like I said. More like the size of a slice of bread, perhaps, but not smaller than that."

"You said you've some notes. I assume that includes something about the shape or size, even if it's coming from lore or assumption?" Farran had started to fiddle with something, his fingers, a stub of pencil.

"Yes. And the general properties. We know it was carried sometimes, that sort of thing. Moved around, fairly easily, from location to location."

"Right, so not a large stone. Not the London Stone, either." Farran said it as if it were a joke, and Vega tilted her head. "Do you not know that bit of lore?"

Vega shook her head. She expected him to make fun of her for that. But then she took him in. Farran looked cheerful, not the way people did if they were about to hold something over your head. Not the way Thomas Vandermeer had made her feel. She took a deep breath, letting it out slowly. "What sort of thing is it?"

"It's a reasonably accurately named bit of lore. It is actually a stone. Some tales are similar to the Stone of Scone, but this one has been part of London for much longer. 1100, if I remember right, the earliest documented date. I'd have to look up what it's made of, but it's been there for a long time. You can see it marked on maps. People would visit it. By the 17th century it had iron railings around it, perhaps three feet high?"

"So, not the sort of thing you'd move around casually." Vega saw the connection now. "Or the Stone of Scone, I gather, though I don't know much about it."

"Exactly. There're some legends about Jack Cade —" Farran paused and glanced at her, and this time Vega shrugged and let him see it. "Led a rebellion against Henry VI. When he got to London, he came and struck his sword on the stone, declaring himself lord of the city. That's not how it works, obviously, even if the current demesne wasn't quite the same then."

Vega snorted. "Well, and imagine if you could change the Lord of the Land for the city just by taking a sword to a stone. There'd be chaos. At least the tales of Arthur pulling a sword out, it's clearly only one person who does, no matter how many people try."

"Exactly. I do like, what's the word, plausible results from my legends? Anyway, like any other mythical object of long standing, it's acquired a lot of theories and ideas. There's rather a well-devel-

oped one that suggests it was brought by Brutus
when he came to Albion and established us here. Or
there are tales about King Lud. The tale I like best is
about the stone being married to a water fountain,
the Bosse of Billingsgate."

Vega tilted her head. "The earth and the water.
That's something from Albion, surely. Or—" She
waved a hand. "You know what I mean, before the
Pact."

"Exactly. It's moved a few times since those early
maps, but always in the same immediate area. The
Church of St. Swithun, these days, with a rather nice
Victorian grille keeping people from chipping bits
off it as souvenirs." Then he shrugged. "We've gone
astray. May I ask a question you probably can't
answer, but that might be good to bring to your
family?"

"Yes?" Vega said it cautiously, because she wasn't
sure what made him put it that way.

"Is there a chance that this Thomas Vandermeer
might be looking for it specifically? People seeking
items is far more than a staple of pulp literature,
though of course it doesn't look like it does in the
serials."

"I have been wondering about that. You're right.
I should ask my family, who else might know about
it. It seems very odd to bring an American here,
though, like that. I mean. There's an ocean. And
while this matters to me, to us, it's not the sort of
thing that would be of interest to most people. Or
that most people would even know about. You
don't."

"No, but I am not a specialist in lost or misplaced
magical items, particularly. That's a long list, but also

a relatively finite one. I'd be interested in whatever your family knows about any sources that might have talked about it. I can probably figure that out myself, if I know what it's been called over time, a better description." Farran held up his finger. "Which I know you will not tell me now. Just laying out the option, if you don't want to do the research your-selves. Also, I can see how someone not bound by the Pact, here a brief enough time they only make the visitor's version, could be useful to a certain sort."

Vega put her hands in her lap, mostly to cover how she felt, a shiver of something powerful that she didn't understand. "You can't have access to all that sort of thing."

"No, but again, there's a finite number of items on those sorts of lists. If it's entirely unknown, then that suggests some things about Mister Vandermeer. And there are only so many items that are on those lists that fit particular ways. The age, the locations it's been in, the approximate size."

"And I suppose it is neither a gigantic sword possibly named Caliburn, or whatever the grail looked like, or any of those," Vega said, though she put it that way mostly to give herself more time to think. "But you're saying the next step would be a fair bit of research?"

Farran shrugged slightly. "Well. As I said, not an expert in this sort of specific thing. But wandering around London hoping to trip over it seems rather poor odds. Being able to narrow down both where it might be, and if there's anything that might allow someone to focus on it. Thaumaturgical identifica-tion by some specific feature, if the object has a name— though honestly, the research on that is dubious, I think. Triangulation in a defined area might work, but that involves knowing where it might be."

"That is definitely not in the pulp stories. Not nearly so many libraries." Vega shook her head, feeling more and more out of her depth, now. These were reasonable points. That was the thing. What was her family doing, just handing her this project with absolutely no further detail or support, or much of anything?

"Exactly." Farran fell silent, and the silence drew out, increasingly awkward. "Are you sure this isn't a matter for the Guard or the Penelopes or something of the kind? I could put you in touch with, well. My uncle's lady friend."

"No, thank you." Vega drew herself back, moving to stand. "Look, I need to talk to my family. I'll let you know if I want to proceed." She hesitated. "It's fine if you're at the club, it's not mine, after all. And you have good manners. Just— I can't. I need to."

Farran immediately stood, perhaps because of those quite good manners, but he didn't crowd her. "Of course, as you wish. You can write me here, or in the journal, whichever you prefer. I'll see the post promptly, except for Saturday or Sunday." He didn't move to help her with her coat, which was just as well. She shrugged into it, then went out. Farran followed, but only so far as to see her to the door.

CHAPTER 14
FEBRUARY 29TH

"Well, now, I thought this afternoon went rather well. And privately, I had several compliments about your work. I am not at all surprised, but it is pleasant to hear one's own evaluation proved out." Master Philemon settled down in his hotel room, gesturing for Farran to take the other seat. They'd just come from a tour round three of the four key auction houses in this project, and Master Philemon had declared it time for tea.

Tea in private, of course, which meant conversation to go with it. On the other hand, the tea looked delightful, a combination of tiny sandwiches and a tiered display of sweets. Farran nodded, taking one chair while Master Philemon poured out the tea. "Sir."

"To be specific, because we do revel in the details, don't we?" Master Philemon was in a good mood, apparently. "You were commended for your attention to those details. Also your ability to discern the line between when you should speak up and when you should defer. And particularly your ability to deal with several of the more difficult personalities with grace." He set the cup down. "Did Alastor Higgs really have three people in tears last week?"

"Three that I know of. Might well have been four or five," Farran said. He'd had that sharp tongue turned on him. But his first failed apprenticeship with Master Tambleton had apparently given him the gift of enduring that with grace, despite everything else it had been.

Being scolded and torn to shreds for something that wasn't actually his fault or his doing didn't have the same effect anymore. He hadn't argued, of course. That was a way to make everything worse, and with people other than Mister Higgs besides. But it meant Farran hadn't needed to go hide in a hole or a box room or the very back corner of whatever storage room was furthest away.

"I gathered he didn't get a rise out of you. An appropriate apology on that one piece about the vase." Master Philemon chuckled agreeably. "That's far better than most manage. Here, take your sandwiches first. You didn't have the lunch out."

Master Philemon had indeed had lunch out, a rather sumptuous one, at one of the clubs. He'd been hosted by one of the heirs of the estate being auctioned off, and they'd come back from lunch a good forty-five minutes later than expected. Forty-five minutes later than the buffer Master Philemon had planned, that was. Farran shook his head. "I hope I am seen as open to correction on matters of fact or evaluation, sir. But simply being shouted at..." He shrugged, and then said what he'd been thinking of. "After Master Tambleton, it's harder to get a rise out of me." Then he reached out for one of the small plates and took two sandwich halves to start, one salmon paste, the other ham and mustard.

Master Philemon considered. "Well, I'm glad there was some benefit then. Having the fortitude and the grace to deal with the difficult personalities will get you remarkably far in this line of work. I know I've said that, but it continues to be true." He took his own sandwiches. "How do you think things are going?"

"There's certainly plenty to keep me busy, and for weeks to come." Farran considered. "I have some questions about specific pieces after talking through it today. That silver."

"I'd noticed you were biting your tongue. Go on, then, or does it need your notes and sketches?" Master Philemon looked amused. "And I'd like to talk about the spoon, too."

"I can talk through it, sir." Farran took long enough to finish the salmon paste half, then cleared his throat. "I know the current analysis, and what we know of the provenance, suggests Dutch, sir. But it is possible it's American, instead?"

"What makes you say that?" Master Philemon leaned forward slightly. "We agree it's not actively magical, yes?"

"Yes, sir. Though there's one aspect," Farran caught himself before he digressed. "The maker's mark is badly faded. Or damaged." As if someone had tried to obscure it previously. "But the feel in the hand is much closer to that piece from Lewis Feuter we had through Ormulu eighteen months ago." He shrugged slightly. "There's an echo in the metal. It sounds in the head more like New Amsterdam than Amsterdam." Punning, of course, on the original name for New York City.

Philemon nodded. "I haven't been able to decide, and we got precious little time with it today. I'll see about asking if it can have some further scrutiny. Do you think it's anything that would dramatically change the value? Other than, I agree, that having an accurate provenance is important."

"I think it would depend on the buyer. And some of the American buyers might be interested, if there's a tie there. They do have money to spend." Farran pointed that out.

"And the other part?" Master Philemon gestured for Farran to eat, obviously about to go on. "Your touch on that is a great help. We can't just tell them that the resonance of the materia suggests something else, of course, but it gives us an excuse to dig further into the records."

Farran took advantage of that to have a bite of the ham and mustard sandwich before setting the plate down. "The other part, sir, is that while it's not inherently designed as a magical object, I'm fairly certain it's been used in ritual magic previously. There's that tremolo." That was the best way Farran had to describe it. Master Philemon had been clear that each person had their own preferences in such things. Farran heard it, an echo of it, a sound so faint that any background noise could disrupt it, and yet it was always there for any object of note. Master Philemon got waves of colour, a synaesthesia effect.

Master Philemon tilted his head, considering. "I could see that. I'd need to handle it more. I can do that tomorrow. Not recently, though? The ritual, I mean."

"I don't think so. I don't have enough points of comparison, though." That was the trouble. It was a nebulous feeling to start with, and the strength of it changed over time, depending on the material, the circumstances of the making, the history of the piece. "Maybe fifty years ago? Maybe a century."

"Which also raises the question of the actual provenance." The piece had supposedly come into the collection seventy years ago, via a dealer whose name had been lost. "I'll have a look at some of the records. The spoon? Or did you have something to ask first?"

"I did, sir, but not about my current assigned work. I don't know when you'd rather talk about it." Farran hesitated for a moment. "A private commission."

"Go on." Master Philemon moved to take a couple of the petits fours.

"It's a continuation of what I'd already mentioned, that matter with Vega Beaumont. I gathered some background on her, but there's not much before she began performing. She didn't attend Schola, or any of the other Five Schools, but of course most people don't. She has been building up her career, and she's well respected, it seems like. But she'd been singing on the continent most of the last couple of years."

"And you said she had a family request to find an object that might recently have been moved or come awake?"

"Exactly. I've a bit more in the way of specifics, but precious few details. And then I started wondering if I should continue. We talked yesterday, but when she left, she was frustrated. And there's someone else, a man, who turned up, and she can't tell if he's focusing on her for this reason or for the others."

"His name?" Master Philemon pulled out his small notebook.

"Thomas Vandermeer. American, she thinks, he gave her a card for the Hotel Cecil." Farran shrugged. "I haven't asked Vivian about him yet. I wasn't sure it made sense."

"She might also have ideas. What did she tell you about Mistress Beaumont?"

"Magistra Beaumont, I'm fairly sure. Even if that's not documented, either." Farran shrugged once. "Hearing her sing, it's quite obvious." He couldn't quite repress a small sound.

"What do you think of her as a person? You're getting quite deft at reading people, you know that. Your evaluation, please?"

"I like her. She's like something that's been touched and worn down a little, the touches of affection. A statue, a bit of bronze, worn smooth and shinier. Does that make sense? Or something where the handle's shaped to fit the hand comfortably, that level of attention to detail." Farran said it before he thought through the implications of saying it. But this was Master Philemon, and they'd long since established the habit of direct speech and honesty with this sort of evaluation.

"You like her. As a person." There, that was just naming it.

"Yes, sir." Farran wouldn't deny it. "And I don't think she has a lot of people to talk to about it, besides her family. I pushed her a little, about whether it was a matter for the Guard or the Penelopes or something of the kind. That's when she got frustrated and left."

"Huh." Master Philemon leaned back, taking a minute to think through it. "All right. You have a point. And honestly, the Penelopes might have a lot of fun with the problem, the useful sort of fun. But you do not yet have an obligation to turn it over. What did you tell her?"

"Before that, I said I'd check with you about the legal aspects. I know the basics, but I've largely dealt with things where we know when they came from and who is supposed to have ownership. Or where the question is obvious if we don't."

"Like our silver." Master Philemon nodded. "British law distinguishes between a treasure trove and other items, like a burial. Or an item that was dropped but not buried."

"What's the difference, sir?" Farran leaned forward, finally reaching for a pastry.

"Common law holds several factors. First, gold or silver in any form, it could be coin, plate, bullion, jewellery. Second, that it had been hidden deliberately and rediscovered. Third, that no person could prove they owned it. Fourth, the trove itself has to be more than half silver or gold. Less, and it's a different law in play."

Farran let out a small cough of a noise. "So a piece dropped, not buried, that's not a treasure. Or, I suppose, left in some underground room and not retrieved?"

"Exactly. Now, as it's magical, Albion's Ministry would certainly like to know about it. And for certain classes of item, there are requirements about that. But I don't think you know enough to be sure of that here? Did she share anything more than you told me about what it does?"

"Amplify. Or something of the kind. But how can you tell with an object from that long ago? Even if her family has more notes, hasn't the, I don't know, shape of magic changed rather a lot since then? As much or more than the vowel sounds have?"

It made Master Philemon laugh. "Well, yes. Yes and no. There have been many changes, and I can recommend a history for you, Roman and Anglo-Saxon artefacts, including some talismans and ritual pieces. If you wanted to do a bit of study on it, that would be a nice additional speciality for you to pick up. We're seeing more treasure hoards turning up here and there as the metal detection is refined, and you've already got the expertise in classical art pieces."

Farran nodded. "I'll think about it, sir. But you think I should continue?"

"I think it comes down to whether you wish to continue. You think she is an interesting person. You do not perceive a sense of harm or discord. You have some relevant skills. Then there's the question of this Vandermeer. I'd take sensible precautions, of course, but if you want to continue, I see no reason to stop now. With a conversation about what point bringing in the Guard might be necessary, so you are both clear about where that line is. You're hardly the sort to go putting yourself in danger for the sake of adventure."

Farran blinked, then snorted. "No, sir. Not my likely failing." He took a breath. "I'll see about talking with her more. You had questions about the spoon?" The spoon was both interesting and relevant. It was a bit of deft silver work with elaborate enamel on the back of the bowl. Master Philemon set into explaining the particular query he had, which was about whether there'd been a repair and how they might go about proving it one way or the other without risking damage to the item.

CHAPTER 15
MARCH 5TH AT ASTRALIS

In the end, Vega could not make it out to Astralis, the main family estate, on the Tuesday. Then, of course, she was working. After some back and forth via the journals, she arranged to go on Thursday once she was awake. The family did not particularly care about St David's Day, though the Cousins in Wales certainly kept it. Tradition did matter, and leek soup was tasty.

But there was a fuss for March second, and the tending of the wells on the property. All the wells, because all their wells had healing properties. If they hadn't when the family moved there, they did now. Also, that was just good sense, on a remote estate in the midst of Salisbury Plain and miles from any other settlement unless you went by portal.

When Vega came out of the portal— there'd been slightly less of a queue at Bedford Square than she'd expected— one of her younger cousins was there to meet her. Chara was in that liminal age. At sixteen she was old enough for tasks requiring some patience, but not yet ready for the larger world, not the way the Cousins aged.

And she was patient enough to wait quietly while Vega made her proper greetings to Aeterna, the current tree guardian. She'd been there as long as Vega had been alive. Her conversation these days was mostly done in shifts of a branch and leaves, rather than words, but that was no reason to neglect an old friend. Then Vega turned back to smile at Chara.

"The aunts and uncles are in the conservatory, please." Chara made a slight bob, the sort of gesture that Vega had not remotely earned, but which suggested that the seriousness of the visit had made an impression. "And I'm bid to ask if you would like a moment to wash up."

"Oh, don't fuss, please. And I'm fine, thank you for asking. Tell me, how are you getting along in your lessons? And did you want me to see if I can find any additional records for you when I get a chance? It might not be for a fortnight." It rather depended on how the meeting went and whether she, or possibly she and Farran, could make any headway on the problem.

That, though, got a cheerful babble of music that Chara would like to hear, given the chance, and it was a delightfully eclectic list. Vega made a note to see if they could arrange for Chara and maybe a couple of the others that age to come out to London for a day or two. They could see a play, hear music, have the fun of peering at museums and deconstructing the errors on the labels later. All very traditional amusements for their family, and they were old enough to start figuring out who had a head for time in the city besides.

Chara led her deftly through the various buildings of the estate, from the barns and workshops and sheds. They went along past the proper observatory with the domed roof, around one edge, and toward the main manor. Then it was down the hall to the east and the dawn, and the glass-covered conservatory. It was large enough in every dimension to hold full-grown trees. There was a seat waiting, and she saw four people. Not her parents. She hadn't expected them. They were not senior enough, and after all, it was Aunt Ancha and Uncle Thuban who'd arranged for this problem. The other two waiting were Aunt Mera and Aunt Helia, both among the eldest of the Cousins in the line who were still active in the world.

Now it was Vega's turn to make a bob to them, then a nod to Aunt Ancha and Uncle Thuban. "Thank you for the time, Aunts, Uncle. May I sit?"

"Please." Aunt Mera gestured at the chair waiting, which also had a writing desk pulled up close enough for notes. "Chara, dear, thank you. Can you stay for tea or supper, Vega?"

"Tea, thank you. I need to be back in London by half-six at the latest." This time of year, the family would be eating closer to six than ten, the times shifted with sunset. But she really did need a chance to gather herself before performing.

"If you'd tell the kitchens, Chara, thank you." Aunt Mera nodded once, and Chara went off promptly.

As she left, Aunt Helia nodded approvingly. "She's growing up nicely, I think."

"You think that of all of our line," Aunt Mera teased, amiably, another sign of adulthood, or taking Vega as a proper adult. "Now, you had questions, Vega. Begin there." Adult, and presumed competent to launch into what was needed with no fuss, the clear clean lines of a well-drawn chart.

Vega took a breath, because that was a part of her training too. Know what you were doing before you opened your mouth. It sounded better that way. Being a singer left no room for false starts. "I have been considering the problem that Aunt Ancha and Uncle Thuban brought to me. But it is unyielding in several directions. I cannot see a way forward without confiding in someone with more expertise. Also, and this is the other reason for the visit, I am concerned that someone else may be seeking it."

That certainly had their full attention, though of course she'd mentioned that much by note. Briskly enough, the sort of explanation that would be a working song with a strong beat, she moved through what she knew. Twined in was the much longer list of what she didn't know. "There is nothing I can pin down about the man in question, beyond the fact he is obviously magical, or he'd not be at the Crystal Cave, and also likely American."

"And we have fewer resources to inquire about an American. Certainly quickly." Aunt Helia tutted softly, mostly under her breath, as she thought. "We might have someone make inquiries. Vivian owes us a favour or two of about this size."

"We can certainly do that. If he is harmless, we should be able to determine that. If not, we may learn rather more. Once is chance, twice is worth noting, and three times makes a pattern." Aunt

Mera tapped a finger on the arm of her chair. "You do not like how he makes you feel."

"No, aunt. Too smooth. Not slimy, that would be a more deliberate feeling. Like there is nothing to grip onto, everything slides away." That got a brief digression between Uncle Thuban and Aunt Helia about the proximal causes of that sort of feeling, magically.

The main options were, apparently, a talisman, half a dozen learned techniques that were not terribly common, or more rarely an inherent nature. And of course, him being American complicated things. Albion had societies, and one could often trace the ways people taught each other through those and through the Five Schools. America tended to little knots of compatriots, much smaller groups.

No one had any better answer or idea than to try a spot of investigation. That meant that after a couple of minutes of making sure of that, Aunt Mera nodded. "You said you were consulting someone."

"Farran Michaels, of Ormulu. Apprenticing under Master Ettis, in the final years of his training. He is in London assisting with a large and varied auction being coordinated by several houses. Focusing on the magical items, of course, without drawing attention to them."

Something in the name made Aunt Helia's eyebrows go up, but Vega couldn't figure out what. She considered bluffing her way through it, but that was exhausting and her aunts would win, anyway. They would certainly wait her out if needed. "May I ask if you know him, Aunt Helia?"

"Ormulu has an excellent reputation, of course.

And Philemon's apprentices are reliably competent. The name's come up previously, nothing to concern you."

That was, frankly, even worse than an enigmatic silence. And it certainly reminded Vega why she normally kept her visits to the estate to the celebrations. They had their own mysteries, both in the religious sense and in the casual use of the term. But usually they also had somewhat less in the way of comments with more layers than a bushel of onions. Also, Aunt Helia had not really given her much to respond to. Vega took a breath, let it out, and waited.

There was a substantial silence. The sort that in an orchestral score would have been some poor player who had only a handful of measures at the climax of the piece, and spent the rest of the time waiting to play. Vega had patience for that kind of silence, though, at least for the moment. They sat, fingers and bodies shifted just slightly. After a good three minutes, Aunt Mera sighed. "We're aware of him. He does not know you're a Cousin, though." It wasn't really a question, because Vega would have said that already.

"No. But he's aware we exist?" Most people weren't, ordinary humans. Privacy was a protection, and in the aftermath of the Pact, the Cousins had needed a lot of protection. When the Fatae had retreated from the world, into magical spaces, away from humans, the Cousins had been the doorway. Some tales said they were too human to go where the Fatae themselves went. Other tales, and plenty of songs, told of how the Cousins had chosen to stay, to make and tend the doorways. The tree guardians were part of that, and the estates, and most of all the various work of the estates.

Aunt Helia nodded once. "We are asking you to take on a colossal task. If you decide to confide in him, that is your choice to make. But knowing that he is aware of us, that is necessary information. Now, you had questions?"

"Many, honestly. This isn't remotely enough information to work with. London is a vast city. A magically noisy city, Farran showed me some of that, directly, when it came to buildings and artefacts. I certainly can't wander around hoping to identify one item among thousands. Tens of thousands. And they're everywhere, magically imbued objects, who knows how many just below the surface." Vega let out a huff of a breath. "Well, fewer than there were a century ago, I suppose. They have dug more in the way of tunnels."

It made Uncle Thuban chuckle at least, and now he leaned forward, tapping his fingertips together. "We have been doing some additional research. And —" He glanced at Aunt Mera who nodded once, "I suspect that this Farran Michaels either knows a relevant technique or two or can recommend someone who does. We have what we believe to be a sample of the same metal, or close enough, as that used for the item. Worked, and worked differently."

Vega considered the options there. "Meteoric iron, then?" It was a logical choice for their line, who were not prone to blacksmithing beyond what was required to keep the estate running. Well, less than that, given that other than a meteor, none of them tolerated iron particularly well. Better than many other Cousins, but that wasn't saying much. But the protections that would make it easier to work would also have preserved it from rust more than the usual. "I can ask him, but having the sample would be a help, yes." It would have been a help several weeks ago, but she supposed they'd had to do research as well. "And the rest of it?"

"We have narrowed down places it is perhaps more likely to be, but that's not as helpful as you might wish. And we're not certain of any of it. There is a reasonable chance it's below ground, and coming to light because of new building or some changes of that kind. It is more likely to be associated with a place of both expansion and beginnings. Oh, and there's a chance it was gilded."

"Oh, like that's not everywhere in London," Vega said, before she thought better of being so outspoken. "Farran was showing me the statues in the Guildhall, and how they've been remade several times. The impact of the Great Fire, among them. The symbology is rather obvious, isn't it?"

"Beginnings and expansion." Aunt Helia nodded. "But there are some places more likely than others. And we think it was lost earlier rather than later. Before the millennium. That suggests some places over others."

"It does." Vega let out a sigh. "Any idea why, if Vandermeer has heard of it, he might be interested?"

"No. Not without more, mmm. Points to make the chart. Two is not sufficient. Two faint stars, especially so." Aunt Mera considered. "But perhaps you might come along to the library. We can show you what we have for notes, and see if you have your own ideas. Give me your arm, dear, would you? And then we can have a pleasant tea and talk about other things."

"A private sort of request, then?" Vega hadn't been sure.

"Your parents know what we asked you, but keeping it quieter, yes. That you're working on a task in London for us, you may share that. We do not keep quite so many secrets from each other."

"Aunt, you know perfectly well we all keep more than a few secrets, and enjoy doing so." It was, honestly, one of the only ways for at least half the family to manage living in such close quarters. The illusion of privacy and things in one's own head mattered a great deal. "But yes, show me the notes, please."

She stood, waiting for Aunt Mera to push herself upright, cane in one hand as the other took Vega's arm. Uncle Thuban offered his elbow to Aunt Helia, and they made a slow and stately procession along to the library. That was curiously empty for this time of day, which just made it clear how thoroughly the aunts had been plotting.

CHAPTER 16
MARCH 6TH AT VEGA'S ROOMS

Farran knocked on the door, a bit warily. Not that the building was that imposing. It was tucked into a small magical street near Bedford Square, where people without magic wouldn't think to look for it, even without the warding and illusions. The street was narrow, with houses and shops on both sides, but this was an ordinary house, more or less. Later Georgian, which made sense given the history of Bedford Square, but of course not nearly as posh.

A moment later, the door was opened, with an older woman peering out warily. "I'm here to see Mistress Beaumont." The woman stared at him, and Farran added. "Farran Michaels. Consulting about a piece of art."

"Oh. She said you'd be by. Up the stairs, door on the right. No visitors after half-eight. My ladies need their rest." Farran didn't argue. Lena had trained him better than that. Though he wondered what

Vega's schedule at the club did to that orderliness.
He nodded again and went up the stairs.

At the top, one door had a neat label in the bronze
holder, saying "Vega Beaumont" in beautiful copper-
plate print. Farran knocked just once before the door
opened. The rooms were small, and surprisingly, not
terribly cluttered. Why Farran had assumed her rooms
would have a lot of stray items around, he wasn't sure.
She wouldn't have chosen the wallpaper, of course, or
the furniture, but he could see a few things out on the
shelf and desk that had brighter flashes of colour.

What he could see was a sitting room with a
phonograph, a small sofa, a desk by a small window
that faced out to the street, and a small setup for a
magical tea kettle. A hallway led away from the door,
and of course he wouldn't pry. Even if he rather
wanted to know how the rooms were set up, since it
was the sort of thing he thought about a lot because
of Thebes and their residents. Vega had stepped
back toward the hall. "Thank you for coming here. I
hope it wasn't too much of a bother."

"No, not at all. A pleasant walk." She looked a
little surprised, and Farran said, "I take the Tube or
a cab or a bus, but I enjoy walking. Seeing different
parts of London. Each street has a different view."

"Oh." Vega seemed a little off-balance at that.
"Tea?"

"If you'd like." Farran couldn't tell if she'd find
making some soothing or not. "Where would you
prefer I sit?"

"Oh, there, the sofa. I'll pull over the chair."
Vega turned away, and the next couple of minutes
were spent with the kettle coming to a boil and Vega

putting leaves in the pot and setting out two cups.
She had only three, but Farran supposed she
couldn't fit more than three people in this space
terribly comfortably. Finally, she poured the tea and
sat down on the edge of the desk chair, her knees
together, looking definitely nervous.

"May I ask, um." Farran stalled. "Something's
changed?"

"For one thing, I have rather a lot more information from my family." Then she took a breath. "I beg
pardon, can I ask if you know someone? Or is that
inappropriately personal?"

Farran considered. The network of people he
knew was, in fact, a professional skill and something
of a professional secret. On the other hand, it was
his knowledge or his application of knowledge that
she was paying for. And he was sitting in her sitting
room. "We are not entirely proceeding in the ordinary way of an auction negotiation. Why don't we
agree that asking is fine, and I may or may not
answer? Or you, for that matter. Both ways round is
fair."

She blinked at him over the cup of tea, a delicate
set even if in an odd number. He thought it might be
one of the Staffordshire magical potteries. Porcelain,
with a deep purple design, but not one he knew by
sight. Turn of the eighteenth century into the nine-
teenth, most likely, but he could be a decade or three
off. It was in excellent shape, but it was curious that
she had this here, in lodgings. He took up his own
cup, peering at it, but of course the tea obscured the
cup itself, and he could scarcely peer at the saucer or
the maker's mark.

"Yes." Now she sounded more decisive. "My

question is whether you know Vivian Porter." She said the name evenly, but Farran had to catch himself before dropping the teacup and set the saucer down carefully.

"Yes? May I ask why you ask?" It was the sensible question, honestly, because there were multiple reasons someone might ask.

"Her name came up when I was talking to my aunts. Older aunts, you understand, with connections to many people?" Vega met his eyes briefly, then shrugged. "Through work, or something else?"

"Multiple ways. I knew about her for quite a while. A good friend of mine's older sister is her assistant. Runs the office, all that. And then I asked her to help with something, hired her. I was not yet twenty. I had no idea what I was doing."

Farran considered whether to say the next bit, but he had that instinctive feeling that it mattered. And Master Philemon had trained him to trust that, not fight it, if he couldn't see a logical problem with it. "She and my uncle Cadmus have been seeing each other since. Five and a half years or so. They don't live together. Uncle Cadmus is tied to our house in Oxfordshire. But she visits regularly, and he comes into Trellech to see her." Farran shrugged. The way they sorted their lives sometimes baffled him, but Uncle Cadmus was happy, and Farran was fairly sure Vivian was as well.

Whatever Vega had expected to hear, it was apparently not that. He got a glimpse of her surprise, before she formed her face back into something smoother, as any competent performer could. "Oh. All right. That explains something, maybe, that my aunts said." She looked as if she might ask something else, then shook her head. "They gave me more information. So I suppose the question is whether you're willing to continue helping. We can pay your fee, of course, and work around your other obligations."

Farran considered that 'we' and the implications. He couldn't quite fit the pieces together tidily there, but there was something lurking just outside his scope. Some detail of the piece he hadn't spotted yet. Or, more likely, didn't have the right angle on just yet. "To be frank, I am not sure how much I can be of help. But I am glad to try. And if you decide I am not the right person, well, we can part ways amicably."

"Who would you suggest, if not you? You've a sense for the feel of the magic. That's not something everyone has." Farran was about to say something else, but Vega raised one finger. He was caught by how fluently she used the gestures of the stage. It was her own particular mode of sign language, that framed what she was doing as smoothly as Lena's hands said what she was thinking. "I can scarcely go down to a high street shop and ask for an archaeologist of the appropriate period. Whatever period that actually is."

"And to be honest, there's not a lot of people doing work between the fall of Rome and Edward the Confessor. Some, but not so many." Farran scrunched his nose up. "Some of them are not very easy to be around, either." He'd met a few. One of the things about his work was getting invited to a range of parties of people who wanted to talk about their latest discoveries or their collections or both. "All right. How do we go forward?"

"Look, let me put out the notes I can share." Vega considered, then moved a small table over. "Still smaller than a breadbox, but possibly a plate or something like that, rather than something worn. Or possibly something worn." She went on, going through each point deliberately, which Farran appreciated. But it also seemed a more orderly way of managing information than many artists he'd met so far, no matter their art form.

"And this, here, is that an indication of materia?" He tapped one particular symbol. "I don't know that one."

Vega flushed. "It's not terribly common. Meteoric iron. Maybe gilded, but they're not sure."

"Higher chance of rusting if it's not." Farran said, automatically, then he looked up to see her seem startled. "Er. Is that, did I say something wrong?"

"Not the reaction I expected?" Vega hesitated, then moved to sit down on the sofa, still a couple of inches away. But here she could look at the papers if she needed to, without bending over.

Farran considered her age, the fact he hadn't heard her name in any of the usual places. That could mean she was using a stage name, but she appeared in various public records before she began singing. He'd checked, like Vivian had recommended. "You didn't attend Schola, I think? Where should I start with the materia explanation?"

That, somehow, made her relax a bit, visibly. "I had a thorough education in the subject, privately. My family. Begin where you like, and I'll ask questions."

"Well, meteoric iron has a number of properties

similar to terrestrial iron, but the balance of the ores. Much more nickel, as I understand it. Not my specialty, mind." Farran shrugged slightly. "Uncle Cadmus likes a bit of blacksmithing, though I don't think he's ever tried that. Anyway, I know it's much softer, it won't take an edge well unless you alloy it with something that will, or do a lot of work with it. Possibly magic. The temperature is a factor."

Vega was staring at him by the end of that explanation. "How do you know that much?"

"Part of my job? Oh, not meteors, yet. But identifying metals, yes. One thing I turn out to be surprisingly good at is getting a sense for the materia of an object. Of course, I can't just tell someone that a piece is a fraud, based on that. There's no way to prove it on my word. Even the truth-telling magics wouldn't help enough, they'd just confirm I thought it was true. But it means I can get a feel for an item, and then do the research more efficiently to prove what I already know."

She blinked at him now, as if he'd done something unexpected. Not bad, it wasn't that kind of reaction. And besides, Farran had got a little more comfortable talking about this the last few years. "I know someone who can tell you the publication date of a book within a three year period, just by picking it up. Odd but amusing party trick, but also very helpful given he specialises in books."

"What if something's been rebound?" Vega asked it, as if she were thinking about other questions.

"He stares at his hand and looks rather confused, and then he sorts through which bits go together. The faces he makes are particularly good when they kept the book boards, of course, especially if he can't actually touch them. A core of something older, the newer binding..." Farran gestured at the pile of notes. "The problem with your question is there is a great deal of possible material to sort through. But if it is meteoric iron, that feels different."

"Tastes different, I'm told by someone." Vega said it without explaining. "All right. Could we begin with that premise, especially if it'd help us narrow things down? Be open-minded about other options, too, but we have to start somewhere, right?"

"And it is a large, venerable, and busy city." Farran leaned back as he thought through the implications. "I think so. If you can give me a couple of days, I can probably put together something that will make it easier to sense that or, mmm. Make that louder? That's probably the metaphor. A soloist, not one of the supporting chorus."

CHAPTER 17
THAT AFTERNOON

Vega sat back at that. She had not expected him to attempt to put whatever it was they were doing in her particular idiom. And he was not doing badly at it. He'd do better, she suspected, if he weren't working solely off her public face. The way Farran went about the world intrigued her. It wasn't the same way her family would, but it had a deliberateness that she liked. And he didn't hurry over the details. Though, she presumed, an interest in the visual and tactile sorts of art objects would encourage both the details and taking time.

"A charm, then, or a ritual, or something of the kind? Or do you have a different method?" She considered, then poured some more tea for herself, and a little more for him when he nodded.

"I was thinking of something you could carry in your hand. I haven't done it recently, but we've used something similar at home, for spotting the places in a house that are having problems before they're visible." Farran spoke about it comfortably, but Vega realised he hadn't said much about where he lived.

"In Trellech? Or no, you'd said Oxfordshire." She searched back through her memory, but she hadn't paid a lot of attention to the chat that happened. Social lubrication, one of her aunts called it.

"My family's had a home for centuries, a few train stops from Oxford. Quite a large place, with two side wings, plus the family wing. It's called Thebes, the family tends toward appropriate names. My Uncle Cadmus, my father was Cilix." He shrugged. "My parents died before I went to Schola, and Uncle Cadmus—" Farran paused, the sort of pause that meant there was something complicated coming. "I mentioned we took in lodgers. It was a help paying the bills. But it also meant that both of us, and Lena, our housekeeper, got quite good at that sort of thing. Listening to the house and the property. Where the wood is rotting, that that railing really needs to be replaced."

Vega nodded slowly. "And that applies to this sort of thing, too?" She gestured at the maps.

"Well. That's the part where having more to narrow it down is helpful. You said your family thought it was made around 588 now. And that there's that alignment with Jupiter and Uranus in Aries. Those are particular definitions we can use for the charm. You probably know that?" He looked up, and Vega found herself looking into earnest blue eyes. She could not tell, not for all the music in the world, whether he knew who her family was, what her family was. Or if he was just that dedicated and determined and earnest all the time.

Only her training as a performer made it possible for her to match that mode, at least well enough to get by. "Private education, again. But we did talk about thaumaturgical definitions. So you'd do something with, oh, the sigils for the planets and the zodiac sign, and all that?" Questions were safer than statements, on the whole, especially when she didn't know what he knew.

"Exactly. I'm no particular artist about it, but I can do a bit of inscription on silver or copper. Enough for this, at any rate. Whatever we could define reasonably. Oh, I've done one when I was going to a market, with all sorts of shops, things that might be antique but weren't, actually. That sort of tool helps you sort out the fakes fast so you don't waste time on them. Or Master Philemon knows someone who has one tailored for ancient Egyptian artefacts, where there are a lot of fakes. If you get very specific, and you're willing to have a whole set of them— they take some particular storage— you can do them for specific materials, combined with time periods or places of origin."

Vega let out a small breath. "So here, we know when it was made, within a few decades. We know where it was made, at least within the city. We know what it was made of, enough, and that's rare enough to actually be a useful filter. We know it's more likely been underground than not, but we probably don't want to assume that's where it is now."

"And so we can narrow down millions of items to something a good bit more reasonable. The problem is, though, getting near enough to feel the pull. Or hear it. Or whatever sense we're using here, I think I've got tangled."

It made her laugh. "Which do you prefer, when you're not being polite and putting it in my mode?"

"Oh, touch, maybe. There's something about the feel of something? That's part of what got me working with Master Philemon." His tone changed a little at the end of the sentence. Not so much most people would notice, but Vega was trained to listen as well as to sing.

She considered whether it would be rude to ask, then said, "A problem before, and less of one now?" That could cover quite a lot of ground.

"Yes." Farran seemed relieved and sounded less strained again. "I originally apprenticed with a talisman maker, and it went exceptionally badly. Vivian has an extended commentary about it. He wasn't handling it well? But what he knew was that whenever he gave me something to do, it went oddly. Anything beyond the basics of shaping metal and stone, and sometimes that too."

He turned one hand palm up. "That's why I can do the sigils, though. If you don't need them to be tiny and gorgeous at the same time, the actual inscription is the first stages of the apprenticeship."

"I suspect you can manage smaller and more beautiful than you just implied," Vega pointed out. "Oddly? Badly, or just not what was expected?"

"Both. And he was getting more and more annoyed with me when Vivian, well. When I asked Vivian for some help, and Uncle Cadmus met her, and she was quite willing to help arrange something better. Master Philemon thinks the knack's quite useful. It's not predictable, always. It's a gift, not a skill, if that makes sense? I can't be sure how it will come out, with any given object. But I've learned how to judge what's going on much better, once something is in my hands. Or, sometimes, near me."

There were several dozen implications in that, starting with why no one at Schola had noticed it well before his apprenticeship. And it explained why he was a hair older, maybe, than the usual apprentices, and why he was willing to take a chance on this. But she didn't want to push him. They didn't know each other well enough for that. A change of subject was in order, theme and variations. "All right, so where do we start with this? A tool to help us, but then we need to figure out where to look."

"Yes. That's where the maps come in." Farran shifted a little, so he could pull out the main one. "We're probably talking about the City of London proper. Maybe from the Middle Temple to the Tower, maybe Southwark. Maybe a little further afield. But what would be sensible is to sketch out a series of walks that would take us through the more likely areas first."

"I can see the sense of that." Vega considered the maps. "And I suppose we don't know as much as we'd like about what buildings were where, at that point. Or what had been there. I know there's all sorts of tales about underground London."

"Well, some of it is logic. We might, for example, see about hiring a boat along the Thames and back, and see if there was anything. If there is, that's a mudlarking problem, and I certainly don't know how to do that sensibly. But we could probably figure out how to talk to someone who did." Farran looked up. "I am not fantastic with tides. Thebes is well away from the Thames in Oxford. It's on the other side of the rail line. And it's not like the Thames is tidal that far up."

It made her snort. "All right. The boat is a good idea. I can probably find someone for that who won't ask odd questions." She could, too, the family connections would be a help there. "Where else?"

Farran took a good minute to consider, then tapped several places. "The City, as we said. The Tower, though I think that's a lower priority? Both because I think it may be a good bit more confused, to try to understand. I'd rather do it when we've a better sense of the tool and working with it together. But also, it's been built and rebuilt and such quite a lot."

"And it has very visible warders. Rather trickier to just wander around." Vega agreed. "Where before that, then?"

"I don't think it's terribly likely to be in Greenwich." Farran said slowly. "But it strikes me that Greenwich would be a good place to try everything out. Fewer people, there's an extensive park, wandering around it is the expected behaviour. And there are some interesting spots there. Roman coins turn up, there are former palaces, there are caves."

"Caves, really?" That last one caught her off guard. She looked up to see Farran grinning broadly.

"Oh, yes, caves. Quite a few stories about them. I think they're blocked off now, but that doesn't necessarily have to stop us, maybe. I can do some more research."

Vega felt she was supposed to be a modifying influence, but the idea of things hidden in caves was entirely appealing. If the caves were safe enough to explore, anyway. "Find out more, then, so we can decide?"

"Then there are spots that some people think are cursed." Farran tapped on the map. "Cleopatra's Needle. Blackfriars Bridge. The Embankment might be relevant."

Vega shook her head. "Don't tell me you believe in curses like that?"

"No. I mean, I do believe that curses are possible. And that cursed objects certainly are, since I believe the evidence of my own eyes and hands. But do I think large pieces of urban infrastructure are? No. Not like people talk about, anyway. And while I would entirely believe Cleopatra's Needle might prefer her native bedrock as a foundation, it would take a fair bit of work to anchor a curse on that. Don't you think?"

"Wait, you've handled cursed objects?" That was Vega's first thought. Then she managed a nod. "The rest of it is good logic, I suppose."

"Some people have exceedingly odd ideas about what to do with their art. Or what to make into art." Farran said, his voice decidedly neutral. "We don't handle those sorts of items, but sometimes they turn up in an estate, and someone has to figure them out. The magical part is usually one of the Penelopes. They like the puzzle, and they are much better set up to undo it safely. Our part is talking about the object itself, and how much it mattered to the curse." He hesitated, then added, "I might tell a few stories, sometime, when we're better - more comfortable with that." It was a tentative gesture at something beyond a purely business interaction.

"I'd like that. I mean. Hearing you talk about

how you handle it." She laughed, a little nervous now. "All right. So we should wander by those, but it's probably not that."

"Exactly. And then there's figuring out what might have been disturbed or changed recently. There are closed Tube stations, for example, maybe someone got into a side tunnel and found something. Or that's the point at which we might start criss-crossing the City, as deliberately as we can manage given the way the streets actually go."

"All right. That's sensible. Is there anyone we ought to be consulting about, um? Where to look, or historical maps, or something like that?" Vega had not kept track of the Research Society for some years, other than vaguely remembering there had been something unpleasant there recently.

Farran, thankfully, gave her the information she couldn't recall. "Were you around in the spring of 1926?" She shook her head no. She'd been in France most all of that year. "There was a dreadful mess with the Research Society. More sensible people are running things now, but they're still stretched thin. Also, none of them quite have the right focus for this, I think, though I'll double check the directory just in case. You might know how they are, people get into tiny specialities. Carved horn buttons of the sixteenth and seventeenth century, but absolutely not the eighteenth. Books by a particular printer. That sort of thing. There's the other part, where it might alert someone who'd be interested for the wrong reasons."

"Like Mister Thomas Vandermeer."

"That is an entirely distinct problem, hopefully, but yes. I am not sure what to do about him, but that's why a plan that starts with us wandering around Greenwich seems sensible. If he turns up, we can be significantly more suspicious, or something like that." Farran sounded dubious. "I don't suppose your family had any thoughts about what he's after?"

"Not many." Vega thought back to the conversation in the library. "But one of my aunts was wondering about, you know how there's quiet discussion about making sure the Great War was the war to end all wars. But just in case, maybe it's good to remind people of that? New weapons and tools and all that. An amplifier would be relevant, surely, for a number of magical things."

Farran grimaced. "I suppose. Or there's still a lot of America to be developed and bought up, in terms of sheer land mass. It could be a purely mercantile desire. I suppose we shouldn't waste too much time about why he might want the thing, but focus on how to find it first."

"I'll talk to my family about how to manage some of that. They were already thinking about the problem." Vega glanced up and saw the clock. "Goodness. We've gone well beyond tea. I'm sure you want your evening, and I need to do a few more of my vocal warmups, or tomorrow will not please the listener."

"Of course." Farran stood up, then bent to gather up his various papers. "I'll write in a couple of days, when I have a timeline for the piece and ideas of where to go in Greenwich."

"Excellent." Vega waited until he had all his things, walking him not just to her door but downstairs and out to the street. When she closed the door behind him, her landlady appeared from the parlour.

"I hope Farran visiting wasn't a bother, Mistress." It never hurt to be polite, and while this set of lodgings was too prim for Vega's preferences, they were otherwise far better than many places she'd lived. The food was excellent and not stodgy, the other lodgers were interesting. More importantly, the sound charms were good enough that Vega didn't wake anyone coming home, and they didn't wake her being cheerful in the morning.

"Consulting for you, then?" Vega nodded once and the older woman coughed. "Well. I will say he was polite. Didn't track mud in, either."

He'd spoken not only fondly about the family home, but about the housekeeper, so that didn't surprise her. Not that she'd say so here. "He seems considerate, indeed, and I'm glad he could come here. A bit more privacy for a consultation of some delicacy. He may be by to meet me in the future, but I'll let you know if there's anything that might affect anyone here."

"Mmm. Yes." Her landlady looked her up and down. "You are also considerate, I'll give you that. I'll have something set out for breakfast for you tomorrow. Have a good night." That was a firm dismissal, and Vega had her own things to do, so she nodded, murmured the same, and went back to her rooms.

CHAPTER 18

MARCH 10TH AT GREENWICH

"Here we go." Farran stepped out of the boat they'd taken down from further upriver. It was apparently the sensible option, rather than weaving through the limited number of roads. Greenwich was very much of the water, and the Thames in particular. He turned to offer his hand to Vega, who was dressed for a sensible walk in the grounds.

It was a Saturday, and Vega was clearly not particularly a morning person. Not that Farran could blame her. She'd mentioned not getting home until nearly two that morning. He'd met her at eleven with a cab to take them to the river, and then the boat. They'd decided that it was better that rather than trying to juggle his own daytime obligations on a weekday. She'd yawned twice on the way out, but she promised she'd perk up. Farran had also made a point of bringing a small picnic in his satchel, or at least strong black tea and some sandwiches in wax paper.

"I thought we'd start here, where the old palace was," Farran said. It was an entirely ordinary sort of thing to say, given the history, but that was not actually his aim. Anywhere under the former grand palace of Placentia or Pleasurance, whichever name you used for it, had certainly been dug up and turned over dozens of times. But not terribly recently. On the other hand, there was always a chance that some item had come to rest in a vault or cellar or crypt, or whatever underground architectural feature might apply.

Vega nodded, following along with him, walking beside him but not terribly close, as others there to see the park split off into their own particular directions. Farran, however, had prevailed on some acquaintances, and thus they had permission to walk through the grounds of the Royal Naval College that had taken over the space..

The porter at the gate looked at the written invitation, back at both of them, and then shrugged. "The young men have their ways. You won't be a bother, then?"

"Of course not." Farran put on his best and most practised expression. "We appreciate the chance. I'm trying to confirm if a particular illustration matches the building sufficiently. We won't be terribly long. Should we come back out this way, if we want to go into the park, or just walk up?"

The porter considered that judiciously. "You come back and let me know, if you would, sir."

Farran agreed that was sensible, and then they set off on a walk, glancing around at the buildings. Farran waited until they were around a corner, then paused. "I've the talisman, or whatever we call it. It might work better if you carry it? An ungloved hand. Or your hand on it in a pocket."

Vega nodded once and held out her palm. Farran pulled the piece of his pocket, and the silk bag he'd stored it in, slipping it onto her skin. It didn't feel like it was doing much to him, but he had actually tested it in the auction house storage vaults on Friday, and he was confident it reacted to both meteoric iron and items made in the right century or so. She slipped it into the pocket of her skirt, then considered. "May I have your arm, then?"

When he blinked at her, she leaned in and whispered, "It'll make a better show from the windows, if anyone looks out. A couple having a pleasant time."

"As you say." Farran nodded. "My thought is to make a serpentine circuit, loop back through the middle. Then we can let the porter know we're done and go by the church, then up into the park. The older sites I'm most interested in are up there, but, well. There have been people here for a very long time."

"Lead on." Vega said. They made a steady round of it, down along a path beside the Thames, looping back through the main paths between the college buildings, around the other side, and back. The second time through there, Farran made a point of pausing and sketching something, a vista that had buildings at interesting angles.

The porter looked them up and down, as if they had actually done what had been asked, and that might have been a pleasant change in his day. Farran gave him a small tip in thanks. The right amount meant he'd be pleased, not curious. Farran followed up promptly by asking if there was a pub or tea shop nearby they should choose over others. That got them directions— he knew the publican, of course— and then directions to the St Alfege's Church, not far up the street.

"Who exactly was St Alfege? I'm afraid I'm not very religious." Vega kept her comment until they were out on the street, a bit shy.

"I'm not either, not like that? But in this case, it's a historical reason, as much as anything? He was archbishop of Canterbury in 1012, and he was martyred, as the official hagiography says, by the Vikings. There's an entire story about how he wouldn't let himself be ransomed and so they eventually killed him. And then, there's a tale about a cut piece of wood, immersed in his— pardon, are you delicate about historical murders?"

Vega blinked, stopped walking, and then stared at him. "I get enough crudity in other places. People lose track of their tongues sometimes. Historical murders? I mean, obviously there was one. Is this the sort that involves objects where they oughtn't to be?"

"No, actually. There's a tale about someone putting a cut stick in a pool of his blood, and fresh blossoms and leaves coming from it. Though, as the tale goes, he was stoned to death. You can tell him in iconography by the fact he's carrying stones in his chasuble, at least in some sculptures."

"Again, not my forte." Vega considered. "Like St Sebastian and his arrows?"

Farran beamed. "Just like that. It's rather useful, actually, if you're looking at manuscripts. Both for identifying who's portrayed, but also for dating them. Sometimes the depictions focus on different things at different times. It's a bit like dating maps."

"Dating maps?" Vega sounded startled. "And the church?"

"Supposedly where he was killed. Built on the site, rather." They were almost there. "As to the maps, there are lists of how you can date a map, narrowing down which names are used for what. You start one place, check an earlier spot on the list, until you find a beginning and ending point. Then you work back and forth until you find the spot in the middle." He shrugged and gestured up at the church just ahead. "Rebuilt in the 18th century, if you want the architectural history, I have notes. Also, where a number of the Tudors were baptised." He found that less interesting, though it made sense, given the proximity of the palace.

Vega shook her head. "Thank you, no, unless there's something particularly striking. You like the history, then?" Farran couldn't tell whether she was making pleasant conversation or whether she might actually want to know.

"The thing that interests me about objects is that someone made them in a particular time and place. Often for a particular reason, even if that reason was 'I broke my plate and I need something to eat supper on'," Farran said. "This, though, this is a new bit of history to me. I know a fair bit of Oxford and the countryside, and I've picked up other places." He carefully circled around naming Trellech directly. He didn't think anyone was close enough to hear, but caution was sensible.

"And St Alfege?" They had come to the doors, then, which were open. Farran held one for her, and let her go inside.

Speaking quietly, Farran offered the explanation.

"He's buried in Canterbury Cathedral. He has been since 1023. There's a story that Thomas Becket was praying to him, when Becket was killed. A saint for martyrs. And there's a tale that the killing blow was given to him by a Christian convert, to end his suffering. I don't know what I think of that, honestly."

Vega shook her head, then shivered. "I don't either. I am not much made for martyrdom, certainly." She hesitated. "Well, not for most of the ordinary causes."

Farran considered her and the things she'd said. "For your family, if they needed it?" He added, "I would. I'd rather not, of course. There's no after, then. You can't do things for them."

"Yes." Vega's shoulder twitched once. "Your family line. Are there others?"

"Uncle Cadmus has no children. I was an only child. There are some more distant cousins, but they don't know the house and the land." Farran shrugged. "I feel like I ought to make sure there's another generation, if that's what you're asking. If I can. Not the way some families do, but maybe not as different as I'd like to claim."

That made her laugh softly and relax a bit. "Like that for me, but I do have many aunts and uncles and cousins, so it's not a particular weight on me in specific. But making sure the family can go on, yes." She glanced around the stonework. "There's nothing here that particularly calls to me, but I can feel the history of it, if that makes sense."

"Well, there's a spot further up where they found some Roman artefacts in 1902," Farran offered. "Or do you want to sit down and have something to eat or drink first? Once we're into the park, it's just what I brought."

"The park, please. We can stop for a drink on the way back, perhaps, if there's time." Farran appreciated Vega knew her own mind about that sort of thing, and wasn't shy about making her preferences clear. Some people, men and women both, dithered no end about it, until everyone was starving and upset.

Together, they made their way out of the church, through the curve of the street, and to a great wrought-iron gate. "St Mary's Gate," Farran said. "And we just follow the path up from here." They walked for a little, following the main path diagonally south east through the park. Part way there, though, Vega stopped. "Can we go this way?"

"Of course." Farran let her take the lead, turning right, back toward the rest, along a smaller path. They ended up in a stretch of meadow, with low bumps of what might, a long time ago, have been more in the way of hills.

"Do you know what this was?" Vega's question sounded more urgent.

"There are some notes about it being an Anglo-Saxon or maybe a Roman burial site. There were some excavations in the 1700s, but nothing was kept safe." Farran disapproved of that, and he let it be obvious. "But yes, possibly the right period."

Vega nodded, turning to better speak quietly. "I can feel the tug. Is that the age? Would it be different if it were the right metal?"

"Pass it to me, do you mind?" He held his hand by his side and she pressed it into his fingers, holding it there until she was sure he had it safely in his grip.

Then he nodded. "The age. Erm. You might hear it as a different pitch? There should be something distinct. For me, this is sort of rumbly, like the bark of a tree, and the metal is smooth. In my head, I mean, not my fingers."

"In your head." She shook hers, then added, "I believe you. All right. Not here, then, but it's an excellent test. Where were we going?"

"There's a bit of a Roman temple that way. Or we can go up toward where the caves are. I don't know how much walking you want to do." Farran did some calculations, quickly. "About a mile and a half up, if we do both. And then maybe a mile back to the dock."

"Oh, that's fine." She sounded amused, and Farran glanced at her face. "I like a walk. Not as much when I'm in the city, but when I'm in the country, ten miles is a light day."

"Well. All right. This way, then." He gestured to the path that would take them back across the park.

CHAPTER 19
A LITTLE LATER

Vega picked her way along, looking around. More than looking, though, she was feeling. Or, as Farran had said, hearing. She understood how he could have a sense of it that way, but for her, definitely, it was hearing.

That meant it was an excellent thing she had trained both her ear and her mind's ear. People talked about a mind's eye, but Vega felt that went for all the senses. The odd part was hearing the sounds overlaid. Underneath everything, she could hear a faint sense of the music of the park around her. It was so soft she couldn't pick out any specifics, but enough to give a sense of the underlying musical tonality. Definitely in some major key, though not an army's march. The water wasn't nearly so strictly organised as that.

Then there was the musical layer of the talisman in her pocket. It had a comfortable sort of weight there, actually. She didn't have to be encouraged to touch it, her fingers wanted to. There were little

ridges - smoothed, but identifiable - that were satisfying to touch, in a way that was like her body
vibrating as she sang. That was tactile, but also it
wasn't. Now, it was a low hum, something that went
with the land around them, but a third up, or something of the kind.

Finally, of course, there were all the sounds
around her. Farran, intriguingly, didn't chatter. He'd
certainly been pleasant to talk to all through this, but
she was paying attention now to the fact he didn't
feel the need to fill the silence. Or demand he be the
centre of her attention. It was a pleasant change
indeed from many of the men, and many of the
women for that matter, she saw at the Crystal Cave.
She thought they were afraid they'd vanish in a puff
of smoke if people didn't perceive them in some
form, all the time. Personally, she found that
exhausting.

As they got closer to what must be their destina-
tion, Farran drew them along a properly angled
path, rather than the slightly winding one they'd
been. "This stretch, the path here..." He gestured up
and down a long path, laid out with straight lines
and lined by trees. "Has been known as Lover's Walk
for a long time. We won't be on it long, if that's—"

"It doesn't bother me if it doesn't bother you."
She said it, and it was true, but then she almost
stopped. Her skills on stage carried her through. The
thing was, she rather liked walking here with him.
Particularly, that he neither made assumptions about
what she wanted, nor assumed she had all the
answers because she was his client. And perhaps she
didn't just want to be his client, or not whenever this
was done.

That was complex, and she'd have to think more about that. It wasn't as if he were a Healer or a solicitor or something like that. If he knew Vivian Porter, well enough, as he did, the fact she was also a Cousin might not actually be a problem. At least it wasn't automatically one.

Now, though, she paid attention to what he did. He hesitated, then smiled at her. "Right then." It was not an informative answer about his emotional state, but he went right on. "Now, there was an excavation up ahead here. Take the left path." He'd been right. They'd only been on the Lover's Walk for maybe two score steps. Maybe a few more, not many at all. There were fewer people on this path, not that it was crowded, and a little further along they came out in a meadow again, with some rolling small hills.

As they got closer, a hundred feet away, maybe, from where they seemed to be aiming, she felt a shift in the talisman. This was a different pitch than before, which made her think it had something to do with age. Probably not material, unless these particular Romans had been working with meteoric ore. "Roman, you said. Earlier than we were talking about?"

"Just so. And coins, fairly ordinary ones for the period, but still exciting to the archaeologists and numismatists." Farran steered her up and around, making a little circuit of the paths so they could stop once no one was near them without being a bother. "A different pitch?"

"A third lower. Ordinary sorts of metals, then, too? What would you guess the meteor would sound like?" Vega kept her voice quiet as well.

"I'd guess either something rather higher or

rather lower— a low bass to what you have now? Or a soprano. Or, alternately, something of a different timbre." He hesitated, as if considering something. "I admit, I'm curious how you'd perceive a range of items now, given the chance to experiment."

"Perhaps when we're done with the immediate question, then." Farran had been about to say something. Then he blinked at her, startled. Vega smiled, the honest smile, not the performer's smile. She made sure of that. "I was thinking, walking here, that I like your company. You're both restful and interesting to be with. Most people don't manage both, never mind at the same time."

It got her another blink, this one slower, before he smiled, and she liked the smile even more. "That is a rather specific and pleasant compliment. Thank you. I'm glad you think so." There was a tiny hesitation, the sort that was properly a semi-demi-hemi-quaver, before he went on. "I've been enjoying today, too, and your company. I don't think we're going to find out more here, not without a shovel. Shall we go along and see what else we can find?"

This time, he did actually offer his arm, keeping on her left side, so she could keep her fingers on the talisman in her pocket. She slipped her hand through his, letting him take the lead. They walked clear across the park, steering for a particular path. "You seem to know your way. Have you come out here before?" She wondered, actually, what he did when he wasn't working or at home in the family estate.

"I spent a lot of time looking at the maps, and I've a good sense of direction." Farran admitted it, then glanced at her. "I'd have come out myself, but of course there hasn't been a free day I wasn't working."

"Wait, you feel—" Vega could tell by the sound of it. Guilt, or something close enough to be going on with as a theory. "Don't feel guilty about that. I'm taking your time, your free time." She wasn't actually stealing his time, she was paying him for it, but still.

"Honestly, if we weren't doing this together, and I was in London, I'd be doing something like this, anyway. By myself, probably, which is rather less pleasant." He gestured with his free hand. "If I'm going to be in London for a time, why not take the chance to get to know it?"

"Are you here for very long, then?" That was another thing. She was committed to London for a good bit, and her career wasn't easy on spending time with someone who worked during office hours. She had suspicions that Farran woke up at dawn to birds singing outside his window and liked it.

"A few months. And if this goes well, there's no reason I couldn't establish myself here, more. I hadn't been planning on it, but I don't have to decide right now. I can see which path makes sense when I get to the turns." He gestured ahead of them, where the paths were illustrating that. "Here, that corner goes out of the park. We're going to call on someone to make use of their back garden."

"Wait." Vega didn't quite stop. "What?"

"The caves are closed off. But one of the houses — someone of Albion, conveniently, though that's also how they stay sealed— has the rights to open it. If they like. I knew who to ask to know who to ask, and what to send round. Not a bother." Farran grinned at her, entirely boyish. "Part of the service."

"A bottle of wine or— not wine, up here, I suppose." Vega considered the houses she could see.

"A bottle of mead, and a particular green tea that Vivian helped me with." Farran shrugged, the movement shifting the arm in hers. "I like that sort of puzzle, honestly. Half of my work is the art. Half of it is the history of the art. And half of it is figuring out how to get the people involved to find something mutually agreeable."

"That is three halves," Vega pointed out.

He laughed, comfortably. "I leave the maths up to the accountants. Anyway, Mrs Allerby will let us in. There's a ladder down from her garden shed. And she'll alert someone if we don't come out the same way in a reasonable time. I am not highly skilled at the charms involved in caves. But these are supposed to be stable, and not the kind of thing we'd get stuck in, so the real risk is bad air."

"That," Vega said, "is rather a particular risk." She did not like that sort of problem at all. She was entirely used to air being at her command. "I see why you said sensible walking shoes, though." She was not enamoured of the idea of a ladder in a skirt, but wearing trousers was still a particular kind of statement. But her skirt was on the longer and sturdy side. And, well, she didn't think Farran was the kind to leer. Not unless she actively encouraged him to, anyway, and that was an entirely different category. Vega did like men appreciating her, if they had manners and good taste. It was hard to make a living as a singer without liking the idea in principle.

Now, they crossed out of the park, over the street, and then along a row of houses. Almost down at the end, Farran dropped her arm and went to

open the gate, obviously following particular instructions. "Here we go."

Vega could take a cue as well as anyone, and she
came into the garden; it was not much at this time in
spring, but what must be some lovely roses come
summer. Then Farran went up to knock on the door.
There was a brief exchange, and a woman in her
middle fifties came out. She looked Vega up and
down, nodded once, not disapprovingly, and then
motioned them inside. It was a terraced house. Of
course there was no way into the back garden
without going through the house. Or perhaps whatever alley ran between the sets of houses.

Vega cleaned her shoes off carefully on the mat
— they'd picked up a bit of dust on the way— then
added a charm to help. That got her a far more
approving smile from the woman. "I'm Lily Allerby.
Come through this way." It was a well-kept house,
but Vega tried not to pry. Also, the nuances of this
form of domesticity were almost entirely foreign to
her. She wasn't really able to evaluate them properly.

Give her a dress, a performance, a pair of people
dancing, and she could make informed judgements
about the state of things. A house, she was baffled by
whatever the precise angle of the cushions on the
sofa, the choices of pictures on the walls, or the
colours might mean. Except that Mrs Allerby apparently liked cats, though none were currently in
evidence.

Once out in the back garden, there was a tidy
little shed, a small terrace, and more in the way of
plants. Vega offered a bit cautiously, "You must have
lovely roses in the summer?"

"Oh, yes. Proper blood and bone meal, of

course, I'm a traditional sort. Now, here we go."
That seemed to have thawed her mood a bit. She
went straight to the shed, held the door open, and
motioned them inside.

There was, in fact, enough room to stand, but
there was also a trap door taking up a good half of
the floor, with shelves around on three sides. She
closed the door, and Vega could feel some charms,
likely those muting sounds. Farran nodded. "We're
just about when I hoped we'd get here. Two
hours?"

"Two hours." Lily Allerby nodded once. "You
can leave anything you don't want to take with you
here. Swear it'll be safe."

"I want what's in my bag, just in case. And I have
a journal, so if we have a bother, I can tell people
where we are. Here." Farran passed her several
folded pieces of paper. And, she thought, some
coins. "The paper will let you write to us, or see a
message. Vega, that's in the outer pocket, here, if I
can't write."

"Sensible young man, then. Enjoy exploring. Oh,
and there are lanterns there, they take a charmlight
well. I'll leave you to." Lily Allerby was apparently a
woman of few words, because she didn't wait for an
answer.

Once the door closed, Farran looked at her, just
the light from the shed windows. "Ready? You don't
have to come?"

"As if I'd turn down this adventure. This sensibly
managed adventure. Shall I take one of the
lanterns?"

"Please. May I go down first? I'll let you know if
there's any problem with the ladder." Farran did not

quite insist, but Vega was clear she might have an argument.

It would mean he'd see her climbing down awkwardly, plus whatever the light showed under her skirts. But it also made sense. She nodded once. "You first, me next. Go on, let's not waste time."

CHAPTER 20

IN JACK CADE'S CAVES

Descending the ladder took all Farran's focus until he was on the ground. It was sandy ground, not entirely firm. The lantern he'd clipped to his satchel stayed lit, and the air didn't seem too stuffy. "Just a moment." He called it up the ladder, then he turned to get a better look.

The ladder came down into the end of a tunnel, which led off to the northeast, he thought, if he hadn't got too turned around. From what he'd understood from the surviving records on these caves, they were one long chain. It shouldn't be too difficult to keep track of where they were and how to get back. Also, he had both chalk and a spool of sturdy black thread in his bag.

Now, he took a few steps back from the ladder, then tested it again with his hands. "Steady, come down when you're ready." He was going to stay there and hold the ladder when he realised that might well be improper. Farran stepped back, behind the ladder, giving her more room. Vega climbed down nimbly enough, making him wonder if she'd spent time in the wings of a theatre or perhaps up in the rafters for some part of a performance. When she was on the ground, she scuffed one toe into the sandy floor, then looked at him, meeting his eyes. "Shall we? Do you have a map or anything like that?"

"Some descriptions. The caves are supposed to chain together, one leading into the next. Do you know the charm for bad air?" He unhooked the lantern from his bag and held it up so the light illuminated much of the area.

"To identify that it's there, yes. To save us from it, less so. Shall I?" Farran nodded and waited for her to cast it. She spoke it like a proper incantation— of course she would, that must be part of her training as much as her singing voice. Then she nodded, obviously confident it had worked as it ought.

"Does that come up often in your life?" Farran asked.

"Paint fumes are a thing in a theatre. Or some of the materia illusionists use, or dyes for costumes. Mostly, I don't enjoy trusting to someone else's idea of what's safe for me to breathe, given that my voice earns my living. Even too much smoke can be a problem." She shrugged one shoulder, then took her own lantern off where she'd clipped it to the belt of her dress. "My. No one tidied up, did they?"

It was easy, given two lights, to see the gleam of broken bottles along the edge of the tunnel. There weren't so many that they littered the path itself, but they were two or three deep along the walls, every so often one at a different angle. "There must be rats down here, maybe other animals. Probably not people." He'd worried about that, before, but the benefit of the entrance being hidden by magic meant that was less likely. People from Albion did apparently come down here occasionally, a couple of times a year, for one reason or another. A ready source of chalk, for one. "Do you feel anything from the talisman?"

Vega opened her mouth— Farran could see the shape shift in the shadows— then closed it. "Maybe. It's hard to tell. Perhaps because we're underground?"

"That way, then. The histories I could find talk about three chambers, curving around, but all connected. The smallest, at the end, has a well, apparently, or did." Farran took a few cautious steps, then heard Vega coming behind him, a little back. That was good. If one of them slipped, they wouldn't both tumble into each other. Farran definitely did not consider himself a brave and valiant knight, and he absolutely was not much use in a brawl. But he felt it was more chivalrous to go first.

The path led straight for a bit, then curved the other way, forcing them to turn right and follow a semi-circle around to the left until it opened up into what looked like a new room. A vastly larger room. It was a good ten feet high, likely higher. More than twice Vega's height, so far as Farran could tell in the lantern light, and then some. And it was long, much further than they could see in the light they had. He could not tell if he heard anything moving, rodents scurrying away or not.

Beside him, Vega came to a stop. "I can do a

charmlight that will light the room, most likely. Would that be a help? Or a problem?" Her voice was breathy.

"It shouldn't be. Unless there's some magic here that we don't know about." Farran took a breath, considering. "I feel like there might be something around, but nothing, nothing that we'd be disturbing, if that makes sense?"

"And I feel a slight tug that way..." She gestured along the wall running off to their right. "That direction, but further. I'd like to see where we are, though."

"The light, then. And we'll be prepared to dash back to the ladder, if we have to." The thing of it was, Farran didn't feel unsafe. Not beyond the slight inherent nerviness of being underground. But it felt more like being in the vaults of one of Albion's banks, with a custos dragon at one end, and a series of small caverns cut into the hallway for storage. There were layers of magic here, and age, but not danger. "Oh, wait. Does it involve sound?"

"Yes. Why?"

Farran gestured. "There were comments about cave-ins, when they closed the spaces off in 1854 or whenever it was. The records are a little unclear. Let's back up under the tunnel here. A bit more protection?"

"And be prepared to dash back, if we have to," Vega said. "Right." She waited until they'd rearranged themselves, then Farran nodded, and she sang.

It was not the same as when he'd seen her on stage. She'd had no warmup, either. Some part of his mind had to point that out. This was what she was like all the time, what her voice could do, any time she chose. It was a rumbly sort of sound, well in the lower part of her range. Then, interval by interval, she climbed up. Not thirds, always, sometimes a second, sometimes a fourth, once a fifth. Farran had enough music and ear training he could identify it, even if he couldn't always sing it cleanly. The whole built up until she held a note at the top. She wasn't singing loudly, not enough to make anything vibrate, but he could feel her wanting to. He could feel the space wanting her to.

Vega had, he thought, far more discipline about her magic than he did. She held the note until the glowing light lit up the central cavern. There was a chandelier, hanging a little crooked, and it glimmered in the light. So did the many glass bottles. Farran looked around, rather awe-struck. It was one thing to have heard about the cave, seen some of the commentary. But he could see why people had come here for parties and gatherings. It had a majesty to it, even without the chandelier.

"Can you tell me more about what's down here? Or what's that way, specifically? Oh, wait. People wrote things on the walls!" Vega sounded delighted. She only took a step before stopping. "We should go together, obviously."

Farran chuckled. "We should. Let me tell you what I could find out. There are rumours, first, that it was used by Jack Cade for Cade's Rebellion in 1450. Possibly also used during Cromwell's Protectorate. Then people lost track of them until around 1780. They'd bring very civilised tours down here, but of course it didn't stay like that for long."

"I was thinking how grand a place it would be

for a club and dancing. And the acoustics— I'm not going to test, I remember what you said about cave-ins— must be superb."

"I was thinking the cave rather wanted you to sing, honestly. I don't know that I should say we chance it but..." Farran admitted, in his heart of hearts, that he might want to hear her sing somewhere like this, just for herself. Or maybe also for him, not that he'd ask her about that. "At any rate, the later gatherings, someone built a bar, there are the chalk pillars, you can see those, holding up the roof. And people would scratch their names or drawings in the chalk walls, or soot above."

Farran shrugged. "Down that end, there's supposed to be a well. With the flood in January, I'm wondering if it has water in it." That had been before Farran arrived in London. There'd been considerable worry about damage to the ground floor of the Tate in art circles.

"And then they sealed it up, at some point?" Vega asked before she nodded. "I'm curious about the well. And how far this goes back. Do you think it goes back to the Romans or the Anglo-Saxons?"

"None of the sources I looked at were sure, but I didn't have that long to look, just an hour on Thursday. They used a different entrance then, and they sealed it up. Go on, let's go around the wall, maybe, to the bar and the chamber behind?" Farran gestured for her to go first, if she wanted.

The cavern had many and rather intricate moments of amusement. There were sprawls of graffiti, of course. As was the usual way of graffiti, or at least as Farran understood it, most of it wasn't terribly exciting: partial names, initials, and such.

But he saw one recommending the ginger brandy at the bar, written, so it said, by one J. Johnson the day before Queen Victoria's wedding. The walls had drawings, too, some decidedly verging on the Hellfire club sort of Satanic design, a few crude.

By the bar, there was far more clutter of bottles, but also some hanging lights. Those had a faint sense of magic to them, enough to make Farran fairly sure they'd been lit that way at one time. The smaller chamber beyond felt rather like Uncle Cadmus's forge, honestly, like the closeness was a virtue. But also that it was not a place Farran wanted to linger, like there was something sacred there, but not for him. "The well?" His voice came out a little unevenly.

"The well." Vega turned to look at him. "This way, right?" She gestured across the cavern in the correct direction. He nodded, and they picked their way over the layer of uneven rubble on the ground, to an archway and another tunnel. Once they were there, she asked, more quietly. "Problem with the space?"

"Oh, no. I like enclosed spaces, actually. Just that, there, felt more… I don't know. Like it wasn't mine to disturb." Farran shrugged, trying to pass it off as a minor fit of nerves.

There was silence for several steps. "You too? Oh, good." Then she added, more conversationally. "I feel a tug from here, definitely. Do you know where the well is?"

"Yes. I don't know how much water is usually in it." They went along, the path twisting a couple of times, but with no further openings. Maybe fifty or sixty feet along, they came out in a room, about

twice as long as it was wide, with a well shaft visible.
Vega stopped about five feet from the well.

"May I sing? I don't think— I don't think what
we're looking for is there. But I think something is.
Does that make any sense at all?"

"Enough." Farran considered. "What will the
singing do, please?"

"Bring up what's down there, the specific thing
that's tugging a little. It's not dangerous, it won't shift
the water around. Just, um. Make whatever it is float
like wood. Or, I suppose, if you like the image better,
a bit of cork or a barrel?" Vega shrugged. "And just
listen. Not the right time or place to ask you to keep
a drone for me."

"Of course." Farran took a step to one side, so
he could see both where they'd come from and the
well, without twisting too much. Without further
comment, Vega took a breath and cleared her throat,
and then she sang. It was not in any language Farran
knew, and he had that same feeling of something
that wasn't his to touch. Some people, that would
have made them want to grab tight. He just wanted
to stay where he was, not breathing, not moving, and
experience it. It was a soap bubble, beautiful and
fragile and momentary.

Whatever the song was, wherever it came from, it
worked. He could see little ripples in the surface of
the well, glimmering in the charmlight from the
lanterns. Then there were more bubbles, something
rising from the bottom. Vega kept singing, but now
she took steps closer to the well, something out of a
processional or maybe a particular dance. It
reminded him, suddenly, of Vivian, the way she
moved when doing particular magic. Farran shoved

that thought down and away for some later and safer
time.

When Vega reached the well, she bent over, a
straight-backed bow from the waist, and then
scooped something out of the water. She brought the
song to an end, at what was obviously the conclusion
of a chorus or something of the kind. It was as if
everything shivered once, back into ordinary time
and less magic, then Vega was coming back to him,
as if this were an entirely ordinary Saturday
afternoon.

"A ring." There were still pitches in her voice, not
quite sung, but not quite speech, either. "See, there's
the stone. May I take this back to my family when I
have a chance?"

"You are the one who could get it back, so
certainly." Even if the laws about treasure troves had
applied here, which he was fairly sure they didn't,
Farran would not argue. "If it needs to go somewhere else, I trust you'll see to that?"

"Oh. Yes. That's fair." Now she seemed
distracted. "We should— we should get back, surely?
I don't know how long it's been."

"And the air's been well enough, just the two of
us here, but I don't want to test that too far."
Farran agreed. "This way, then." Going back was a
fair bit easier. Now it was just following the wall,
keeping it to their left, until they wove back through
the first passage again, and came out by the ladder.
This time, Farran let Vega go first. It was a matter
of a couple of minutes for them to make their
farewells, and to find a cab to take them back to
central London. An extravagance, possibly, but
Farran certainly didn't feel he had the stamina to

navigate a walk to the river or to find the train or the Tube.

He left Vega at the corner nearest her hidden street, before telling the cabbie to go on toward his own rooms. Once back there, he washed up— the chalk dust had caked on his hands and around his ankles something awful— before falling into bed.

CHAPTER 21

MARCH 13TH IN TRELLECH

"I don't entirely understand." Vega, frankly, was feeling rather dense and not at all in control of anything. She was standing in Trellech, which was fine. In a workroom at Ormulu, which should also have been fine. The ring they'd found on Saturday was sitting on the marble work-table. On the other side stood Farran, in the centre, and to one side, Master Ettis.

The older man opened his mouth, then considered. "You explain, please, Farran." He glanced at Vega, then added, "I think you were doing a better job than I was managing, actually." That was another sentence that Vega couldn't decide how to weigh properly. If it had been one of her aunts or her own apprenticeship, it would have been at least partly a test. But Farran didn't seem to be concerned. He shifted his weight, glanced at Vega, and then focused back on the ring.

"The ring is similar to a number of surviving Anglo-Saxon rings, though simpler in design than some. Made of bronze, it has a knot work pattern, and a small garnet. I am not a talisman maker, obviously. We can refer out to a specialist for appraisal. But I think it might perhaps be that which caused the dual sensation of the ring in the well. It is both from the time period under consideration, and a combination of metals that would fit within the parameters." Farran hesitated, then added, with good humour, "At least if you squint. Thaumaturgical definitions are always a hair imprecise."

The way he put it made Vega feel better. She'd been staring at the ring once she'd got home, because she had felt something from it, down in the cave. And yet, once it was cleaned up, it obviously wasn't iron. It didn't feel like iron, even under the gilt layer. And so, by note, she'd asked Farran to arrange for someone else to appraise it, properly, with the tools that would best suit.

Master Ettis nodded. "We would be glad to do some additional conservation work. There's a standard fee scale for that, I can give you a card. We'd also be glad to inquire if there might be a suitable auction or private buyer interested. Such pieces have a certain body of those interested. Especially given the location and provenance."

"I would like to think about it, first, please. And to check with my family records, before making any decisions. Beyond, of course, today's consultation fee." Vega gestured. "Would you be able to wrap it up safely for me? Are there any particular considerations for care?"

Master Ettis flicked a finger at Farran, who stepped aside, going to a side door, and looking for something. A box, presumably. As Farran did that,

Master Ettis said, "There's nothing here that indicates that it should not travel by portal, for example. Though that's relatively rare in the period, there being so few portals at the time."

Vega made herself nod pleasantly. The portals of the time had almost entirely been in Fatae hands, her Grandmothers and their far-ranging kin. The thing that had been nagging her is that the ring had a hint of that feel to it. When Farran came back with a small velvet-covered box, she nodded. "I'll take good care of it, of course. And I appreciate your time and expertise. Both of you. I'll stop by the Scali and have them make the payment arrangements, separate from the work Farran has been doing for me." Vega took a breath, trying to figure out how to say what she wanted. "I have been very pleased both with his skill and his dedication to the research problem. I hope it hasn't interfered with his other work."

"No, not at all. In our line of work, people expect us to have various private projects, as well as the more visible ones. The work he is doing is well within Farran's capabilities. This is an interesting way to use some skills that do not come up as often as all that. I am pleased we give such welcome service to you. And your family." That was ambiguous in the extreme.

Vega nodded once, then said, "Farran, might you walk me out? I don't need to take up more of your afternoon, of course, but perhaps we might talk again later this week?"

Farran nodded, but he said nothing until they were climbing the steps from the underground workroom up to the ground level. At the top— they weren't in the way of the main door— Vega turned to him. "Do you think Vivian Porter might be in her office today?"

He didn't seem to see anything odd about the query. Or if he did, he was an exceptional actor. There was no sign of it on his face. "It's Tuesday, so likely, yes. Though I don't know about her schedule. Eleanor Norton, her secretary, will be there, though."

"Oh, you mentioned, didn't you? Her brother's a friend of yours." Vega remembered that. Honestly, she'd been combing through their conversations in her memory for the last several days, trying to decide what she felt about most of it. "Thank you. What's the easiest way there?"

"From the Scali bank, you want to follow the street north. Her house is on the edge of the parkland." Farran gave her the specifics as if he were used to doing that, clear and concise. He didn't waste energy. That was something she'd noticed and liked already. And even more so since being down in the cave. He'd handled a situation with a number of possible dangers without either being careless or too cautious, and that was entirely too rare in her experience.

Now Vega nodded, then hesitated before leaning forward to kiss him on the cheek once. It was the sort of kiss someone like Vega gave routinely. It didn't mean anything particular. He'd know that, as surely and calmly as he'd known how to appraise the ring. When she stepped back, he smiled at her, which wasn't easy to interpret beyond Farran being just as pleasant as always. Then he turned, holding the door open for her. "Let me know when you'd be free to talk more. Or perhaps take a walk through another part of London?"

"Thursday, possibly. Let me double check my call times." She'd pushed things a bit on Saturday, and they wanted to rehearse a new illusion bit on either Wednesday or Thursday. She'd check. Then Vega smiled and set off through the door, before she had to figure out what else to say. The walk up to the Scali bank was pleasant enough, at least. And they were not terribly busy, able to make the payment arrangements for both today's consultation and to bring the payments to Farran current through Saturday.

From there, she followed the directions through increasingly quieter streets, to find herself before a pleasant house. It was detached, with a path to a small garden at the back, perhaps. Once she knocked, the door was opened by a middle-aged woman. "Good afternoon. May I help you?"

"Good afternoon." There was no reason to be rude, and many reasons to be polite. "I was wondering if Mistress Porter might be available for a few minutes. My name is Vega Beaumont. I'm working on a project with Farran Michaels, and I wanted her advice on an aspect of it." The thing was, she'd have to explain, if this conversation happened, and she wasn't sure how to do that. But she knew that being here, that needed doing.

"Oh, indeed. She's finishing up with a client at the moment, but they should be done fairly soon. May I get you a cup of tea? Fifteen minutes, perhaps, until I can ask her if she has time this after-noon, if you don't mind the wait. I'm her assistant, Eleanor Norton."

Fifteen minutes was quite reasonable, really, given that Vega had just turned up. "Thank you, that would be fine. Whatever tea is handy, please don't go to any bother. And Farran mentioned your name, and that he's good friends with your brother?"

"Oh, goodness, yes. Do call me Eleanor. There's a delicate green in the pot. I'll just pour you a cup. Here, come through here." Vega was shown into a small room, more private, and out of the way of whoever was in the office coming out. Eleanor disappeared into another room on the ground floor, coming back in a minute with a cup of green tea, and then leaving the door slightly ajar.

Vega at least had a book in her handbag, and she pulled it out, reading distractedly. Just about fifteen minutes later, there were sounds, muffled but audible, of someone being shown out, a door opening and closing. And then, after a minute, it opened again. Vega had finished her tea, and she looked up. "Mistress Porter will be glad to have a word."

The office was a deep green, the green of a living and abundant garden. There were different shades, the way the gardens on the Cousin estates were, not the dull sameness of some too-cultivated spaces. Against that, there were flashes of colour. One shelf had a deep purple teapot and cups, though of a different design than her own. There were books bound in all sorts of colours along with small statues and ceramics.

"Please, have a seat, Magistra Beaumont. How may I be of help to you?" The door was closed behind her, and Vega was in the moment where she had to move forward with whatever improvisation was called for. On the one hand, she was trained in

improvisation as much as she was in incantation. On
the other, this was a particular song she'd never quite
done this way. And she noted the title, that Vivian
Porter clearly had an inkling who and what she was,
or at least the level of her competence.

"Thank you for the time, on no notice. I was in
Trellech for some other business." Vega considered
her options. Electra's line, Vivian's line, they had
their own particular magic and customs. Just as Alcyone's line did. Most of the time, it wasn't necessary
for them to mesh and harmonise as precisely, but
they knew enough of each other to avoid the most
unfortunate dissonances. Probably. Then it came out
of her, with no control. "Does Farran know? About
you?"

It was embarrassing, that lack of control. The
older woman smiled, then stood, going to a shelf and
pulling out a small bound volume. "I think you
might reasonably call me Vivian, Magistra
Beaumont."

"Vega, please." Vega took a breath, then
managed to focus on Vivian's face. "I'm sorry. I
didn't mean to blurt that out."

"I suggested, some weeks back, that Farran
might reasonably do some research about you. He
has said nothing one way or the other about what he
might have found." Vivian lifted a finger. "The
common names in your line— he knows the ones in
Electra's line, now. He has been at gatherings at our
estates, along with his uncle. Farran is a thoughtful
young man, with good manners, especially around
the aunts."

"Ah." Vega had to smile at that. "I have found
him polite, considerate, and quite skilled. Though I

admit, I don't know enough about his work to measure it. But he seems, am I right, to have a particular knack for materia?"

"He does. It got him into trouble, his first apprenticeship. Unbalancing the work. Philemon has done a wonderful job of building his confidence and trusting his intuition and sense of a piece. And then, of course, using that to back up his initial impressions with proper authoritative resources and testing. He has a good eye, aesthetically. He's done some work with other Cousins." She didn't say who, but of course Vega didn't expect confidences here. Not of the professional sort. Vivian leaned back, considering Vega. "Are you inquiring in a more general sense? I take an interest in his well-being."

"His uncle, he mentioned. Farran speaks quite warmly of him." Vega almost went on, but she wanted to see if there was any reaction to that.

"They've only had each other as family for some years. Well, and their housekeeper." Vivian glanced toward the bookshelves, a few photographs there. "Are you interested on a personal level?"

Put like that, that bluntly, Vega could only nod. "A curiosity, at least. I— we did some exploration, Saturday. And it was, you must have an idea. A life which has many pleasures in it, my own skills. But it was an afternoon that was just enjoyable, on every level I can think of, except perhaps other people's inability to pick up after themselves. I enjoyed talking to him, I enjoyed learning what he knew. I enjoyed being with him. And I keep coming back to that."

It earned her a warmer smile, so perhaps being forthcoming had been a good choice. "For all Cadmus is something of a hermit, he and Farran are

quite warm to those they welcome closer. Their residents. Me, for some years now. Others, on occasion."
Vivian tapped one finger on the desk in front of her.
"If you are asking if you should tell Farran of your
background, I cannot make that choice for you. I did
not handle matters well when Cadmus learned it,
though I had my reasons. I do not think Farran
would take it poorly, shall we say? His work has given
him an excellent framework for understanding that
different families have their own customs and priorities. He would take lying to him directly badly, but
he understands the art of not saying all the truth and
he doesn't begrudge it."

That was extremely helpful information, and an
even more useful way of putting it. "I appreciate
that. I am— I am inclined to find a time to say
something, when we have space and privacy enough.
I don't know when that will be."

"Not a conversation for a nightclub, no, I
expect." There was a knock on the door, and Vivian
looked up. "A moment. Yes, Eleanor?" The door
opened, and Eleanor put her head into the room.

"Beg pardon, Vivian, but there's a note about
that matter. Marked with some urgency." She
waited, half in the door.

"Ah, I beg pardon, Vega, but I need to see to this.
Come by and talk again, if you'd like. Or write in
the journals, if you need a bit of advice. Or want to
let me know something relevant?" Vega could interpret that. If Farran might turn up needing a
shoulder or a bit of family.

Vega nodded. "You've been generous with both
your time and your expertise. I appreciate it no end."
She added, almost at the last moment, "I'm guessing

you and Master Michaels are not the sort to want to come to London. But I'd be glad to arrange a table and supper for you, if you wished to. While I'm singing there, of course."

It made Vivian laugh. "Oh, the idea. It amuses. I suspect not, but I will ask Cadmus rather than brushing it off. A good afternoon to you, then, and I'm glad I could be of some clarification."

Half a minute later, Vega found herself back outside, and the only thing she could think of to do was go back to London and her notes.

CHAPTER 22
MARCH 15TH EXPLORING LONDON

"What's the timing today? I thought we might walk along the river and Embankment. Then you'd be in a suitable spot to get a cab. Or the Tube, but I know you'd rather not." Farran had met Vega just outside the Blackfriars stop. Now, he wasn't sure about what she was thinking. She'd dressed for the weather and a substantial stroll, but she looked more spruced up than she had on Saturday, in a rather becoming green frock. Not that Farran was the most adept at that sort of thing, since most of the women he knew, other than those at Ormulu, tended to dress neatly, but not. Well, not like whatever that was.

She turned to him, smiling. "Oh, that sounds fine. Further than that, didn't you say, in your note, if I wanted?"

"Several historical sites that aren't strictly relevant to what we're doing, but they're interesting and we're here." Farran gestured. "Longer route this way."

"I don't really feel the need to stand on Black-friars again. I heard some stories about it. Curses and ghosts." Vega tilted her head, then waited for Farran to show where they were going. He didn't want to offer his arm, since the streets were busy enough to make that impolite to everyone else. But she stayed right beside him, and he kept her on the inside of the street, to avoid her dress getting splashed. "Do you think there's any truth to that sort of tale?"

"Ah, that's a question for a less crowded street. Here, let's cross. We're going to the church, there." Farran indicated the church on the other side of the street.

"St Bride's?" Once they'd got across the street, Vega peered at the sign.

"Older than it looks. Or rather, the site is. There's been a church here since the 6th century, but it's the healing well we're interested in. This one is a Christopher Wren, rebuilt after the Great Fire, but there are several earlier ones. And a strong associa-tion with Fleet Street and journalists, of course. And the printing press, before that; Caxton's press was closer to Westminster, but his apprentice set up here. Wynkyn de Worde, appropriately named, don't you think?" Farran peered, then gestured. "Along this side of the church, there's an alley."

The alley was narrow, but clean enough, and at the far end there was a gate. "I gather the well's been dry for some time, but there's likely water deeper. The Fleet is a river, of course, covered over the last century. You can imagine it, though, there were docks along here at one point."

"Exactly how much reading did you do about

this part of our tour?" Vega was smiling as she said it. "Don't stop, please. I'm trying to decide how much I should apologise for your late nights reading up. Or are you getting up early?"

"Staying up later, mostly. Or there's a good stretch between supper and bedtime, honestly, if I don't have to make a show of being social." Farran shrugged. "Not really a morning person, though I can manage it when I have to." And he'd enjoyed doing the reading, knowing he'd share it with her, that she seemed to like the stories and bits of trivia and making the buildings come alive.

"Really? I was thinking Saturday you were the sort of person who'd be up and about and cheerful about it. I, of course, prefer to see morning only from a very late night." That, at least, had been true for a long time. All her family tended to be night owls. It went well with stargazing, and all the associated magics and rituals. Then she took a breath and paid attention to what she was feeling. Farran made no attempt to go into the church, and it wasn't really the church they were interested in. "Oh!"

"The water?" Farran asked.

"Yes. Not just the usual damp of England or of London, but a more purposeful sort of water." She took a step back and forth, as if getting a sense of the changes under her feet, almost a dance. "Especially now we're a little away from the Thames. It's a very loud note in the chord, right at the bank. There must be lore about the river, specifically?"

"Rivers. I could lend you a book about it?" Farran said.

"Bring it round to the club tomorrow night?" Vega offered it quickly, fast enough he wasn't entirely sure she'd thought it through. "I'll make sure you can get one of the small tables, if you like. Bring a friend, or they can seat someone there if we're tight on space."

"I'd not want to keep anyone out of a seat," Farran said. "If you're sure." Then he added, more softly. "I wasn't sure if it'd be a problem. Or a distraction. Of course, you're far too professional for that."

She smiled, so it was probably all right. Then she leaned over and touched his arm. "I am. But I'd like to know you're listening. I mix up the sets, of course. It's different from last time you were there."

"Doing the same songs over and over again, in the same order, that would get boring, I suppose. Even if they're a little different every time. One of my friends thinks that about my work, how can I go look at another piece of silver plate, or another snuff box, or whatever? But they're all different. And their stories are, especially. Who owned them, what else is in the auction with them." Farran wasn't sure how to ask about what he wanted to know, but this would do for a topic, probably. Hopefully.

"That's just it. You can put songs together in different ways. Someone will hear a song one way. And then the next time, you add something that builds on a theme, or a turn of phrase, and the two are more together than they were on their own." She turned her free hand up. "Like constellations and planets, if that makes sense to you. They're in rela-tionship to each other, and we're in relationship to them, but it's also always changing."

Farran nodded slowly as she finished explaining. "I like that. And what will I hear if I come tomorrow, then? Or will it be different Saturday?" That got her into a conversation about balancing the three sets, and what she had in mind. The ballads, done in jazz style, had become decidedly popular. There would, of course, be a set of those, but also some jazz standards. Then it'd depend a bit on the mood of the crowd. He enjoyed hearing the way she laid out the decisions, though he had to reassure her twice she wasn't boring him.

They came around to the next place he'd wanted to stop. "That there is St Dunstan's-in-the-West. It used to have a clock with Gog and Magog beating the chime with clubs, but that's been taken down. But there are statues of King Lud and his sons. And they're working on the restoration of one of Queen Elizabeth, the only one, they think, carved during her reign."

Vega blinked at him. "But she had a terribly long reign, didn't she? Surely there must have been other statues."

"You do ask the sensible questions." That got her to blush slightly, and Farran wasn't sure what to do with that fact. He went on a bit quickly. "That's what the history says. I agree it's implausible. First, you're right that there should have been more. And second, statues take a fair bit of time to make, but they also tend to survive better than many other forms of art. They might shatter in a fierce fire, or crack if something falls on them, but paintings or even objects are far more fragile." He shrugged once. "If we're both still in London, we could come back to see it when it's back on display. A few months, I gather."

"How do you ever know these things?" Vega said. "All right, if we can't see it, where next?"

"I thought we'd wander along past the Temple Church, then down to the Embankment. That's a Templar church, of course, so full of lore, but not actually relevant to what we're doing. Or at least I'm fairly sure. Entirely the wrong period and area of focus and all that. Two blocks that way, though we'll go up to Fleet Street to go across." Farran pointed out where they were going. "And well, the auction house staff know the conservators, and what pieces are getting particular attention. The big one. There are dozens of people working on pieces that were damaged in the flooding at the Tate, though, along with other work. That sort of thing. It's not a very large world, when it's all said and done, and keeping up with the gossip is part of the job."

They walked another block or two before admiring the outside of the Temple Church, including the round portion. "Why is it round?" Vega asked, confused.

"That's the original church. Now the narthex, they added the rest later. William Marshall's buried there, if you want to go in sometime." Farran tilted his head. "That's not the bit I find most interesting, though. Let's walk down a bit and find a quiet spot. I haven't forgotten your other question. About the curses."

Vega nodded, and they walked in silence down through a narrow alley and then down the street, the Thames coming into view, then turned right to follow the Embankment. They made it halfway down the curve of the park, to Cleopatra's Needle. "You said you'd heard the stories about it, some of them," Farran said.

"Some, yes. That there are curses. And ghosts."

"It's a complicated question, really." Now, suddenly, Farran wasn't sure he wanted to get into it in a public space. "But look, see how the sphinxes are facing inwards? They're supposed to be protective. And then there's the whole matter of why this is here now. Which is partly international politics, which means it doesn't make all the logical sense you might want. Then there's what's actually on the obelisk." Farran was about to say more, but then Vega's hand was on his arm, tightly.

"Can we go back to my flat? By some means where he couldn't follow us? No, don't look directly." Farran hesitated, then adjusted his hat, managing to glance in the direction Vega had been looking. A man, one who fit the description she'd given him of Thomas Vandermeer.

"Same man?" Farran asked it quietly.

"Think so. Why is he here? Why would he be here? Is there a way we can, I don't know..." Vega's hand squeezed tighter. "I don't know what to do."

"Take a breath. Do you think he's seen you?" Farran tried to keep his own wits together, thinking about a place where they'd be able to slip into a crowd, and then find another street and get a cab. "If we could slip down to the Tube, it'd be a crowd."

"Not the Tube, please." Vega shook her head. "A cab. Is there somewhere?"

Farran nodded, and then stood up, offering his arm to her. "This way." He wasn't sure exactly what route would be best. But if they went away from the river, there were trees and people. They could cut back up toward Fleet Street or the Strand. There were hotels all along that stretch, but also plenty of offices and government buildings and shops. "Here we go."

They wove through several groups of people, including nannies out with small children, before turning down one street, then another, until they came out on the much busier Strand. Farran immediately managed to flag down a cab, helping Vega get into it with one hand while he kept an eye out. As he took his seat, she gave her address, and the cabbie drove off.

CHAPTER 23
LATER THAT AFTERNOON

By the time Vega opened the door to her rooms, she was freezing. Shivering, the sort of bone-deep cold she hadn't felt in ages. Not since she'd helped several of her uncles with a problem out on Salisbury Plain proper, something where the magic had gone twisted. "Tea?"

"Your landlady?" Farran asked, though he'd come in behind her.

"I need to be at the club by seven. As long as you leave with me, no problem. Most of the others won't be back until around then, anyway." Vega shivered again, more visibly. "Tea." It wasn't a question.

Farran frowned at her. "I can manage the kettle. You go change into something warmer and more comfortable if you want."

It was, hilariously, the opposite of what most people might suggest, alone with a woman in her rooms. 'Slip into something more comfortable' implied many fewer layers, silky fabric rather than

cosy, and vastly more access to skin. Vega couldn't
deny that she wanted to bundle up. "You're certain?"

"Yes. On both counts." He turned to peer at her
kettle. Vega assumed he could sort it out. It was an
ordinary sort of model. She'd learned how to use all
the more common ones in the dressing rooms of
various clubs, and the same probably applied for
wherever Farran did his work. People with stable
places of work got set in their ways, confused by a
different model. Maybe that was why she liked the
way Farran went about things. He had an adapt-
ability that was like hers.

She went back through to the bedroom, closing
the door firmly behind her. After a moment's consideration, she went for a silk step-in, then a blouse,
skirt, cardigan, and wool stockings. She added a
charm or two to the cardigan and stockings for additional warmth. She'd have to change at the club,
anyway. When Vega came back out to the sitting
room, Farran was just setting the kettle back in place,
standing by the table she used for the tea things.
"Just a few minutes for tea. I did it in each cup, if
you want to hold it for warmth."

That seemed like an excellent idea, and Vega sat,
then blinked up at him. "Oh." She didn't want to
banish him to the desk chair. It had quirks, and it
wasn't very comfortable for chatting. "Have the other
half the sofa?"

Farran nodded; he didn't ask if she meant it.
Some people might. And he didn't immediately sit
down right next to her, close enough to touch, which
plenty of other people also might have. It was a
friendly amount of space, not assuming anything.
The fact she kept thinking like this really meant they

ought to talk about it, but she didn't want to spoil, well, whatever it was. It did not help that she couldn't stop thinking about what Vivian Porter had said. And hadn't said, but what she'd implied.

That Farran wouldn't take Vega being a Cousin badly. That he had good manners for that sort of thing. Vivian would never have brought him to one of the estates if he couldn't be trusted that way. They had other things to talk about, though, before that. "Where do we start?" There, that was practical.

"Curses. And I meant to say something about the Temple Church, too, that might or might not be relevant when it comes to secrets. Though I'm scarcely an expert there. And then, of course, Mister Vandermeer." Farran said it evenly enough, until the end, but then he was watching her intently. She more or less repressed a shiver, and he said. "Start there. It'll be better shared. He makes you feel uncomfortable. Physically, magically, something else?"

"Yes." Having to put it into words outside her head was a help. She knew it, no matter how difficult it was. "A sense of cold. He was closer to me last time, close enough to speak, and it didn't feel like that then."

"You didn't have the talisman in your pocket then," Farran pointed out. "It felt warm around things more like what we're seeking, at least for me. Perhaps the opposite here, for something..." He shrugged. "Something that's the opposite of what we want? Or maybe he's got some talisman or device it's reacting to."

"Well, it's not terribly modern, made last week. Vandermeer dressed well, but nothing he wore was brand new." Her chin came up when Farran blinked.

"You get used to paying attention to that sort of detail. Especially at clubs where people come back, week after week. Who's in good funds, who isn't. How recently someone skilled has polished their shoes. Subtle, especially for people who buy good things to start."

"But there. And I suppose you've a decent eye for paste gems and costume jewellery," Farran said. Naturally, he'd think of that sort of object.

"There's nothing wrong with a bit of costume jewellery. And if I were going to a club, all sorts of people around, I'd rather wear something like that, honestly. Less worry about it." That was the truth. Of course, some of it was about what jewellery she did and didn't own in her own right.

Farran tilted his head, and then, almost as if he'd read her mind, he said, "You don't have much of your own, I'm thinking." Now he was looking at her, not staring, but broadly, as he might look at a large painting before taking in the details. "I'm guessing you're from the sort of family that's particular about their pieces. Fewer, but chosen deliberately. Not for the current fashion, not to suit this week's frock."

It was unerringly correct. Vega swallowed, then nodded. "Old family, but that's not what we care about, no. Passing fashion." Then she asked, "What do you think is going on with Vandermeer?"

"Ah." Farran considered. "I asked Vivian to see what she could find out, as well as Master Philemon. Well, someone else in the office who's very good at that kind of thing. What they've found so far is that he's definitely American. He has ties to various art museums in America— the Metropolitan in New York, the Museum of Fine Arts in Boston, the

Smithsonian. But he's also well known to private collectors. The sort of person who goes looking for particular pieces, then sees if he can make a deal to get it."

"And in this case, it's not like he can make a deal with us. And I wouldn't if he asked." Vega frowned.

"No, because you're interested in it for reasons other than fame and glory and putting it on display. Or money." Farran said it fondly, she thought, as if he approved. "The sensible assumption is that he's hoping you— we— might give him a hint about where it is. Or a hint about where something interesting is. There's no word, not yet, and there might not be, about if he's looking for something specific in the period."

"Or made of meteoric iron and magical." Vega grimaced. "That's not much help, even if it is more information."

"And I was hoping we wouldn't see him. How does he make you feel? Magically?"

"The first time? Like he was brash. A hair too noisy, out of balance with what was going on? But now? Like nails on a chalkboard." There, that was an excellent description, and it made her shiver again, but not from the cold. "Dissonant in wrong ways, not the jazz ways. Something that won't resolve properly. Something selfish. Something changed in him, and I don't know what or why, except that I don't like it."

"Jazz is a conversation, isn't it? Not a lecture. Opera, now, a good aria can be a monologue and that's fine. But not when you're trying to have several people all at once." It was an interesting way of putting it. Now Vega very much wanted to see if she could convince more of her family to try her style of music and mix it with some of their rites. The ones they did often enough they could experiment once in a while. Of course, she wasn't a fool. "Is— no, he has done nothing obviously wrong, has he?"

"He hasn't." Farran shook his head. "Vivian said if he turned up again, let her know. She can suggest some options. But he's allowed to be in a public park in London. So are we, but."

"But if he turns up again, that's certainly suggestive." Vega let out a long puff of breath. "I don't like it. And we're not really any closer to finding the object. Other than knowing some places it isn't, and having a tool that might help. Right. You were going to say something about the Temple Church?"

"Oh, it occurred to me it's interesting magically and legally. It's a royal peculiar. It has been since the beginning. That means it isn't part of a diocese or archdiocese, it's subject directly to the monarch." Farran's shoulder shrugged. "Less relevant to Albion now, maybe, but it was founded in the late 1100s."

"Before the Pact." Vega considered that. "Wrong period for what we're looking for, but I see what you mean. Are there other pockets like that?"

"London, I gather, is full of that sort of thing. But not always well documented." Farran shrugged. "Curses? It's related."

"As you wish." Instinctively, she shivered again, and moved a little closer to him before she thought about it. A moment later she felt his hand on hers, cautiously, like he might pull it away at any moment. When she looked up, he was watching her, as if he weren't sure what she was going to do.

"Curses." His voice got softer, but he didn't move

his hand. "I do think they exist. I've seen examples of cursed objects. We've worked with them as part of training. I've been able to observe, twice, while one of the Penelopes dismantled one. People keep the oddest things in their bank vaults. Do I think Cleopatra's Needle or Blackfriars Bridge is cursed? No. Is it possible that, historically, some horrible things have left a mark? Maybe. I'm less sure about that."

It was pragmatic again, though now Vega had dozens of questions about the process of undoing a curse on an item. "We have some family stories, though I haven't seen the objects myself." She took a breath and let it out. "I don't know why I'm afraid."

Farran hesitated, then he cleared his throat. "May I speak, um? Directly?"

"Yes?" Her voice cracked on the single syllable.

"What my fingers tell me, what my magic tells me, is that you're nervous. And talking about a curse isn't helping, but I don't think that's all of it?" His mouth turned up slightly. "I'm not as good with people as I am with materia. Probably better for everyone. But— you, it's helpful for me to be here?"

"Very." That came out before she could think about how to put it better. "I like your company, rather a lot. But particularly after— well. That was a shock seeing him. Feeling him."

"Then I'll stay until you need to leave, if you like. Or take a cab with you. I'm assuming there's good security at the club?"

"Oh, yes. Thankfully. They'd keep him out if I needed, but I don't know that's the right choice. As you said, he's allowed to be in a public park, he's allowed to be in a club. But I can make sure he leaves me alone, if he's there. Maybe better that you don't come tonight, but some other night?"

"Some other night," Farran agreed softly. "I am very interested in how your sets go together in practice. Now I know more about how to listen to them. Tomorrow, maybe."

"Tomorrow would be excellent. If you don't mind a later night. I need to go out and talk to my family again, Monday or Tuesday, I think. But we can talk after that, when you have a chance?"

"My time, beyond my other work, is yours." It was a bold statement, a sweeping one, but when she looked at him again, he seemed utterly sincere. There was no false face there. "Let me know. I've appointments until five on Monday, but I'm free after that. If you wanted supper together or something of the kind."

Vega swallowed and nodded. "Thank you." Then she glanced over at the clock and simultaneously realised her tea had steeped far too long and also gone cold. "I should get ready for the club. It will take me a bit, if you don't mind coming with me?"

"Not at all. I've a book. Take as long as you need." It was only then that Farran moved his hand, letting her stand. She took her mug back with her to the bedroom as she began going through all her ordinary preparations.

CHAPTER 24
MARCH 16TH

" It's not the sort of thing I can ask Uncle Cadmus. Or Lena." Farran was sitting on the sofa in his rooms, feet up. In a little, they'd pile into a cab and go along to the Crystal Cave. Vega had arranged a table for them, after Farran had learned that Tony and his next oldest sister were going to be in London for a day or two. Talking about this with Tony was odd too, but Tony had been his best friend for a long time. And if not Tony, who? It was near enough written as a law that this was a thing a best friend was for.

"Well, that sounds mysterious." Tony shrugged and glanced at Maddie. "If you want to read, Maddie, that's fine."

"Oh, I might have thoughts!" Maddie looked positively eager to hear the details, even though Farran had barely sketched anything out. She was working on a research project for a private employer, which involved looking at books in libraries. As well as, apparently, a tour of every bookseller she could find, or at least all the ones she could visit in two days. Tony had come along to carry the books, or so he kept joking.

"I told you I'm working on this private project. That's why I have the tickets to the club." Farran shrugged. "I will not get into all of it, because the work's not the part I want to talk about. And client privacy."

"Client privacy." The other two echoed it. They'd grown up with that near enough. Their eldest sister, Eleanor, had married young and been widowed not too long after, right around the time their parents had died. She'd raised her younger siblings to adulthood, with a string of sensible but clear rules.

Farran and Tony had found themselves some-what at loose ends at Schola, not quite fitting in with other people. Not posh enough, and certainly not rich enough, for the snotty sorts. Not outright bril-liant enough to make a name for themselves doing something else. They'd both been good students. Now they were building solid careers. But they, all three, had an odd view of the world sometimes, compared to the people they worked with and for.

Tony shrugged. "So, what can you tell us?"

"I want to be all moony and go on about how I just like being with her. I mentioned we spent the day at Greenwich, and it was just—" Farran consid-ered. "I mean, you heard all about my first appren-ticeship. How every time I turned around, it felt awful. Gummed up, not even just dammed." It was sticky and messy and felt awful, even just in memory. "This was the opposite of that. Cool clear water in a stream. Or not cold, I mean, also warm, friendly."

He was babbling now, and he closed his mouth rather than keep going with it.

"So." Tony considered. "What's she like with you? Besides continuing to make time to see you. What's the rest of her life like, other than the club?"

Farran considered that. Or rather, came back to considering it, because it wasn't like he hadn't been poring over their conversations in his head the last day or two. Or before that. "She talks fondly about her family. A large family, aunts and uncles, not just her parents. This is something she's doing for the family, but she doesn't seem to grudge that. They're giving her a fair amount of freedom in how it gets done, from some things she's said. They're not being grasping or anything."

"How would you tell the difference?" Maddie tucked one of her feet under her other leg, obviously interested in this part.

"Oh, we see that with art often enough. Someone feels they need to sell a piece, and the family disapproves. Or they need to get an appraisal and there's difficulty with that. 'How could you dare question what Grandmama said about it', you know?"

The tone he gave the quote made both Tony and Maddie laugh. "All right, so that's like researchers. Or the people we do research for, anyway." Maddie considered. "Do you have professional ethics about that sort of thing? I mean, there's a certain sort of novel where one person doing work for the other ends up with the two of them in the library doing things that mess with the proper arrangement of books."

"Can't have that." Now Farran was laughing.

"Also, our locations have not been the most promising. The cave was private, but desperately needed a
good cleaning, and we weren't entirely certain about
the ceiling staying put. Tuesday, we were out and
walking around, and it is March. Well, before I got
her back to her flat." He said it and then realised
how that sounded. "Not like that. She was..." He
stopped. "I could maybe talk about this part. You
might have some ideas."

"Go on." Tony leaned forward. "Now I'm
curious."

"You're always curious." Farran pointed out. It
was part of what made them good friends, finding
the world endlessly interesting. Tony had gone into a
line of materia work, finding specific items on
request from a small set of clients, and he was excellent at it. It also brought him into a wide range of
sometimes unexpected situations. "All right. She had
an odd experience, someone talking to her by chance
on a bridge."

"In London? I thought that sort of thing was
forbidden here. Speaking to strangers without significant encouragement."

Farran snorted. "You see the initial piece, yes. An
American, mind you, and they tend to be more
extroverted about talking to strangers, statistically."
Farran considered how to put the rest of it. "He was
polite enough, at least overtly. But it struck her as
odd. She didn't know then that he was magical, but
he turned up at the club a couple of days later. Tuesday, we were out walking through a few spots, and he
turned up again on the Embankment. I don't know
if he spotted us, but she felt quite queer after, cold
and... you know, that sort of cold."

Tony winced. "Yes. Hence going to her rooms, and tea or whatever." He chewed on his lip, which meant he was thinking hard. "Does she seem to be level-headed about other people?"

Farran raised an eyebrow. "Tony, do you really think I'd be interested in her if she were all fluttery nerves over every little thing? Actually, I'd been thinking about how skilled she was at evaluating a situation. It must come up a lot as a singer, both the people she's working with and the audience. Getting a sense of the mood quickly, being able to collaborate. You'll see what I mean."

"No, I can't see you being interested in someone who was flighty. Or..." Tony tilted his head. "How much have you talked about Thebes so far?"

"A bit. Fairly sure she's got a sense of how I feel about the place. But it's— I mean, I'm not living there full time as it is. And Uncle Cadmus is thrilled being there and keeping things running. I don't know. There's no point even having that conversation until there's a reason to."

"And yet, if you are actually on different ends of it, if she can't abide Oxfordshire, for some reason, you'd want to know that before getting serious." Tony held up a finger. "Don't say you'd see each other without being serious. You don't know how to do that. You've never done it yet, and I don't think you're going to change all of a sudden."

"How could anyone not abide Oxfordshire, in particular?" Farran said, leaning into being mock-offended. It got Maddie grinning. "A month ago, you'd have said I wasn't the sort of person to go to a nightclub either, but here we are."

"There we'll be, you mean." Tony waved a hand,

fingers inscribing a circle in the air. "Honestly, you should just find a time you can talk privately and see what she says. Maybe she's not interested, then you'll know. Maybe she is in the future, but not while you're working on this project together. Or maybe she has some secret swain she's seeing, I don't know, at three in the morning, when she's done at the club."

"Don't think it's the last one." Farran felt he needed to be loyal here, and that was something he'd have to think about more, how he immediately wanted to stand beside her. Not protect her, exactly. She didn't need his protection. But be her company in the truth. Now he was coming up with entirely overwrought and rather Victorian metaphors. That wasn't a help. "Anyway. You're right that talking's probably the sensible thing. Do you want to wash up and we can go along?"

"Sure." Both Tony and Maddie tidied themselves. Farran went and found one of his better jackets and a pocket square to go with his tie, then made sure his hair was behaving. The cabbie dropped them off just a few feet from the club, and they piled out.

One of the men at the door nodded. "You expected, sir?"

"Miss Beaumont arranged a table for us. Michaels." Farran tried to say it as if it were the sort of thing he did all the time, never mind that it wasn't. And to do it in the way that didn't sound odd if someone non-magical went by on the pavement.

He knew that a good two-thirds of this sort of social challenge was simply acting as if he had every right to be there. He'd done it in auction rooms and museums and art galleries more than often enough. Dressing right, talking right, and acting the way people expected, anyone could get away with a great deal.

Somewhat unexpectedly, the man smiled. "Ah, excellent." He gestured at someone inside. "Jack, could you take Miss Vega's party back?"

Another man came out onto the steps, then nodded. "This way, sirs, ma'am." They handed over their overcoats and Maddie's cape to the coat check, and Tony tucked the claim tickets away in his inner pocket. The table in question turned out not to be front and centre— those were for larger groups— but with a direct line to the stage. Once they were seated, Jack nodded. "I'll be bringing a bottle for the table, at Miss Vega's request, and our chef's suggestions for the evening. The performances will begin in about a quarter hour, with dancing between."

Maddie inquired about where the loo was, and was directed off to a door in the far corner of the room. Jack went off to see about those unexpected offerings. Tony leaned back, taking the place in. "Nothing quite like this in Trellech." Then he added. "She thinks well of you, and the people here think well of her."

"I'd noticed that." Farran hadn't made note of it the first night, of course, but he could see the little shifts now he was watching for it. The staff moved smoothly, waiters bringing drinks and plates of food, women in bright dresses began circulating. "Those are the dance mistresses, if you'd rather not dance with Maddie. A few men, too."

"What would you do if I made a bet about you getting a dance with Miss Vega, then?" Tony said.

"She needs a break between sets. For her voice, if not for her feet." Farran would not push. "If she offers, I'll certainly say yes. But this is her work, as well as her joy. She gets to measure out how she spends herself."

Something in the way Farran put it made Tony blink and lean forward. But before he could say anything else, there was a bottle of wine on the table. Maddie reclaimed her seat, and they needed to focus on what the chef recommended. Farran went with those suggestions, because he suspected Vega had a hand in the idea. He wanted to tell her what he'd thought.

That done, Tony let the subject drop, choosing instead to watch the other people, and hear Maddie's comments on the various frocks and jewellery on display. It was a pleasant chatter, and it let Farran think more about what he wanted to say to Vega when he got a chance.

CHAPTER 25
LATER THAT EVENING

Vega peered through the curtain. Her first set had gone smoothly, and now she could watch Farran and his friends at the table. The beginning of the second set had started well. They'd worked out how to build out the introduction, so that there wasn't a jarring contrast from the chatter of the pause to a full on performance.

Kevin Stafford, the guitarist, would come out. He'd slide from tuning his guitar in little arpeggios that twisted deftly into a tune, his blond head bent over the guitar, entirely focused on what he was doing. Then Harry, the drummer, would take his place, then the others in the band, one by one. They moved into the music like they were picking up a conversation that had been going on for twenty years. It had a friendly feel to it, comfortably worn in, without being either bored or boring.

Once they'd gone through a song or so, the dancers would come out, the dance mistresses and masters. They'd had a few minutes of a break from dancing with guests. This bit of the show wasn't entirely choreographed. For one thing, Madam Helena wanted each dancer to have time to show off a bit of their own particular talent. It had them whirling in different patterns. Then they'd find a place where Pasco could shift lights to illuminate couples pair by pair in the centre. From there, they swooped off to take their place along the edge of the dance floor, keeping time with small but graceful movements.

Then it was time for the others. This time it was Ivy and Charles, coming out in a swirl of her skirts as Charles got her spinning across the dance floor. They had more space to move, being the only couple dancing, and their set was full of lifts and twirls, getting delighted sounds and applause from the audience. Farran seemed to enjoy it, but the woman next to him leaned over and touched his arm, so he turned and grinned at her. Vega pulled back from the curtain.

Of course, he had friends. People did. Should. She did, even if she didn't get to see many of them often. Her family, the cousins she was close to, weren't in London much or anywhere else she'd performed recently. Her performer friends moved about in the peripatetic orbits of comets, coming near each other now and again. And of course, it wasn't as if they could go out for an evening on a weekend. It was impossible, what with that being both their busy time and different contracts varying their nights off.

After Pasco's illusions, there was this week's special contract. Vega enjoyed watching the trio of dancers, all sisters, who did acrobatics and high kicks. Now, it was Vega's turn. She strolled out toward the stage from the back, letting people take her in. And letting the band play her up to her best face, too. Once she turned around, Pasco's light charm on her, she took a breath, and began to sing.

This set, she was doing a number of jazz favourites, with the illusions complementing the music. They were impressionistic, but precisely on beat, making the underlying rhythms pop for even the most tin-eared listener. She loved the added dimension it gave to a performance, the way it made people lean forward, all their senses engaged.

The only problem was that she saw Vandermeer. He must have been seated since the last time she'd checked, at one of the small tables at the back. Vega refused to let it throw her. She could have asked for him to be turned away, and she hadn't, quite. Not without talking to Madam Helena about it. Vega should have done that after the note, last time, or this afternoon, or, well. No use mourning the past. She put her all into the last two songs, not with her magic but with her heart, before retreating off the stage.

This time, instead of peering through the curtain, she went up to Madam Helena's office, which had an interior window that overlooked about half the room. She knocked once, then heard the quiet "Come."

As soon as Vega entered, Madam Helena looked up. "A problem, dear? I hope not with your particular guests?"

"No." Vega took a breath. "The man who sent the note a bit ago now. Thomas Vandermeer. Table 10."

"He ought not to." Madam Helena raised an

eyebrow. "He must have an illusionist on tap, or something of the kind. I gave instructions he wasn't to be let in, and a clear description."

"Oh." Vega should have asked, but she sank into a chair. "You did?"

"I did not much like the feel of him, either. Or his magic. Something odd there. Besides, I value you rather more than such a guest." Madame Helena stood, peering out the window, then glancing across. "Hmmm. That's your particular friend, yes? Who's the woman with him?"

Madam Helena was not looking straight down, it turned out, but at a mirror. It was angled to make it possible to see the entire room, at least with the help other mirrors. Vega blinked. "I hadn't realised..."

"Oh, there are charms, too." Madam Helena gestured at one wall, which suddenly had an image — fuzzy, but enough to make out individuals— projected on the blank white wall. "How else am I supposed to seem omniscient?"

That, especially Madam Helena's tone, made Vega laugh, despite the seriousness. "So, um." She glanced at the mirror again. "Farran asked if he might bring a friend and the friend's sister." The sister of a friend was, by some counts, a prime target for romance.

Farran's note had mentioned the name, but nothing much about her. Though the same last name as the brother, so presumably unmarried. And the last name suggested it might be a Cousin line, though nothing she'd seen of Eleanor Norton had made that entirely clear. "What will you do about Vandermeer?"

"See if one of the sensible women will dance

with him. Or..." She was about to say something else, before gesturing. The current dance song had come to an end. Farran made a slight bow as Maddie stalked off. She had the walk of a woman with a purpose, toward where Vandermeer sat. She said something to him, tilting her head, and then held out her hand. Vandermeer stood a little more slowly than someone who actually wanted to dance might. But then he led Maddie out on the floor, as the next tune started up.

"Have a chat with them. I can send drinks around to your dressing room after your last set. You're early in the set, yes?"

As if Madame Helena would let that detail slip her mind. "Third." Vega agreed. They had maybe another song or two of the ordinary dancing, then they'd segue into the individual performers again. "Lucella wanted the last spot, and I didn't feel like arguing with her about it." She was the other singer at the moment, and certain that there was some trick that would mean people remembered her better than Vega.

"I do appreciate that you're not grasping about it." Madame Helena said it amiably. "Lucella's rubbed a few others the wrong way." That was a neutral statement, but being given the information certainly wasn't neutral. "I'll send your party back once you're done. You can talk until we lock up." It would give a couple of hours if they needed it.

"Thank you." Vega ducked her chin. "I'm sorry to bring a bit of trouble."

"You didn't. The trouble brought himself, and I'm sure he ought to know better. But I'll see if I can find out anything else. If so, I'll let you know." She waved her hand, a little dismissal. Vega went back down to her dressing room to freshen up, do a few vocal exercises, and prepare for the last set of her evening. It went well enough, though she felt it wasn't her best performance. Fortunately, they'd already agreed on the mood and songs. This was a series of jazz numbers of Albion itself, with some clever and demanding puns on various bits of magic. It got a reliable laugh, and it sounded good without being too much of a strain.

Seven minutes after she'd made it back to her dressing room, there was a tidy knock on the door. "Miss Vega? Your party."

"Please come in." Knowing they'd be coming, she'd quickly wriggled out of her performance dress and into something comfortable and not nearly as decorative. Then she'd pulled one of her more voluminous and slightly gaudy wraps over it. People had expectations. The door opened, and Farran came in, stepping to one side, followed by his friends.

The woman was perhaps a little older than Farran, and rather lovely in feature. Seeing her close up, Vega was more certain the brother and sister were also Cousins, though of a more distant generation than Vega herself. They had that edge of vitality that sometimes made Cousins a hair more eye-catching, which Vega certainly had herself. Now she nodded, glancing at Farran.

"Anthony Sturgis, Tony. My best friend since Schola. And his slightly older sister, Maddie. They've several others." Farran closed the door, then said, "Maddie has some new information for us. We didn't want to discuss it out among everyone."

"Oh!" Vega shook herself out a little. "There's

wine here, or if you want something else. We've a bit of time. I'm done for the night, though they'll want to lock up eventually. An hour or so. Please, sit." The two siblings took the small sofa, leaving Farran one ottoman, and Vega for the chair.

"That is not a man I would want anywhere near me. And he's a lousy dancer. Stepped on my feet twice, though I admit he was a bit distracted. Farran's much better. You should dance with him when you get a chance." Maddie's commentary came out like a burbling stream, and with several points that Vega wanted to think about later. Including the fact that Vandermeer was not the sort of smooth dancer she'd expected from him. Or at least not with Maddie. "There's something definitely off about him."

"What sort of off?" Tony asked, in the sort of tone that Vega knew from her cousins, someone patiently getting someone to explain something obvious to them. Well-worn. He added, "Maddie's a researcher, usually working with a client for a few months on some project. She's met rather a wide selection of slightly creepy academics."

"This was different." Maddie sounded insistent, and she leaned forward, elbows on her knees. Vega rather liked the determination. "I think he is looking for something. That sort of looking, maybe more active sorts. Farran didn't explain what he's helping you with, other than that it's some object, and because it's him, some sort of art object. I don't think Vandermeer is an art historian. And while he tried to come off like a businessman, I don't think that's it, either."

"Why?" Tony asked before Vega had to figure out how to word it. "Explain yourself, please."

"He's American, yes?" Vega nodded. She could clarify in a minute. "There might be differences in terms. But he didn't speak like a businessman. More like there was a face he put on."

"We believe he used an illusion to get into the club. The owner had taken some precautions," Vega offered. "Previously, he's said he was American, and he sounds like an American."

Farran nodded, focusing directly on Vega. "Look, I can ask Vivian to do some more research and see what she can find out. But I think we can assume he's quite likely interested in whatever you're looking for. Or something closely related. And that's a problem."

"What about leading him on a bit of a false trail?" Tony suggested. "Go somewhere that's not relevant."

"It's London," Farran pointed out. "It's actually rather hard not to trip over something the right period without meaning to. Even if it's not actually the most relevant period, most places."

"Well. Somewhere you're pretty sure isn't the right place. The Tower, maybe? You said you were focusing on earlier, didn't you?" Tony was quick, Vega realised. Also, it was interesting to see the way he and Farran went at things. Like Farran had with her, but also a little different.

She cleared her throat. "I think the Tower might be a good idea. There would be plenty of people around. There are Beefeaters if he tries to do anything odd. A museum might do, but that's more complicated. If we wanted something in a museum, we'd go about it differently."

Farran met her eyes for a moment. "As you like. It's Thursday night. Saturday, perhaps? It's something we can do in an afternoon."

"Saturday." Vega nodded firmly. "We can sort out where to meet." Then there was a knock on her door, and a murmur that the performances were done. "If you want to get out the stage door without too much fuss, this is a good time. Or if you could give me a little cover."

"Of course." Farran said. "Get you into a cab safely, your favourite cabbie."

That, naturally enough, got Maddie asking how that worked, a series of interested questions about the process. It took up the time until Vega had changed stockings, into comfortable shoes, a jumper, and an ordinary coat. As the others went out, Farran paused, holding the door for her. "I'd love a chance to talk a bit, Saturday, too. When we get a bit of quiet?"

"Me as well." She offered a smile, the best she could give him, to be reassuring. "And I like your friends."

The smile she got back, now, that was worth having set aside her nerves about whether Farran might already have an interest in Maddie.

CHAPTER 26

MARCH 17TH AT THE TOWER OF
LONDON

Saturday at noon was, of course, a relatively popular time to visit the Tower of London. It made it a less than optimal time for their visit, but needs must. It was cloudy, though maybe a drizzle would have kept the crowds down. Farran was waiting for Vega when she came down the path. "I've already bought our tickets."

"Oh." Vega cleared her throat. "You needn't have? I owe you expenses, don't I?"

Farran shrugged slightly. They'd agreed on terms, of course, at the beginning. But he didn't entirely want money getting in the way. "We can discuss later. It's not much, and I kept an account. And see, the line's got longer, no need to wait in it." The line was indeed longer, partly because of some rather larger family group, or perhaps multiple families. Children kept spilling out of line like the tentacles of some giant ocean creature, then getting pulled back.

Vega glanced over, winced, and said, "Well, all

right. Where are we going first? Do you have an idea?"

"I also have a guidebook," Farran said cheerfully. "Last year's, but there's not been a new one yet, I think. This was in one of the bookstores, the used shelves, when I went by this week."

"Do you also like a bookstore, then? I enjoy browsing, when I've an hour to spare. Or more than an hour, depending on the size of the shop." That topic occupied them for a good few minutes, until they had crossed over to wander by the Traitor's Gate, from the inside of the walls. There, in a patch of quiet, with no one too near them, Vega paused to stare at the gate and ask, "What is our plan today?"

"Wander the Tower, admire the architecture, talk about the history, see the jewels, and see if a certain person appears. If we want to see the chapel, we should request a tour from the warder on duty before 2pm," Farran said promptly. He knew that part of it, at least. Then he cleared his throat. "And maybe tea, after? Somewhere quieter?"

"I'd like that." Vega said it immediately, then she looked away. Conveniently, there was rather a lot to look at, Farran thought. Most of it was stone walls, of course, but exceedingly historical stone walls. "Did your friends get home safely?"

"Yes, thank you. And they very much enjoyed the club. Maddie, especially." She'd enthused about it in the cab back to their hotel, in fact.

"Oh." Vega considered, now with space before she spoke. "You looked happy dancing with her."

Farran had been about to step back onto the path, and he turned. "Did you think?" He cut off, then tried again. "It's not like that, with her. Probably not a topic for right here, but it's— it's not like that."

"You said you'd known her brother for ages. Since school." Vega then closed her mouth. "Not for here, no." Farran nodded, because of course any details of Schola might get into topics that shouldn't be overheard by the non-magical. "All right. Which of these towers do we look at first?"

"We've a ticket for the jewel room in…" Farran paused to peer at his watch. "An hour. Do you prefer ghosts, chapels, arms and armour, or the White Tower?"

"I'd be interested in seeing the oldest to the newer, if that made sense?" Vega shrugged. "If it's a bother, though."

"No, no, that's probably a sensible way to do it. With an intermission for the jewels." He took a moment to open the guidebook to the proper page. "The White Tower is the oldest part, built by William the Conqueror in 1078." He went along talking about the inner ward, pointing out the various towers as they walked through.

"Wasn't there a Lion Tower?" Vega asked, sounding more relaxed.

"With lions," Farran said. "That was more or less where the ticket booth is. A menagerie, though. I read a book— I don't have it in London— that talked about the menagerie. Lions, gifts from some foreign king. And a polar bear. They used to take it down to fish in the Thames on a rope."

Vega stopped walking. "I don't think that would have done anyone much good, do you? If the bear had other ideas."

"Probably not," Farran agreed. "There was, oh.

An elephant. There are drawings of it, I've seen a print. There were superstitions, of course. They'd name one of the lions after the king. The lore was that if the lion died, the king would follow. There's raven lore, of course."

"That one, I've heard," Vega said. "Do you think there's truth in it? That if the ravens leave the tower, England will fall?"

Farran walked on for a few steps, because putting what he thought into words was delicate. "I think that people have believed that one for a long time, and that gives a thing strength. Also, it's certainly harder for ravens to leave if they have their wings clipped. I'm a bit more curious about some of the associations with Bran, whether his head is buried nearby, all of that."

Vega stopped again, tilting her head and looking at him. "You think the time passing matters that much?" Then she shook her head and smiled. "Later topic. What's over here?"

"That was, let's see. Mint Street, for a long time. Imagine all the coins that anyone used, being minted all in one place. It's not a big bit of land, considering. Though it's also interesting that way. Technically, part of it is in London, and part in Middlesex." Farran made a note to figure out more about that what meant for the demesne estates, especially since the Pact. It was an interesting problem of magical identity.

"Is there art around somewhere? I mean, art that you'd know about?" Vega asked it suddenly.

"Not much on display, other than the armoury and the jewels. Here. The White Tower?" There were more people around, so as they went in, Farran focused on talking a little about the architecture. It was not remotely his speciality, but of course knowing about the buildings where art was mattered sometimes.

Besides, he had always rather been interested in the buildings themselves, what it meant about the people who made them or lived in them or fought against them. He had Thebes to thank for that, really. And Schola's keep itself. Here, the guidebook had been usefully informative. "Did you know that it's not actually a square? Each wall is a different length, and three of the four corners aren't right angles. But you can't tell by just looking."

"Huh." Vega peered at the White Tower suspiciously. "I don't suppose we know why?" That was not something Farran had found, and he admitted he wasn't sure.

They took their turns walking around and admiring the vaulting where there was vaulting, and the somewhat austere chapel. "It feels..." Vega pursed her lips. "Has it been a chapel the whole time?"

That made Farran muffle a laugh until they got back into the main area of the tower. "No, actually. It wasn't complete when William died, and then they built other spaces. It was storage for records for quite a long time, apparently. A different kind of temple, at least I like to think so, to storing the history of the place. Now, though, I believe it's a chapel in regular use again. I rather liked it. There's something about the plain stone. But if you want to compare, there's St Peter ad Vincula."

Vega turned and peered at him. "Is there some-

thing odd about that one too? Like you showed me
before?"

"Also a royal peculiar. But it was built for the
people who lived and worked here, not as a royal
chapel? Originally twelve hundreds, I think. I'll look
at the guide when we get outside."

When they got outside, however, they both were
turning to move toward the church at the northwest
of the inner ward, when Vega elbowed Farran. Diagonally across the parade ground, up near the far end
of the Waterloo barracks, she nodded with her chin,
and Farran saw a recognisable figure.

"Chapel? One of the towers? There'll be more
space in the chapel," Farran offered. "Probably more
other people. Certainly a warder right there."

"That, then." Vega curled her arm through
Farran's, and he felt like he should be more protective. Except, of course, he was not the sort of man
who did that naturally. And he wasn't trained to it,
not like some people had been. He took a breath,
though, and led off bravely.

"Do you think he's the sort of man who avoids a
church?" The question occurred to Farran when they
were most of the way there. They were passing by
the marker that he knew from the guidebook marked
the site of the private executions in the Tower.

At the door to the chapel, the warder agreed to
let them in, giving a brief tour to them and another
handful of sightseers. People murmured, but it felt
good, to Farran at least, to have others nearby. He
felt they couldn't trust an American of unknown
desires to behave properly, but at least other people
might be a deterrent.

When they came out again, Vandermeer had disappeared again. "It's just about time for our Jewels ticket," Farran said. "Perhaps he went in there, but there will be both people and guards."

Vega nodded. When they entered the Wakefield Tower, and climbed to the second floor, the lighting focused on the jewels themselves. Those were splendid, of course, both the gems and the settings.

Farran thought a few times that Vandermeer might be some people ahead of them, but it was hard to tell. When they'd made their proper circuit and come back downstairs again, Vega drew him aside, under a tree. "Shall we, I mean, do you want to see the Beauchamp Tower? I gather there are some rather interesting carvings?"

"I think we've more or less proved our point," Farran said, keeping an eye out. "But I admit, I'm sort of curious to see if he approaches. Or what he says."

Vega blinked at him. Then she squared her shoulders. "Onward, then. A promenade, around the grounds, then the tower? And if we don't see any sign of him after that, reconsider?"

"Just so." Farran offered his arm, and they went along again, down the south side, through one of the arches through the inner wards, and then into the central area again, up a broad cobblestone path toward the Waterloo barracks. Those weren't open to visitors, but it made a pleasant circuit.

They did not see anything out of the way until they were almost at the doors. Vandermeer appeared from around the corner of the White Tower, on the other side. This time, he absolutely saw them,

touching his hat and coming over, his coat
behind him.

"Miss Beaumont! A pleasure." He beamed at
Vega, whose hand tightened a bit on Farran's arm.
"And you, sir?"

Farran had a sudden shiver, reminding him of
the way one wasn't supposed to give a proper name
to the Fatae. Vivian had explained where those tales
came from, and of course, it was more complicated
than that, but still. "Michaels." He cleared his throat.
"Anthony Michaels." It was a common enough last
name, and Tony never minded Farran borrowing his
first name. Farran was uncommon enough it stuck in
the memory far more.

Vega, thankfully, picked up on it evenly.
"Anthony and I were just thinking whether we'd call
it a day. Such a pleasure to see the history, but I'm
afraid I ought to get back."

"I won't keep you. Not today, then." That also
had an edge to it, to Farran's ear. "Perhaps I'll see
you at the club again." That definitely was half a
threat or warning or something else of the kind.
Then he took a step back.

Farran nodded once before gesturing. "This way,
then. I saw the cabs lining up down the road. It will
be easiest to catch one there." They walked, not too
quickly, but briskly enough, across the bridge, up the
slight hill, and away from the Tower.

"I did not care for that." Vega's voice was tight.
"Can we go somewhere and talk? I'd rather not my
rooms, in case, well."

"Your landlady would disapprove of him. I've a
serviced flat, a small one, but private, and there's a
porter. If it wouldn't bother you, come to mine?"

"Oh, that's no bother." Her voice brightened. "I'm curious to see how you live, actually. You've seen mine."

"It's not much. I wasn't set up for entertaining. But Uncle Cadmus taught me to be tidy. Besides, you might want a look at some of my notes." He nodded and then gestured. "I meant it about the cabs. And we can ask the cabbie to take an unusual way back, just in case."

"Grand. I dislike the feeling there's someone watching me behind my back."

When they got to the row of black cabs, Farran looked back, as he was guiding Vega into the seat. He thought he could see Vandermeer— or again, someone very much like his silhouette— standing on top of the walls, looking out toward them.

CHAPTER 27
A SHORT TIME LATER

"Here, come in. Let me put the kettle on." Farran showed her up into the flat. "Do you need something to eat?"

"Oh, don't go to any bother. I can get something at the club before I go on." Vega wanted to rub her hands up and down her arms, but that would mean letting what she was feeling show.

"There's not much of a kitchen, but I have some makings for sandwiches." Farran considered. "Also some scones."

"A scone, then." Vega glanced around, shifting nervously. "Scones are rarely a bad idea. Unless they're lumps."

"These are not lumpy. The woman who sees to the flat has a wonderful touch with the baking. Or knows someone who does. She hasn't been clear when I've asked? But I try not to question excellent baked goods. Anyway. Sofa there. Or the chair. I'll get the tea on." Farran disappeared into a hallway.

It left Vega in the front room. The flat wasn't large, she thought. It was about the size of her rooms. Though she thought from the width of the building that he likely had his own loo and bath, rather than sharing one in the hall like she did. He had a sofa, two chairs, all in the sort of inoffensive colours of a hotel. Farran had said this had been let by Ormulu, so she assumed, like so many places she'd lived herself, it only had a few personal touches. The more portable ones.

The desk had a few photos out, with a small bookshelf beside, and she couldn't resist looking at both. The photos were more or less what she'd expected. A much younger Farran, but visibly himself, with a man and woman, presumably his parents. There was one of Farran with a different man, though obviously related to the first one. That suggested it was his uncle. Farran must have been around eighteen.

Third and perhaps most relevant was a shot that made her stop and consider, because she was almost certain that was one of the estates in Electra's line. It was difficult to tell, of course. Trees and hedges and gardens were all over the place, and the angle on the photo had very little that was distinctive. But Vega was almost certain she knew the line of that statue in the corner, or the way it was casting a clear shadow, at least.

The statue itself was relatively recent, but in the classical mode, a haunting image of a woman turning her face away, pulling a length of fabric over her face as a veil, weeping, as it was said Electra had wept at the destruction of Troy. The statue's other hand was outstretched. That was the part that showed in the shadow, as if she were reaching back to grasp something that was no longer there and would never be there.

Before Farran could come back and catch her looking at the photos, Vega moved to look at the bookshelves. Those were about what she'd expected, given that Farran had seemed well-read. There were a range of materials that were likely related to his work, a few biographies of artists and a few reference titles. But there was also a mystery, the spine well-worn in a way that suggested it came from a used bookshop, and a magical title related to architecture. And of course there were several guides to London and a space where the guide to the Tower he'd bought was likely meant to live.

Farran came back, carrying a tray, and then he snorted. "Vivian says that it's a sign of a good mind if someone looks at your bookshelves."

"Also telling, though? I can't imagine she likes that much." Vega said it before realising that might give something away. She coughed. "She has something of a reputation for discretion."

"That is why Vivian has two offices. Well, and a library room," Farran said, then he set down the tray before considering. "There are books in her private office, but they're the sort of books you'd expect for her work. The Gold Book, various other family histories, business directories, that sort of thing." The Gold Book laid out all the Great Families of Albion over the generations, and that would be useful for a number of reasons.

Something about how he put it made Vega sure she needed to come clean with him. She wasn't used to that. Either people knew she was a Cousin, and of

Alcyone's line, or they didn't need to know. But she wanted Farran to know. And honestly, she thought he needed to know. There wasn't any way to talk about some of why Vandermeer worried her without it. Not that she was at all articulate about it.

She sat, and Farran did immediately after. He'd been waiting for her to sit, then, an attention to manners that seemed entirely instinctive for him. He'd been raised well, both by his parents and his uncle, in that case. Though, she supposed, Ormulu would also have put a polish on that sort of thing. "Please pour." There, she could give herself a little more time. "Every pot has its quirks I've found. And I, erm." She was supposed to be gifted at words coming out of her mouth. There were certainly songs and arias and bits of opera lyrics she could quote here, and all of them caught in her throat. "I'm trying to figure out how to say something. Several things, related."

"Well, then. Tea might help." Farran set about pouring, not rushing it. Vega liked that he didn't rush, that his movements were all measured. They were like one of her aunts working at a loom or with an embroidery frame. "Is there somewhere that's easier to start?"

"Your friends?" Her voice cracked a little at the end. "You mentioned a little, but."

"But you saw me dancing with Maddie." Farran looked up at her, meeting her eyes as he set the teapot down. "I've never had someone react like that before. So you know."

"Haven't, um. Walked out with anyone else?" Vega wasn't sure how to ask this.

"Oh." Farran laughed, but it wasn't mocking her.

"Tony keeps setting me up with people. Or Maddie, actually, she gave it a good try, too." His shoulder twitched, which made her think there was a bit more pain there than he was admitting to. "None of them worked out. Pleasant enough. The most recent was six months ago. She wanted to be in Trellech, all her spare time, and I wanted to be at Thebes. That's not actually the sort of thing you can compromise on. There's a portal that's not a bad walk, or the train, but it's not like we have one in the front garden, like some houses. Never mind the wait at the Trellech end sometimes."

"Oh." Vega looked down at her hands now. The tea was still a bit too hot to fiddle with. "I've been so focused on taking contracts, it doesn't make for a good partnership. Unless there's someone you're doing it with, but that's different."

"And most of your music, I can see how a duet could work for some of it, but a lot of it wouldn't." Farran said. "Yes?"

"Yes." She swallowed. "That's part of it. But there's another part." Now she couldn't look at him, and she needed to look at him, because every hint he gave her would help her figure out what to say. "If I said I was a distant relation of Vivian's, would that mean anything to you?"

Farran looked back at her. He'd been reaching for his own teacup, but his hands stopped. "Ah." He closed his mouth and he continued to be measured. It was both reassuring and terrifying, a combination of melody and harmony she couldn't untangle fast enough to find the right beat. "A different, um. Grandmother? Is that the correct way to put it?"

She swallowed, then nodded again. "The photo-

graph, there, there's a statue, just to the right of the
image, isn't there?"

That made him laugh. "There is, yes. And the
statue has an interesting history, actually, but that is
for another time. Are you asking if I've seen where
some of Vivian's family live?" Vega nodded, just
once. "She has invited us— me, and Uncle Cadmus,
and Lena, who's our housekeeper— out several
times. The larger gatherings, where they can. I
couldn't go last time. There was something else I had
to be at." He then leaned back. "Were you afraid of
telling me?"

"We don't, generally. For many reasons." Vega
gestured incoherently at the door. "Vandermeer,
maybe, for one reason. But people have assumptions.
Even people who know one Cousin. It's not like
knowing all of us."

"I haven't asked for details. It's not the kind of
thing where that seemed appropriate. But I have
paid attention when Vivian has talked about it.
There are different lines. Some of you are all right
being in a city with a lot of metal, but not all of you.
Or specific foods. She doesn't eat red meat, for
example." His eyebrow went up. "Relevant when she
came as a guest at a boarding house with shared
meals."

It would have been, yes. "I'm fine in a city,
usually. I prefer not to take the Tube? That's a lot of
metal, and underground? But a cab's fine." She
glanced upward, the way that was instinctive. "We,
my family, we care about stars. And some of the,
what's the right word, flashes of performance? Every
generation, there's one, two, maybe three of us who
go out in the world and do what I do, or something

like it. Singing, dancing, acting. Eventually we go back and settle down, but I think I've got a while yet. Maybe long enough that my age starts to show. Or lack of age." Her chin came up. "I— um."

Farran waved a hand. "Vivian explained that. You look younger, longer. I wouldn't be so rude as to inquire about a lady's age, mind." He added after a moment. "I'm twenty-fo— no. Twenty-five. Last week." Now he flushed, charmingly. "Last Saturday."

"Wait, that was how you spent your birthday? Without telling me?"

"I had an entirely delightful day with you. And getting to see something new, something not that many people have seen, not in decades," Farran said. "I also didn't have other plans. Tony was busy. Vivian had something she was doing. I couldn't have gone back to Thebes easily. And I really enjoyed the day with you, the way I..." He stopped and swallowed. "I think that the way you spend a day like a birthday, it tells you a lot about your coming year. Or it can. Who you spend it with, what you do. If my year has more time being interesting places, being curious, that's grand. Or, well, I don't want to presume. But if it had more time with you, I'd like that very much."

"Oh." Vega had to rapidly rearrange half a dozen assumptions. "Even knowing that I'm a Cousin?"

"I am entirely sure that if I decided against you on that ground alone, Vivian would give me a look, and thank you, no." Farran gestured. "Tea. You want some tea."

Vega shook her head, trying to clear it, but tea

was a good idea. It was a delicate green, in fact, just lightly fragranced. She peered at him over the rim, once she'd taken a sip. "And the rest of it?"

"I enjoy spending time with you." Farran repeated it firmly. "But there are some practical things to talk about. I'm only in London for so long. And I love Thebes. I don't want what happened with Lucinda, where both of us were unhappy all the time." Vega heard it, more than saw it in his face, that there was an ache there.

"You really like your home, don't you?" She considered. "I need to visit my family regularly. I mean, besides the part where I'm working on this for them. But I don't need to live there. I have an awful schedule for spending time with people who aren't working at a nightclub."

"I like a quiet evening on my own," Farran pointed out. "Or there are portals. For sometimes." He took a breath. "I think it's something we'd need to talk through. In more detail. Not just when you're actually working, or when I'm working, but all the things around that."

"I might be able to get Sundays off, too." Vega offered after a little. "It would depend. But they are quieter, and Madam Helena might like to have a night to give people a trial more simply. It'd be worth talking through."

"Let's set that aside then, for the moment. We think there's a possible solution. It will take more information, and we have other things to talk about."

"We do." Vega let out a huff of breath. "What else?"

"Vandermeer. And then, depending how much

time we have, a bit more of what we'd like together. Or do you want to save that part for when you don't need to be at work?"

"I'd rather save it. I'd hate to, erm. Have to stop."

CHAPTER 28
A LITTLE LATER

Farran had to look away at that comment about not wanting to stop. He felt the same, or at least, as much the same as those words could convey. He was certain that if, when, somehow; they got onto the topic of each other, of creating something together between them, stopping would be the worst thing ever. And the thing was, talking was necessary. The logistics, even with both of them trying their best, were messy and complicated, and there'd never be enough hours in the day. At least not as long as Vega was performing.

Farran was not the sort of man who would ever suggest someone he cared about give up what she loved for convenience or even for love. That wasn't love, that was a cage, and he wanted no part of that.

It was part, he thought, of why so many of his previous relationships hadn't worked. The women he'd walked out with had ideas of what a relationship looked like, who was responsible for what, and

all of those chafed. As much as his first apprenticeship had. Even if it hadn't bothered him, he couldn't
do that to someone else.

Now he cleared his throat. "Might I join you on
the sofa?" It would be easier than craning over the
table, and he wanted, well. He wanted to be closer.
Even if they were still figuring out so many things.
She blinked at him, then smiled, the sort of smile
that was all invitation, and nodded. Farran moved,
sitting next to her, not quite touching, but almost
immediately her fingers moved to thread through
his. "There." It sounded inane.

"Vandermeer." Vega seemed to force herself to
focus. "We should lay out what we both know. Oh. I
should apologise, maybe? Tell you, anyway."

"Apologise?" Farran wasn't sure what she'd be
apologising for. "Yes? If you feel the need."

She squeezed his fingers once. "I went and talked
to Mistress Porter about you. After we had the
meeting at Ormulu. I don't know if she'd have
mentioned."

"Vivian is extremely thorough about her discretion, so no, she didn't. Not about anything that
might be any kind of consultation." Farran was,
actually, encouraged. "What did you ask her?"

"If you knew about her being a Cousin. And she
said..." Vega gestured with her free hand. "That
you'd been out at one of the estates with her a few
times."

"Doing research in advance of your questions,
then." Farran shifted to look at her. "Do you think
I'd be upset by that? There are excellent reasons for
doing a bit of research before going out on a limb.

And especially with something that you, all of your family, keep private for excellent reasons."

Vega let out a huff of breath, loud enough he could hear it. "Most people don't understand." Her chin twitched. "People at the club don't know. Though maybe Madam Helena does. I haven't told her, though."

Farran nodded. "She runs things well, from everything you've said. And she's been around in the larger community for a long while, I know that." He considered. "May I ask about that? And then about Vandermeer."

"Yes, of course." Vega twisted slightly, so now they were more or less looking at each other, their knees barely touching, hand in hand.

"When you sing, obviously, you're using some magic, but I'm curious about what kinds. Not least because I'm wondering if Vandermeer has picked up on something related." Also, Farran was curious, but he'd not have asked, not here and now, if there hadn't been an actual reason.

"I'm trained in Incantation, the same as many people. Well, most performers in Albion at my level or a bit below, honestly. It's the obvious choice for us. The use of the voice, the body, spoken enchantment." Vega considered. "And you think that's relevant?"

"What we know about Vandermeer is - not as much as I'd like. That he approached you, initially. That he's turned up at the club. Vivian did a little checking for me. He's registered as a guest at the Cecil. He's been in town for a month or two, and he's been having the sort of business meetings that

suggests import and export trade." Farran added
after a moment, "Which can often be a cover for
people with rather less legal interests. She was
working on some American connections, but that's
tricky." He paused. "Would he recognise you as a
Cousin? Even potentially? Or know about the object
you're— we're— looking for?"

Vega bit her lip, and then let go of Farran's hand
so she could reach for her tea. Farran was glad she
liked it. It was a blend Vivian preferred, and it had
seemed the right mix of something with flavour and
something ephemeral. When Vega spoke again, it
was not an answer, but rather a question. "What do
you make of him, first? Besides what little she found
out."

"If I were looking at him as a client?" Farran
considered that. "Nicely dressed. A hair too sharply,
actually, the sort of sharp dresser where I wonder
who he's trying to impress, if that makes sense. It's
not always a terrible reason, and some people do just
like being entirely up to the minute. An American
tailor, obviously, though I think a magical one."
Farran thought through the rest. "If he showed up at
Ormulu, I'd be wanting a profile of his background
and accounts. His likelihood of paying his bills, not
that we'd ever put it that crassly."

It made her giggle, and that was worth the phras-
ing, definitely. "Is that something you have a system
for, then? I'm not used to that, I don't do private
parties. That's a lot of bother and people groping
you or thinking that because they've paid for your
voice, they've paid for other things." Vega met his
eyes. "I'm no untouched maiden, but that's not a

path I have any interest in. For one thing, it's as easy to be quickly discarded as quickly taken up. The current sort of man inclined to take a mistress doesn't have the staying power of men in the eighteenth century. Or earlier."

That was not a way anyone had ever put the problem to Farran. "If you were going to be a mistress, you'd want it to be the sort that had an agreement. A cottage or whatever for you whenever he was tired of you. A way to make your own life."

"That." Vega set her teacup down again. "Vandermeer."

"How does he make you feel? Like I said, he makes me feel like I'd want more of a solid background on him before any sort of business arrangement. He has the feeling of someone who'd pass off a fake, though there's only so many times you can do that."

"Do people actually try often?" Vega reached for his hand again, and Farran twisted his wrist slightly to make it easier, enjoying the warmth of her fingers.

"Often enough. Sometimes they don't know. Someone a generation or two ago replaced a stone in a family piece with an excellent replica, for example, or a painting's been duplicated. There are some ways to check, now, if you know. Ormulu has talisman makers and a few others on retainer. If it's a matter that might touch on legal issues, there are things the Penelopes can do. And there are a fair number of fairly easy tricks, if you know what to look for." He looked down at his hands. "That's part of what I'm good at. Realising something's a bit off, even if I can't pin down by myself what it is or how to prove it. One of the seniors at Ormulu, he can do it by looking at something. At least in the periods he's expert in, he just says he knows if something's a fake or a replica, he can't ever explain why."

"So what— I mean. It's a help to know something's wrong, but what happens then?" Vega asked. She was speaking softly, as if she were working her way through a particular thought while asking.

"Then we do more investigation. Or we hire someone to. Or the person skulks off with their object and we pass a message along to the other auction houses to keep an eye out." Farran shrugged. "We're not the courts, but we also put our own reputation behind what goes in our sales. We'll get it wrong sometimes, but we try to do it as rarely as possible."

Vega nodded slowly. "And Vandermeer feels that kind of wrong. Like he's claiming one thing, and he's being another. Too sharply dressed, like you said. Is that just because he's American?"

"Here's my question. Are there Cousins in America? There must be."

"Some. But it's different other places." Vega frowned. "It's not something I'm used to explaining. Give me a minute?"

"Of course." Farran settled himself, shifting one foot so his toes didn't fall asleep, and thinking through what else might be relevant.

After a good two minutes, she spoke again, carefully, feeling her way through it. "Here, we have the Pact. The Fatae aren't entirely gone, but nearly so. All the interactions are either very private, on our estates, or mediated by the Council and the Pact itself. Mostly it's just the Cousins. And most people in Albion don't even know about us, never mind the Fatae."

She took a breath. "But in America, it's more complicated. There are Fatae of those places, and they never agreed to the Pact. There are Fatae from Europe who came to the Americas at various points, and settled in, not bound by the Pact. And while people in the United States and Canada make the Pact, it's sort of a, a holdover from being a British colony. So he might well know about Cousins. Or how to identify us. Me. Or how to find a particular object of interest. Is there any sign of whether he might work for a client, something like that?"

"Nothing that was obvious. That was part of what Vivian was trying to figure out. But if he were hired by, I don't know, some railroad magnate or whoever has the money, we wouldn't know that, unless we got lucky. Or even someone in the magical community. It's not like people publicise that sort of thing. We might hear it through a contact with an American museum or collector or auction house. Often we do, but it's not the kind of thing we can just ask about. Especially the Cousin part. Or the Fatae part, whichever applies." Farran let out a sigh. "I think that fits the observed situation. That he's looking for something specific, that he thinks you— we— are looking for the same thing, or something close enough. And if he follows us often enough, he might get a lead."

Vega nodded. "He makes me feel..." She glanced off at the corner of the room. "A bit like a fox or a hart must feel, being hunted. Something predatory."

"Foxes slip through the hounds often enough, I gather. In song and story, as well as in the flesh,"

Farran offered. "I like that about them, as long as they're not going after our chickens." That made her smile and relax a little, he could tell through her fingers. "Do you feel safe enough? If you think he's a danger, then that's something to take to the Guard, at least to consult. And Vivian knows who to talk to there. Several people, actually, depending on the actual problem."

There was a long pause. Farran liked that she took her time, that she didn't rush, not about important questions. "I don't know. He's not done anything obviously dangerous. He just keeps turning up when he oughtn't to. It's a big city, so many people and different things going on. How is he doing that?"

"There's a chance he's following your magical signature a bit," Farran said. "Having heard you sing at the club, that might be enough for a thaumaturgical enchantment. I can ask Vivian if there's a simple enough way to block it. That's where some of the old Fatae lore comes from. Turning your coat inside out, red thread, rowan, things like that. I don't know which ones will work here, but she will. Or she'll know who to ask."

"Will that cause problems?" Vega said. "I don't want her annoyed at me. Or the Guard or anything like that."

"As I understand it, you have a right to go wander around London and look at the sights without someone following you. It won't stop him if he spots you in person, either. But it will mean he can do rather less popping up." He held up his finger. "This building is thoroughly warded, and your flats are too, I'm assuming. The ordinary

protections that keep the non-magical from knocking
on the door do a fair bit, if I have it right. I was
talking over it with Maddie and Tony a month or
two ago." There, he'd slipped in the names
comfortably.

"What do they do?" Vega asked it, a little
distracted.

"Tony finds specific materia for people. You
know the sort of thing, the yellow eggshell of a
particular bird, a plant documented to have been
picked at dawn on a certain day. Maddie's a research
assistant. They were up because she was looking at a
few things in museum collections, and people give
her a lot of bother on her own sometimes. Their
older sister…" He tilted his head. "If you met Vivian
at her office, you've met Eleanor."

"Oh." Vega considered that. "So you're familiar
with— I mean." She swallowed. "Look, I think we've
got back to where if I don't leave, I'll be late for the
club. Or entirely too distracted."

"Can't have that." Farran said promptly, taking
his cue. "We'll find another time for the conversation. Monday evening?"

"Monday, as soon as you're done at the office,"
Vega countered. "And here, perhaps? Well. Less fuss
from my landlady, certainly. I could stay later than
eight, too, when she'd want you out."

"I'll arrange something for supper. Let me know
what you'd like tomorrow, or if there are things you
don't eat. I should be getting some biscuits from
Lena Monday, too, we can share those." He liked
that idea immensely, and Lena wouldn't be baking
them until tomorrow, so he could ask her to decorate
a few particularly nicely. Now Farran stood, helping

her put her coat on, before offering a chaste kiss on her cheek. "Monday. Let me know if you need anything before then."

"Monday." Vega smiled at him, and then she turned, as if she wanted to say a lot more and wasn't letting herself yet. Farran entirely understood that feeling.

CHAPTER 29
MARCH 19TH AT FARRAN'S ROOMS

"Evening!" Vega tried to keep the nerves out of her voice. "I brought you something. Belated birthday present." She held up the gift, wrapped up, but still obviously book shaped. It was half-six, arranged so that Farran would have a chance to get back to his flat after his work and do whatever he felt needed doing.

"Come in." Farran opened the door. He was dressed much less formally than she'd seen him previously, even for their walking adventures that included the caves. Now he was in shirtsleeves, a sweater vest with a geometric design over it, and trousers, just slippers on his feet. There was a fire in the fireplace, which made the sitting room warm, and he had flowers on the table, with two chairs handy. "Your coat?"

Vega let him take it and hang it up, as she took off her hat and placed it on the hook by the door. Then she turned back to him, and he reached out and took her hand, deliberately. It made her blush, even though they'd both agreed on this, it wasn't as if she were surprising him. Not like she had last time. "Where do we— I mean?"

"I've supper waiting, if you'd like. It will hold, of course, if you'd rather wait. There's tea, or I have some wine open." Farran gestured at the chair, or at the sofa.

"I— supper, certainly. If that's not a bother. And I suppose we probably want to talk about some things. Also, I want to tell you about this." She waved the book again.

It made him smile, and that was grand. His eyes crinkled when he was happy. "Have a seat at the table then, and I'll bring things out. Nothing terribly fancy. We're still learning each other's tastes, aren't we? Chicken, potatoes, some roast vegetables, a nice sauce." He glanced at her. "We've not talked too much about food, actually?"

"No, and I suspect it matters to you." Vega offered it a little cautiously, but got another of those smiles. "You mentioned your housekeeper?"

"Lena, yes. Right, let me get the tray." He disappeared into the little kitchenette, or at least what she assumed was one, and came out with a tray, properly done up with silver covers on the food. "There's a proper kitchen downstairs. The food is quite good, as a standard, though I admit, not Lena's." He set it down. The meal was certainly served nicely. The potatoes were the little decorative browned puffs that meant someone had gone to several steps of trouble. They sat beside chicken and roasted vegetables with a cream sauce. It smelled excellent, and Farran pulled out the chair for her before pouring wine and taking his

own. He held up his glass. "To good things to
come."

It was a toast she could entirely agree with, and
so she echoed it immediately. It took her a few bites
to get the sense of the thing. Balanced, with a focus
on things going together. She suspected it was rather
like how Farran went at art. Certainly how she went
at music, and that gave her a place to talk.

"We haven't talked much about it. Some singers
are very fixed on what they eat. This food is good or
bad for the voice, this one bad for the figure. I'm not
like that. Either way round. I like a lot of different
kinds of foods, just like I enjoy a lot of different
kinds of music. Chestnuts from a street vendor, a
meal in an excellent restaurant. I've—" Her voice
caught. "A little less experience with the smaller sort
of home cooked meal. The cooks at home are
cooking for several dozen at the smallest, and often
twice that."

"A different sort of cooking," Farran agreed.
"Lena is cooking for a dozen, maybe, most nights.
Maybe twenty, during the War, we had more rooms
taken for a while. Nothing fancy, soup and chicken,
vegetables, something for pudding some nights." He
added, "We have pudding. That is perhaps a little
fancy. And some of Lena's biscuits, if we need a
nibble later."

His eyes were dancing, which suggested he'd
gone to a certain amount of thought about it.
"That's something I'm enjoying about London.
The range of restaurants. The arrangement here is
that they cook breakfast, supper if I want it, and
I'm on my own for lunch. Or sometimes I've gone
out with colleagues. Smoothing the social connec-

tions, but also a chance to try different places to eat."

"I hadn't really thought how that might be part of your work. Or, I suppose, the sort of meals you have at gallery or exhibit openings?" Vega took another few bites, taking her time.

"Exactly. Though those are often bites, all the worries about dropping a bit down your suit or having something on your fingers or teeth. And not enough food to keep going. Those nights, here, I ask for Welsh rabbit or soup or something of the kind when I get home. Stasis charms at least make that easy. It's not a bother how late I come home."

"When you're in Trellech, are you in rooms there?" Vega asked.

"I was. My landlady wanted to do some renovations, so I moved my things back to Thebes when I took on this contract." Farran shrugged. "We'll see after that. I can always stay at Thebes, or Tony has a spare room if it's just for a night here and there." Then he glanced up and added, "Of course, you might fit into those plans, and that would change some things."

Her mouth curled up. "All right. Let's talk about that. You get your present when we've cleared the table, then." She took a breath. "The thing about being a singer is it depends who hires you. I could set up a fairly steady contract on one of the liners, if I wanted, but that's rather tedious work, unless you really like life on a liner. Or you want to see different places. I did it for a year, early on."

Farran tilted his head. "How much of that was being away from Albion, and how much of it was, I don't know. A small cabin, seeing the same people all the time. People talking through your songs, I'm sure, if you were in a lounge or something of the kind."

"As if I don't get that now." Vega glanced up and Farran had tilted his head, one eyebrow arched. It was a rather compelling expression. He didn't disagree with her. That was the thing. He was just making it clear he perceived something different. "Oh, all right. Not at the Crystal Cave. The people who want to talk are down on the larger dance floor." Then she added, before she forgot about it,, "Can we go to a museum together sometime? Some-where you can talk about the art we're looking at and tell me what you see?"

Farran blinked, and then he flushed an utterly delightful pink. "Really? Most people find me tedious like that."

"I rather think I won't. But if I did, that's the sort of thing we should figure out sooner than later, anyway. So. A museum. You pick. Tomorrow, or next weekend." She swallowed. "Please? I'd like it very much."

"Now, of course, I'm not going to be able to decide which. Probably best next weekend, so I have time to pick something interesting. A little out of the way."

"There." She beamed, glad to have given him what seemed like the best sort of challenge. "Besides whatever other investigation we do, of course."

"You do— pardon for speaking of business over a meal. You realise I'm entirely engaged in the prob-lem, not as a consultant, but wanting to solve it. And make sure you're not alone dealing with Vandermeer."

"Other men," Vega said, carefully, tackling one part of this before the rest, "would talk about keeping me safe."

"First, you're a performer in night clubs. I'm certain you normally have a solid line in keeping yourself safe. Though perhaps that depends on knowing the ground, having others around. But second, I have some skills, but mostly not relating to fighting. Other than the sort of fighting that happens in an auction with bids and counter-bids."

The way he put it made her giggle for just a moment. "Fair. I like that you know your skills and your limits. It's rather rare, actually, in men your age or quite a bit older." She then considered. "One reason I like you enough to talk about something longer-term. Or at least seeing what it looks like."

Again, he took the cue smoothly. "I like time with you, in all its forms. If you want to pay the expenses for whatever investigation we do, that's certainly fair. Or consulting fees for anyone else, of course. But for my part, I would prefer time with you without needing to think about how we're counting the time. The best sorts of puzzles often involve waking up at three in the morning and having a new idea."

"And if, some night, you should do that in my ear, yes, I see how the accounting might become a tad complex." Vega nodded, though she was decid-edly amused at both his priorities and how he put it. "All right. I pay the expenses, that includes relevant meals out. Fair?"

"Fair." Farran leaned back a little, setting his fork down. "Should I clear the table? And open your present?"

"Please." Vega let him stand and clear. He really did have rather lovely manners. Subdued manners, he wasn't at all flashy about them. But his hands were deft. He didn't clatter the plates or the silverware. Watching him walk to the kitchenette gave her a lovely view of his backside, and more than a few ideas about what he was probably like under his clothing. She'd seen plenty of men scantily dressed backstage at various points. She had a wide range of experience to draw on.

When he came back, she pushed the wrapped book toward him. "Present, logistics, pudding, and then perhaps conversation about what we'd like to try together tonight?"

"Followed by the doing of whatever that is? Oh, yes." Farran glanced up, his eyes warm, then looked back down, untying the ribbon and the paper nimbly rather than cutting it off. He peered at the book, then looked up. "Art history?"

"Art history. All the painters in there are Cousins. None of them are still alive, though sometimes, it hasn't been very long. There are people around who collaborated with them, who know their work. I thought you'd enjoy it in particular. And enough of the right period, yes?"

It was one of the privately printed copies, with magical copies of the artworks tipped in to the relevant sections. They were covered with a thin sheet of tissue paper to protect them. She saw his eyes widen as he got to the first of the prints. "Proper prints, so you can appreciate the art. A few of the pieces are in museums, most are in private collections. Not all Cousins, mind."

Farran's eyes got wider. "This is glorious. And

no, I know about a couple of the ones in private collections. Lord and Lady Carillon bought this." He opened it to a page of a landscape, with a group of people with falcons on their wrists. "Two years ago. Painted up near their Cumbria estate, I believe, in Lord Carillon's grandfather's time. Vivian knows them quite well. Lady Carillon worked for her for a year or so."

"Ah, see, I was sure you'd know some of them." Then she let herself smile warmly. "Now, shall we see if I am enticing enough to drag you out of the book for the evening?"

CHAPTER 30
THAT EVENING

"Oh, I think you might manage that." Farran managed to keep his wits together. The book was stunning. It wasn't just the book itself, it was the attention to detail implied by the book. It was a book where he could aspire to the knowledge inside, and make use of it, and also simply enjoy it. And it was a book that danced the line between things she could talk about and things she couldn't, casting a light that wouldn't damage the art in the process. As it were.

Now, he glanced back toward his bedroom. "Pudding? And then we can retire to the bedroom for a little and… well. We should talk a bit about that."

"A fine plan." Her hand twitched, as if she wanted to get up and help, but she waited for Farran to do so. He went off and came back with a smaller tray, with two glass pots of chocolate mousse, delicately topped with whipped cream and chocolate shavings.

Vega's eyes widened at it. "Oh, how charming. Also, how delicious, I'm sure." He set one down in front of her and gestured at the wine, but she shook her head. "I'd like to be clear-headed for the next bit. I drink less than you'd think, on average, for being a singer in a club."

"I'd have thought that's somewhere you wanted a clear head, ordinarily?" Farran offered, taking his own mousse and the tiny spoon that went with it, then trying a bite, letting himself sigh with the pleasure of it.

When he looked back at Vega, she was considering him. "You might actually understand this. People like the ones performing, especially women, and most especially singers, to behave as if they're the only one in the room. Some men get ideas, they get jealous if the singer pays attention to someone else."

"Hence why Madam Helena has excellent security," Farran said. Then he watched her, and asked, because he wasn't sure how else to go forward. "What has that meant for you, personally?"

"Not a lot in the way of lasting relationships or friendships. I get along with people, of course. It's better that way. Some people make a show of being a diva, and I've never found that appealing. Or, fundamentally, a good idea. But most men, there's always this sense that they like me for the me that is on stage. They expect that all the time."

"Well, that's no good." It was, perhaps, not the ordinary thing to say. Certainly, she didn't think so. Her eyes went wide again. "No one could keep that up forever." He shrugged, once. "Or, I suppose some couples do. But I think it involves not sharing a bedroom, only being together when she's all done up and dressed and whatever cosmetics and undergarments and charms and potions."

Something in it made her giggle, and that was an entirely human sort of sound. "That. And I enjoy that fuss, for being on stage. But I also like not."

Farran considered her. "And tonight's somewhere in the middle?" He did not understand cosmetics, even though Maddie had tried to explain the different implications a number of times, and some of the women at Ormulu had as well. Vega looked lovely. He was sure she had lipstick and such on, but it was not overdone or obvious. It suited her. Mostly, it made more of what was already there, rather than how she'd been done up at the club. Of course, the lighting was different at the club too, and he understood well enough what that did to pigments.

She nodded, opened her mouth, closed it, and then opened it to take another bite of her mousse. After she swallowed, she met his eyes. "You don't make me feel like that. That all you're seeing is the me on stage."

"Well, no. For one thing, the you on stage does not dress for exploring caves." It made her smile again, and that was grand. "So, what you're saying is that you've had some relationships in your past, not recently." There was a tiny nod at that. "And that you don't want this to become about just one of your faces." Another small nod. "Then I suppose the Cousin part also has to be complicated. At least with me, you don't have to decide if you're going to explain it in the first place."

"There is that advantage." Vega glanced down at her plate, then ate the last spoonful deliberately. Now he was sure it was to give her time to think. "People make assumptions there too. That it will be particularly magical. Or that they'll be permitted into all of our family traditions. I haven't had that problem, but some of my cousins have. I mean, actual cousins, that generation."

"Not the general term, yes." Farran nodded. "All right. And we still need to talk about scheduling and all that. But I'm—" He swallowed hard now, because this was tricky. "Given that both of us have been on our own, I certainly would rather have a life with some of your time. Even if it wasn't as much as I might like in an ideal world without necessary bedtimes and work to be done and music to be made. Better the time we can have than a life without you."

"That, that..." Her voice cut off, then she tried again. "That is ridiculously romantic. Did you think about that in advance?"

"Oh, yes. I haven't thought about much else the last day or so. Well, beyond work." Then he stood, because otherwise he would lose his courage. "Shall we get more comfortable?" Farran offered his hand, and then they were walking back to the bedroom.

It was a serviceable bedroom. He'd added a blanket from home, and books, of course. At least the bed was a decent size, because sometimes these flats had married couples. He hesitated, then he reclaimed his hand, long enough to pull off the sleeveless jumper. She stepped back, watching him, before she shrugged out of her own jacket, leaving her in a sleeveless dress with buttons down the front.

He sat with more of a thump than he'd meant to. That put his head at her chest height, more or less, a chance to get a good look at the pendant she was wearing. "May I?" He gestured. "The stone?"

"Oh, you would be interested in the materia, wouldn't you? It's a talisman, but entirely safe to handle. Actually, I'm curious what you think." Vega settled beside him, thigh just barely touching thigh, and that was utterly distracting, not much in the way of clothing between them. She twisted, so he could get a good look, her chin up and to one side to give him space. "Go ahead and touch."

The sentence was completely full of innuendo. Farran took a breath and then let his fingers reach. He could feel the magic in the pendant pulling at his fingertips, guiding them, unerringly. A focal stone, obviously, "An aquamarine, pale blue, so much so it's likely clear in some lights."

"Easier to wear it with more things, though I do often have a flash of blue in what I wear." Her voice was even the sort of modulation that suggested there was something tucked away in there. Farran looked at her again, caught her eye, and she added, "Alcyone is also associated with the kingfisher. A good blue, or blue and copper, those are a, mmm. Not a heraldry, but a sort of blazon."

"Thank you for that information." He made a mental note of it, for the benefit of future presents, especially with an eye to colour. Then he let his fingers touch the stone, getting a sense for it, before he let his thumb touch her skin. She was breathing shallowly, holding still, but it had a nervous quality to it before she took a breath. He felt the stone flex, and then everything settled. "Aquamarine is good for confidence."

"It is. Good for performance. This one is

designed for clarity of voice. It was meant for someone who did a lot of speaking, originally. But it works well for singing. A family piece. And the setting isn't so dated."

"No." He let his thumb shift a little on her collarbone. "May I kiss you now?"

"Oh, yes." She turned her head back towards him and made it easy to bring their lips together. However out of practise she might be, she had a delicate and practical attention to the angle of her head, they didn't bump noses. There was the brief taste of her lipstick, then her mouth was soft against his, her tongue inviting. His hand went around her back, to steady, as if they'd been dancing, and hers settled at his waist, making him arch a little at the touch.

Farran didn't want to rush it. There was only one first kiss, one first everything, and he wanted to savour every single one. Like walking into a room and seeing a piece of art for the first time, in all its glory. Not as a print or photograph, but as it had been meant to be seen. There was nothing like that moment, even if all the moments that came later— the deep study, the examination of the tiniest details, the building of an understanding of the work on every possible level— also had their own glories and passions and delights.

When she finally pulled back, breathless, she leaned her forehead on his shoulder, and he let his hand come a little further up her back. "All right?"

"Very." Vega took a deeper breath, let it out slowly, then lifted her head again. "You don't rush."

"No." He'd never talked about this with anyone, even Uncle Cadmus. "The first time, the first moments. Those matter. And with you, even more. I hope we have many, strung out like brushstrokes of paint, tiny specks of pigment, all making some glorious epic painting. But the beginning, it sets the ground for everything else. No rushing."

She pulled back just enough to look at him fully, then she let herself fall back on the bed, tugging his hand along with her. He got the hint immediately and stretched out against her. Some other night, he might have been embarrassed. Surely, she'd feel him against her, that there was a certain rather blatant bit of desire. And Farran wasn't sure what she wanted. Or how to begin to ask.

"I am thinking." Her voice was perfectly pitched, all of her own skills on display, and he could listen to that for hours. Years. Decades. "That tonight is for kisses and hands. If you want to take your time about the firsts. I don't think either of us wants to stop at kisses." She was watching him now, her eyes focused, and then her hand shifted to between their bodies, the back of it brushing deliberately against where he was hard. He couldn't stop himself from grunting, or from pushing, just slightly, into that touch. "No, we don't, do we?"

The next minutes, the next hour, were full of a steady exploration, done the way they'd gone about Greenwich and especially the caves. Both of them were paying attention to the small details, a gasp or a shift of body, or the way skin shivered when the touch was just right. She encouraged him to undo her dress, button by button. He took his time, wanting his fingers to learn how to do it with just the right amount of delicacy. Vega untucked his shirt, working her hand up against his skin, beneath his undershirt. In the end, he was rocking against her, both of them sprawled on the bed. Finally, he got his fingers in just the right place to rub and bring her off. Her fingers curled around him until he exploded.

He let out one last gasp, before burying his head in her chest, feeling Vega stroke his hair gently as he felt her breaths. They lay there like that, neither of them wanting to move for several minutes, before her fingers shifted to his shoulder. "Learning how to sing a duet usually takes some practice." She sounded absolutely amused. "In your case, our case, together, not nearly so much."

"Mmm." He ought to say something more than that, and he couldn't. All of him was warm and happy and content. Her fingers stopped for a second, then picked up in his hair again. In a few minutes, they'd need to move, to clean up, and she obviously hadn't planned to spend the night. But for the moment, there was no reason to hurry, and every reason to soak in the moment.

CHAPTER 31

MARCH 22ND IN VIVIAN'S OFFICE, TRELLECH

"Here, sit. Farran, the sofa." They were settled in the same office Vega had been in previously, but she was fairly sure the space was new to Aunt Ancha. Her aunt was glancing around, taking in the decorations. She was almost certain that Vivian had not been about to suggest the sofa, but had taken in some key detail as she and Farran entered the office.

That was going to take some thinking about. She'd not been able to see Farran for two days. There'd been the equinox rituals out at the family estate on Tuesday, and yesterday had been the new moon, so she'd stayed out there until midafternoon. And then of course, she'd needed to be at the club in good order, not flushed and rushing from a few moments with Farran.

He had, however, written her a lovely note by journal. Actually three notes, at different points. The first to make it clear he was looking forward to more time together. Then two more about various small things he'd come across during his day that made him think of her or continued a conversation they'd had. She'd managed to write back, though not until after she woke up and read the last note which also had included where to meet him. That had been near the Trellech portals, so quite public. They'd not had time to do more than say hello and come directly to Vivian's office.

Now, she glanced at him, settled on the sofa, and made sure her skirts were doing what older aunts thought skirts should do. Farran joined her a moment later, after a brief tussle with Vivian, all done in eyebrows and gestures, over who should bring the tea tray over. Vega rather liked what she saw of that, how he was deferential, but also not too much so. It suggested he'd be able to handle himself competently with her aunts as well. And her parents. That was something she'd have to think about a good bit more, and soon.

Once Aunt Ancha was seated in one of the two easy chairs, with Vivian taking the other, she nodded once. "And you are?"

Before Vega had to figure out the introductions, Vivian spoke, smoothly. "Ancha, I am pleased to present Farran Michaels. Farran, Ancha Beaumont. One of Vega's aunts, as I'm sure you've learned already."

Farran inclined his head. "A pleasure, ma'am. I believe I've read a paper by you, about dating certain artworks by the constellations? Three, no four years ago?"

Aunt Ancha smiled, the sort of expression that always made Vega a trifle wary. "Did Vega tell you to say that?"

"Oh, no, ma'am. I'd not want to place her in a difficult position regarding her family. Also, I'd already read it and made notes on it well before I met her. I'd love to discuss it with you at some point, perhaps by letter? There are a couple of paintings likely to come to auction at Ormulu later this year that feature a night sky. And where the provenance is not as clear as we'd like."

Vega cleared her throat, and Farran spread out one hand to show he was deferring to her. "I gave Farran a gift on Monday of Uncle Belisarius's book." Her aunt's eyes widened.

"Farran has sometimes been a guest on our estates," Vivian said, her voice crisp. "So that we're all clear about portions of the conversation. Farran, please let me know if there's some detail that you feel needs clarification."

"Of course, Vivian." Farran shifted a little, leaning back just slightly. He didn't move to touch Vega. That was the right choice. She would find it immensely distracting. They had particular points to discuss. "Vandermeer, then?"

Vivian snorted, genteel. "You are direct. I appreciate that. Yes. I have been inquiring about Thomas Vandermeer for a fortnight or so. Since Farran first raised a concern with me. My connections are rather less prompt in America, but I have some initial information."

Aunt Ancha nodded. "Go on, then." Not that this stopped her from watching Farran, apparently he was getting all her visible attention at the moment. Vega hoped he wouldn't take it wrong.

"I have confirmed that a man matching that name and description has indeed come to London

for various business dealings. That man hails from a
notable and longstanding family in New York state.
The nature of the business is somewhat obscure. He
is nominally working for at least two of the wealthy
families of New York. New money, of course, by
their standards and ours. Oil and imports, I believe.
He does not seem to have known connections to the
Cousins in America, but I can't be certain about
that. Regardless, he is also known to be making a
point of exploring art. Not directly at the auctions.
Farran?"

Farran picked up smoothly. "He is not listed on
the registers at any of the major auction houses,
though he is listed at Clermont." That was Ormulu's
principal rival for the magical auction trade. The
way she'd heard it put, though not by Farran, he'd
scrupulously avoided comment so far, was that they
were determined in pursuit of the best options for
their clients. Vega suspected that meant a certain
amount of not entirely legal manoeuvring. "But I'd
expect someone working at that level to have a
buyer."

"Explain to me how that works." Aunt Ancha's
voice was crisp, then she added, more gently,
"Please."

"Bidders at auctions can make choices, well-
educated ones, based on who is bidding. The Carillons will bid up on high-quality incunabula. The
Mortons on silver boxes with enchantments,
anything that might be suitable as a gift for someone
they know. The Devon Howards bid up to a certain
point on porcelain ware in sets. If they are in the
room for such auctions, people will bid accordingly.
Some sellers might have a false bidder in the room to

push the bids higher. If, instead, it's someone bidding for them, that evaluation is much harder. The banks all offer it as a service. If you see one of the Scali, you don't know who they're bidding for or how high they might go." Then he waited a perfect beat and added, "Of course, if you know the players and the art, you can make better judgements on this point. But it takes a lot more observation."

"Huh." Aunt Ancha nodded. "So if he were here buying for a client in America, you'd expect him to be at the auctions. But possibly working through someone hired to make the bids according to instructions. Someone better known to the auction house."

"Just so. There are a number of checks and balances. No one wants a sale to go to someone whose agreement turns out to be made of false coin. Coins that turn to crumbling leaves." It was a gesture at some of the old folklore about Fatae gifts.

Aunt Ancha snorted now, and she was relaxing. That was excellent. "I see your point, Farran. And you don't have a way to find out who he's working with."

"No, ma'am. The banks keep confidentiality, barring the proper sort of request from the Courts or Guard."

"People are allowed to bid on art. Even excessive amounts," Vivian said, dryly. "Is there any way to find a list of the actual buyers for recent auctions?"

Farran nodded. "There is, and I brought the lists, but they're not terribly helpful. Obviously, there are a limited number of late Roman or Anglo-Saxon items auctioned at any given time, just due to their general scarcity." He reached into his satchel, pulling out a set of notes clipped at the corners. "The top sheet summarises items from the period, as well as any where they might plausibly have been meteoric iron."

Vivian took them, scanning them. "How long did this take for you to put together?"

"About three hours over the last two days. And I owe two people a dinner out." Farran replied. "About half of it is chargeable to the current work, though."

Vivian raised an eyebrow, and Farran shrugged, though Vega was almost certain he was deliberately not making much of it. "Can you explain, Vivian, please?"

"This is an exceedingly tidy bit of work, tedious to put together. Though I will grant, Farran, that at the moment you have excellent access to the relevant lists. Along with a demonstrated knack for cheerfully chatting to clerks."

"I learn from the best, Vivian," Farran replied, though he was definitely smiling now. Vivian seemed amused, which was all to the good.

"What does that mean about what we do?" Vega asked. Vivian handed her the list summary, and Vega peered at it. There were perhaps twenty different names, stretching over the past few months. Four were starred, with a note that those were not people known to be interested in the period.

"It gives us a possible angle on a business contact or two," Vivian said. "I have someone seeing if she can arrange a casual meeting in the hotel." She added to Aunt Ancha, "Gratis, in this case, given other interests."

"Huh." Aunt Ancha nodded once. "All right. Can we be of any help? Certainly looking at patterns, constellations, is something we have skill in."

"Oh, since you're offering." Vivian stood, crossing to her desk and bringing back a portfolio, held closed around a stack of paper. "These are pieces that might or might not be related, a complete copy of the working files, with some attached notes. Eleanor can lend a hand if you can't make sense of something, by journal. I've told her to keep an eye out to give anything related priority."

"You're taking it seriously, then." Aunt Ancha leaned forward, taking the hefty set of paper.

"I don't like the feel of it any more than you do. You said he made you feel uncomfortable, Vega. Have you been able to give any better label to it? I ask because there are two plausible directions for his background, and the precautions would be different."

"I've heard descriptions of people, oh, on safari, something like that. Someone who turns around and realises some lioness or cheetah has crept close and is watching them. That kind of danger," Vega said immediately. "Then there was something in his magic, but I'm not sure if it was there the first time. Or if he were modifying whatever it was, since it was an entirely public bridge."

"Presumably he didn't want you fleeing, first thing," Vivian agreed.

Farran cleared his throat. "May I ask what the two directions are, or is that the sort of question that won't be answered? At least for me?"

Both Vivian and Aunt Ancha began to speak before Vivian waved a hand and Aunt Ancha continued. "Here, I think we might share the basics to

make certain we all have the same understanding."
She took a breath and went on. "There are lines of
Cousins in the Americas, but they are distinct at this
point from the lines in Albion. The Pact has an
ongoing impact, but it is not the same agreement,
not with the long indigenous Fatae, for example.
Over the years Cousins descended from Fatae on the
continent have migrated to the Americas as well.
Some of them are touchy about certain matters."

"I had explained that, Aunt Acha. Also, some of
us are decidedly touchy," Vega pointed out. "But we
have, what was the word Aunt Mera used? Agreed
on territories. When someone crosses the ocean,
those lines are much fainter and easier to cross."

"Just so. And if there is some reason this Vandermeer thinks he might have some connection to this
piece, or to a similar piece, or the person he is
working for does..." Aunt Ancha let her voice trail
off. "The other option is that he is someone who is
aware of Cousins and our magic, but because he
hunts it out, seeking it. They are rare in Albion,
because the Pact protects us from interference. But if
he is a short-term visitor, he would have not made
the full oath on the Silence, perhaps."

Farran was quick enough to see it immediately.
"Keeping his own magic private is a different matter
than the full agreement with how things stand,
upholding the treaties, and so on. If he didn't seek
out going to Trellech or Dinas Emrys or any of the
demesne estates, he just intended to stay in London,
too..." He shook his head. "I see the problem. May I
ask your recommendations?"

"There's a third option, actually." Vivian cut in.
"There is a chance— small, but real, I think, in this

case— that he is also doing some work for the American government of some form. Or possibly some other foreign government. It's hard to tell. I inquired of a few sources, but my sources for that sort of thing are not strong, and they take time."

Farran blinked. "Well. That would be complicated, yes. Does that change what we do about it?" He addressed that more to Aunt Ancha.

"I would recommend speeding up your research as much as you can. The sooner you can find this piece, the better," Aunt Ancha said. "We are glad to make a couple of protective talismans available to you."

Farran coughed. "We have found they have an odd reaction with my magic unless specifically tuned."

"Oh?" Vivian didn't say anything, but she arched an eyebrow, and Aunt Ancha subsided. "Vivian, in that case, whatever you might recommend."

"I have a friend with a pet creative alchemist," Vivian said, agreeably. "Who should have a suitable potion ready for delivery on Friday. Enough for several doses. It mutes the magical scent like traipsing through a river to put hounds off the scent."

Farran nodded. "I have a few ideas on where we might want to look next, but I'll need to make an arrangement for access for one of them. Or Vivian, you might have a better contact?" He hesitated, then added, "My first apprenticeship determined I've an odd knack for materia, but it also reacts a little unpredictably. It's an advantage now, but it needs tending."

That part of things took a few minutes. Vega did

not try to follow the back and forth, nor did Aunt Ancha. Farran and Vivian went back and forth, trading names, phrases that made sense to both of them. Aunt Ancha was listening, but Vega let her mind drift. Finally, Farran nodded. "Thank you, Vivian. Tell Uncle Cadmus I'll be in touch about when I can come out. Not Saturday, maybe in a week."

"Of course." She turned her cheek, and Farran stood before bending to kiss it. Vega took her cue, doing the same to Aunt Ancha. Farran offered her his arm, and they made their way through the door. It wasn't until they were outside, a good twenty feet down the street, that Farran said, "I'm sure they're going to gossip about us."

"Oh, yes. We should allow them to do so. No sense in making them cranky at a lack of gossip. I am glad they were both forthcoming enough. Shall we get tea somewhere in Trellech, before the portal? I've got an hour comfortably."

"Excellent."

CHAPTER 32

MARCH 24TH AT FARRAN'S ROOMS

"I'm sorry I'm so late." Vega was speaking as soon as Farran opened the door. "I overslept." She'd written a note in the journal forty minutes ago as soon as she'd woken up. It was now close to two, which meant they likely wouldn't get out to do any exploring this evening; they still had to figure out what they were doing. That was the point of today. On the other hand, Vivian had only got information about a connection to Farran that morning. He was meeting the man for coffee first thing tomorrow. Earlier than first thing.

"I was a little worried, but you've had a busy week," Farran pointed out. "Come in. Tea? We can take our time discussing. When's your call at the club?"

"Six, I'm afraid. We've got a new bit to work through. Mostly not mine, but Madam Helena wanted me handy to advise." Vega shrugged one shoulder, then turned so Farran could help her out of her coat. "But I can go straight there from here. I brought everything with me." She spun back to face him. "Including the cosmetics, so you don't need to worry about mussing them."

She was, in fact, not wearing much in the way of them. Or at least Farran didn't think so. He considered asking, then raised an eyebrow. "Oh, I just put on enough the cabbie wouldn't think things too odd. Do you mind? Some people find it—." She was not sure how to conclude.

Farran leaned in to kiss her, taking his time with the movement, so she had plenty of time to decline if she wanted. She did the opposite, arching to meet his mouth with hers, her hand coming to rest at his waist. He took that as a cue to settle his hand against her upper back. When he finally pulled away from the kiss to get a breath, he added, "That clear enough? Why would people mind?"

"A surprising number of people are interested in me only with my performing face on." Vega reached to touch his cheek.

"And that's a reason none of it lasted. If you're going to build something with someone, over time, you're going to see them in better moments and in worse ones. Also, at some point, I do hope to spend the night with you. A number of nights. I'm sure you don't wear all of that to bed." Farran hesitated, then said, "Tell me about your parents, would you? Just a little. Seeing as I've met one of your many aunts now?"

"Will you do the same?" Vega gestured at his desk. "I assume that's a photo with them?"

Farran nodded, then took a step back toward the couch. "You first? I need a minute to work up to it. It's not— it's not something I talk about much."

"Let's start with tea, then. I need to figure out how to put a thing or two," Vega said.

"Have you eaten? I've some sandwiches in stasis." Farran glanced over to find her nodding enthusiastically, and so he went off to turn on the kettle, plate a sandwich or two, and add some of Lena's biscuits. By the time the kettle sang, everything else was ready, and they'd both had a few minutes to gather their thoughts. Farran brought the tray out to find Vega settled on the sofa, and he set the food on the table, before turning to gather up the photo.

When he came back, Vega was a couple of bites into a sandwich, obviously hungry. He let her eat until the tea had steeped, and he'd poured it. By then she'd finished half of the sandwich. "You know the Cousin lines, we interact as much with others in our families as with our parents. We're often raised together with the others of our age. Time with our particular parents, but often they have their own tasks. My parents do some travelling work, both inside of Albion and outside, matters of locational magic. They'll be home for three months or six, away for about as long, back and forth."

"So part of your life, but not always the people who tucked you in?" Farran said, thinking about that.

"Exactly. And from the time I was five, I was up in with the others in the nursery rooms. Stories and hugs and kisses every night, but not always the same person." Vega shrugged. "People find it odd."

"Your family, and the others, have been doing things that way for a long time. Presumably with some reason. I'd rather not judge something I don't know enough about." Farran glanced at her. "It seems both sensible and safer."

That made her laugh. "You know enough to know that not all the tales of the Fatae, or the Cousins, are true, yes?"

"Oh, enough. Though also that plenty of them are sufficiently true to mind my manners and avoid offending." Farran gestured with one hand, and Vega reached to take it when he lowered it. "So you are fond of your parents, and they of you, but they're not, erm, the centre of home for you?"

"That's a good enough way to put it. Not my North Star, is how we'd say it. Or one of the ways, anyway."

"Fair enough." Farran leaned back a little, squeezing her hand, thinking about what else he needed to know about. Not wanted, because there was a fair bit of wanting in there, but most of it wasn't necessary today. "What do you want me to know about them? About what they might think of me? Will they be upset that I'm not a Cousin, or not whoever they might have thought you'd take up with?"

"I think they'll be pleased enough I show signs of taking up with someone steady. You are not a threat to us, or rather, if you're a threat, it's Vivian's fault. And if you've been to Electra's line's estates more than once, that speaks well of you." Vega chuckled. "You are not a frog, you do not think you're a frog, and so on."

"From what Vivian has shared, Electra and her line are most concerned with humans," Farran pointed out. "And also, if I'd strayed, they make oaths about shed blood. Not frogs, so much. Ribbit."

He made the last into a reasonable enough croak. He'd heard enough frogs in ponds in his own earthy explorations.

It made her giggle more, and Farran liked that sound a great deal, and what it did to her face. "The rest of my family... Aunt Ancha has given you an excellent report. She told me that already. They'd like to meet you, when convenient. A representative selection. They will be deliberately intimidating, so it's up to you to decide when it is convenient for that."

"And yet, it's the sort of challenge where facing up to it lets us get on to the next thing," Farran said. "I'd rather be able to meet them to share some success in the project, shall we say? But I defer to you about what that means for the timing. Your family, you know how to judge that."

Vega tilted her head. "The thing I am trying to understand about you is that you're not. What's the word I want here? Competitive. Aggressive. About that sort of thing. You don't need to be best at it."

"The thing about my line of work— the art history, not the magic— is that there are lots of specialists out there. I can't know everything. I'm not even an expert appraiser in more than a tiny sliver of it. Well. Still a journeyman, but I am assured the mastery will come in due course. To do what I'm learning to do well, I need to let other people be experts. Some of whom I want to work with, and some I don't. But insisting I know best, when I don't, that's how to fail. Not listening to my intuition about that, that's a way to fail."

"And that was part of the problem, your first

apprenticeship," Vega said, more quietly. "You mentioned a little of it."

"It made me feel like everything I did was wrong. And when I tried to shove away what I was feeling, everything got even worse. I felt miserable, but I also felt trapped. The trapped of some animal in a snare, deciding whether gnawing its leg off would be a reasonable choice. I didn't tell Uncle Cadmus about it because, because he had enough troubles. My parents didn't set up my inheritance sensibly. Most all of it was locked away until I was of age. Almost all our money that we could spare had gone to the apprentice fees. I didn't think I had options."

"And then, what?" Vega leaned forward, squeezing his hands. "And your parents?"

"My parents." Farran swallowed, turning his head to look away from Vega to the portrait. "That was taken the beginning of that summer. Mama and Papa and me. Uncle Cadmus was living at Thebes, so were they. Uncle Cadmus was younger by three years. They were travelling, and Mama took ill, and something happened, and they both died." He couldn't quite look back. "No one really explained, maybe because there wasn't any actual explanation. Just, they were gone. There was a funeral."

"And you were how old?" He felt her squeeze his hand, longer this time.

"Eleven. At tutoring school. Uncle Cadmus came and told me, and brought me home for the funeral and, and." Farran shrugged. "He was wonderful. Uncle Cadmus has always been wonderful. He didn't really know how to be a parent, not like that? He didn't try, and that mattered. Uncle Cadmus just figured he'd be the best uncle he could be. There was a lot of trying to sort out the money, and then I got into Schola, and Uncle Cadmus kept most of his worrying from me. But then, things started going wrong. That's a long explanation, not really for today? It involves a different Cousin, a different line, and it's sorted now. Vivian sorted it. But I went and asked her for help, because I knew Tony and his sister Eleanor."

"And that turned out well." Vega hesitated before saying the next bit. "I'm sorry I don't get to meet your parents. I suspect I'd have liked them. But I hope I can meet your uncle sometime soon."

"I'm sure Vivian will help make that easier. Uncle Cadmus doesn't do terribly well with change, sometimes? Certain kinds of changes, like the occasional new resident, he's used to those. But I like Vivian, and she cares for him, and that goes a long way. I know Uncle Cadmus just wants me to be happy, so it'll be mostly about making it clear that you do."

"Well." Vega nodded. "All right." She tugged his hand. "Look at me, can you?" It took a moment and another breath, but Farran turned to look at her. She met his eyes, deliberately, before looking at him more softly, more comfortably. "I also care about you. I suspect rather a lot, given a tiny bit more time. I gather that's sometimes a challenge for people who've had a fair bit of loss."

Farran shivered, before he could hide it or do anything else. Then he nodded. "I had a hard time with friends. Tony understood. His parents died when he was a little older, but he understands. And now I get on with the other apprentices at Ormulu, but it took a little to figure that out." His shoulder twitched. "The War sort of helped, horrible as that is. Lots of people losing people. They still say stupid things. The bits that smart and sting. But not as often. And they understand better when they've done it, even if they don't understand why it hurt."

"Huh." Vega twisted to take his other hand now, bringing them both together, next to each other. "To continue listing things I like about you, I like that you understand that people do things for a range of reasons. You don't take that personally when it's not. While not, I assume, wanting to keep on with the hurting bits."

"Less of the hurting, yeah." Farran let out a slow breath. "My life is really pretty good, honestly. I don't, I don't dwell on the harder parts. I don't think it's good for me."

"All right, then. Shall we move onto some other topic?" Vega asked. "A different sort of challenge. What we do next."

"Yeah." Farran paused. "Can I have a moment? Go wash my face? You should have more of a sandwich. You need food for thought." It was mostly an excuse to give himself a little time. Vega nodded, let go of his hands, and deliberately picked up another half sandwich as Farran stood up to make his way to the loo.

CHAPTER 33
A LITTLE LATER

Vega let Farran take the time he needed. For one thing, that was kind, and Vega wanted to be continually kind to Farran for all the obvious reasons and the usual ones, and then some. He was someone who didn't take kindness for granted, not from most people. It made her want to give him something different. Reliably different.

Also, she was still starving, and the sandwich was excellent. Salmon paste, with what must be hothouse cucumbers, thinly sliced. By the time Farran reappeared, his face a little red, as if he had indeed washed it, she was done with that, and considering if she wanted another half of the remaining sandwich. Instead of deciding, she looked up, then patted the sofa next to her. "Do you want half?"

"Oh. I suppose. If you've had enough." The thing about asking him was that it gave a bit of a new setting for what they were doing. Enough of a change that he wouldn't feel like he had to continue sharing the most delicate parts.

"And then we ought to talk about our next steps." That, of course, was the other part of it. The thing about improvising was that moving from what had been laid out into something new, but doing it in a way that didn't feel jarring. "Vandermeer? Have you heard anything further from Vivian?"

"There seem to be two things to try," Farran said, pulling himself back together. "One is to find a direction for our own exploration, and hope he doesn't turn up. Vivian sent along the potions, enough for one outing, at least. Maybe two. 'A swallow' is curiously imprecise as a measurement."

Vega snorted. "Yes. And it depends so much on the bottle." She nodded then. "Do you have ideas about that? Given that 'wander around London' has some logistical challenges?"

"I was wondering if you've had any inclinations. A draw to something, even something like a dream." Farran asked it carefully, rather gently.

Vega was about to deny anything of the kind, but then she stopped. "Now you say it. No details." She hesitated. "The last two nights, a sense of a space. No windows, dirt floors, nothing like a modern building. Maybe underground."

"And we'd been thinking it might be underground. That would explain why it might be more recently disturbed." Farran nodded. "Anything else?"

"There's an awful lot of underground, though, isn't there?" Vega said it, just thinking about the maps she'd seen.

"So." Farran spoke slowly. "Vivian knows someone who could get us into some of the subway tunnels. I'm wondering if that might be some use. There are quite a few just north of the river, and a station that's no longer in service. They use those tunnels for storage, that sort of thing."

"Underground." Vega sucked in a breath. "The Tube."

"This is a time to talk about that. You said you didn't like the Tube. Is it the Tube itself, or being underground? You seemed all right in the caves, but that's rather different."

Vega let out the breath, slowly. "The metal of the cars. I can if I have to. I just really don't like it, and it will affect my magic for a day or two, maybe. Also, my voice. And isn't it dangerous?"

"We'd need to go down during the dark of the night, when they do maintenance. Vivian's contact can get us down, and has some charms to make it so people won't ask too much in the way of questions. He'd like to know if there's something odd there. Especially if other people might come poking around for it. And we won't be in the actual cars, just walking along the tunnels for a bit. Metal, but not all around us like a car." Farran was watching her closely now.

Vega nodded, without saying anything, considering it from as many angles as she could. "What do you think?" That was what it came down to.

"I think it's worth considering about. Maybe doing. I think there will be less, um, background noise there? But it'll be a question of whether there's anything like what we're looking for near enough. Or accessible enough. There are all sorts of spaces down there, some of them mapped, some of them not so much. And it depends how deep you get."

"So there is such a thing as a map?" Vega asked.

"For some of it. There's someone who knows as

much as anyone. I was going to meet them when they get off work, six in the morning or so. If it makes sense, we could try tomorrow night, when you're done at the club. If you want." Farran hesitated. "If you trust me to make the call."

"I don't know that I'd do any better. On the decision, I mean." Vega let out a puff of breath. "All right. Go meet with them, and write to me when you're done, and we'll see. It feels sudden. But on the other hand, I worry that Vandermeer's going to get closer and closer."

"That's the thing, isn't it?" Farran said. "We'd both rather take our time. And that's dangerous, too. I don't exactly want to go rushing underground, but I think it'd get us more information. And I trust Vivian's judgement? Certainly that she doesn't want to explain to Uncle Cadmus if something went wrong. Or your family, for that matter."

"There is that." Vega felt slightly reassured by that part. "All right. That means you have somewhere specific in mind, right? Do we think Vandermeer might also be interested?"

"Well, it's in the City proper. So yes." Farran glanced at the tray. "Let me clear the tray and bring back the map. Do you want to keep your tea?" She did, so she held the mug while he moved the rest of it away and brought out the map. "This is the current Monument station. Under the Monument to the Great Fire. But a little south, here, is King William Street Station. It's been closed since 1900. Ages, now. And it's not on the same line as Monument. Or Bank. But they're very close to each other."

"And here?" Vega peered at the map. "They seem to overlap."

"The trick of it is the depth of the tunnels. King William Street is very deep, one of the original stations that deep. Bank and Monument are roughly the same depth, both shallower." Farran paused, then added. "Don't hold me to this, but something like seventy-five feet compared to twenty at Bank."

"Quite a difference." Vega thought about that. "That's what, five stories of a building between them? Sets of stairs?"

"Yes. But it means that there might be tunnels down at the depth, going away from the river, that are more recently disturbed?" Farran shrugged. "A lot of this isn't mapped out well. That's part of the problem."

Vega tapped at the map. "Wait, what other things are under there? Burial grounds or whatever?"

"Those are mostly not at that depth, as I understand it. That's why Vivian's contact matters. His name is Bill Collins. Or Botolphus, apparently, but Bill among the non-magical."

Vega wrinkled her nose. "Can't blame him, I suppose. All right. So he's magical."

"And his friend. And they'll show us down there, assuming we go ahead. We might get a better direction from there, anyway. Even if we can't get from one point to the other."

Vega nodded. "We talked about it a little more while I was out for the equinox, and I have a charm I can try, something that, um. Aunt Mera said pulls on the familial ties. They weren't too fond of the idea of my doing it if you didn't know about the family. But now you do, officially, and Aunt Ancha approved of you. I can use it. Without explaining to Bill and his friend."

"Frank. Frank's the friend." Farran then ducked his chin. "Your aunt approved, then?"

"Oh, yes. And if we pull this off, that will be a good reason to invite you out, and so on." Vega leaned back a little. "They can't forbid me seeing who I like. But they, the extended family, can make things uncomfortable. I don't want to live at Astralis, not yet. But I want to visit."

"You care about your family, and you'd have a hard time being serious about anyone they didn't approve of," Farran said. "I would about anyone who Uncle Cadmus didn't like. Or Lena."

"Your housekeeper. I would like to meet them, when we get a chance. And do my best to have their approval." Vega hesitated, just a half-beat. "You don't have a lot of family. Their opinions weigh more, I suspect."

"Yes. And the house matters." Farran's shoulder twitched. "If you don't like the house, then we'd have some problems with anything lasting."

"Right." Vega offered him a smile. "We'll see about my visiting then, to make sure everything's fine." Then she took a deep breath. "The underground part."

"We will go down. There's a stair, and along the tunnel on foot. The station is still there, but the lines are turned off. And will be that time of night, anyway. Bill's got supplies. He's told me what to have with me. Lantern for a charmlight, nothing that will make a spark, just in case. A whistle, that sort of thing, if we get separated. Wear sturdy shoes, clothes that can deal with a bit of muck. A pair of gloves to protect your hands, nothing dainty."

"I do, in fact, own clothing that could not possibly be described as dainty." Vega was amused by it, though. "And Vandermeer?"

"He is, we hope, less likely to appear in a closed-off Tube tunnel at three in the morning. I did tell Bill about the concern, and he'll take some precautions on the doors and such. But honestly, it's apparently the sort of thing where someone has to show you. They have to have a key or be included on the warding, and you'd never find it yourself. Even with tracking magic, probably."

"I just..." Vega took a breath and let it out, feeling her nerves rise even just talking about it. "I don't want to be surprised by him."

"I don't either. But we'll have the potions. We'll have the timing on our side. We'll have an option for access he doesn't. Few people do, and it's the sort of thing where you need an introduction to get them to agree to take you somewhere."

"Is there a process for it, then?" Vega was suddenly distracted by that idea. "How often?"

"Something like this? People with a specific project, but private? A couple of times a year, maybe, in a given area. The people working the lines, they have a specific range, of course. As far as they can walk, do the work, and walk back to a safe exit in maybe six hours. Sometimes just four."

"So there are a lot of little jurisdictional fiefdoms." Vega said, thinking through the implications. "And Bill's only goes so far."

"Exactly." Farran stretched a little. "And like I said, different lines. They hire their own staff. It's complicated."

Vega looked at the maps one more time. She was going to have to do something to move this forward. And she was going to have to trust that Farran had some clue what he was doing. "Go have breakfast with Bill, then. And write to me. We can work out the details for once I'm off tomorrow night. Now, though..." Her chin came up. "I've got an hour or so?"

"And we could find something decidedly pleasant to be doing for an hour?" Farran agreed. "Getting more familiar with each other. Is that the way to put it?"

That made her laugh, and reach out to touch his nose with one finger. "Like that. Can I clear the tray for you? Do you need to tidy anything up in your bedroom?"

"Oh, I was hoping we might end up with a little time for the bedroom," Farran said, cheerfully. "Already tidy. But if you'd like to see to the tray, I can do something about the lighting."

The following hour was, indeed, everything Vega wanted and needed out of the time. Not enough time, certainly. She really wanted to figure out when the two of them could have an evening, overnight, and see what that gave them. No rushing, no needing to set an alarm. But in the meantime, some pleasure was certainly vastly better than none.

In the midst of it, what she figured out about Farran was that he had a particular touch. It wasn't just about the usual sorts of touches that came with sex or whatever they were doing. Farran was doing something more aligned with his magic, or at least she thought it must be. It was decidedly something she wanted to explore more when they had time and space to talk about it.

CHAPTER 34
2AM ON MARCH 25TH, BELOW LONDON

The wee hours of the morning were definitely not Farran's best time of day. Of course, he'd done his best to plan. There had been a potion in the afternoon, so he got a good solid nap, and a different one at midnight to keep him up. He'd arranged for a day off, since he'd likely be sleeping most of Monday, even if everything went absolutely smoothly. And then, of course, the potion to make it unlikely they'd be noticed.

Bill and Frank had turned out to be cheerful and somewhat weather-worn men in their fifties. They had that useful mix of competence and also having seen a fair number of things. That Farran wanted to go down in the tunnels wasn't terribly unusual. That he was looking for something magical was more so, but still didn't bother them. They'd only wanted to know if the thing was dangerous.

Over their breakfast when they'd gone off shift at half-five on Sunday morning, Farran had explained quietly. The item wasn't dangerous as it was, but it might be if the wrong people interfered with it, and they knew of someone who might be looking for it. He'd explained that he and Vega wanted to see if they could get more information about where the specific item might be. It had taken a bit of back and forth chat, and several roughly drawn maps on the copies Farran had brought. But by the time the plates had been cleared and Farran had paid the bill, they had a decent plan.

Now, here Vega was. She'd wrapped up for the night a hair early, and Farran and Bill had met her near the door at street level. She was wearing entirely sensible clothes. Brown trousers were tucked into calf-high boots with a good tread, a jacket over a blouse and her hair up under a scarf, with only a few wisps showing. There had been a long and nerve-wracking climb down dozens of stairs until they came out a door onto a disused station platform. All the signs were still in place, even posters and such, though those were peeling in places and faded. There was a smell of damp, but not too much like the worrying sort of flood.

"Had a fair bit of water in here, January." Bill was scanning the station. "Now, off this way. The track's not on, but avoid it anyway. Good practice. Stay single file, follow me. There's a bit of tunnel I think's where you want."

Vega cleared her throat. "Can we try something here? A little singing, nothing loud."

"It's a tunnel, luv. Echoes." But then Bill shrugged. "No one to hear, though. Just the rats."

Farran caught Vega wincing at that. Rats were, he assumed, not her usual sort of environment. Nor his, other than that Thebes certainly had some, and

mice, like any old estate that also farmed grain did.
He reached out to touch her arm, and she nodded
just once. Then she took a half step to the side,
cleared her throat, and sang.

It wasn't in English, whatever it was. And it
wasn't in Latin, either. Farran knew that well enough
to be sure. It wasn't even the same language she'd
used before. It had vowels like something out of
Chaucer or the Pearl Poet, great rolling things that
had depth and space like the tunnel beside them. But
if it had been Middle English, even Old English,
he'd have made out a word here or there, and he
couldn't.

Maybe Vega would tell him if he asked. Or she'd
sing it again for him, so he could listen. Now, though,
it was like the music made a space around them, and
then flowed. She moved her hands, as if trying to
feel for it, the way Farran felt for the flow of magic
in a piece. The charms were anchored, everything
else shifted around it and made a new pattern. Only
Vega was doing it with space in three dimensions.
She brought the chant to an end, a long held note
that echoed down the tunnel a little.

"That way, yes." Her voice was suddenly crisp
and entirely different from the singing.

Bill looked impressed. "Didn't know you meant
like that, miss. Ma'am." There was an instinctive
sound of respect, even if Vega was— well, she
looked about the age of Bill's children, Farran
suspected. "Frankie's up this way, by the door."

They went along the platform, to the end, then
hopped off the platform to land on rocky ground,
covered with gravel that shifted under their feet. Bill
had a charm lit lantern. He held it out and then

nodded for Farran to set a charmlight in his. They kept well to the left edge, away from the tracks, following the surprisingly sharp curve of the tunnel until there was a door. Bill knocked on it once, then two more times in quick succession, and someone inside opened it.

Farran felt that sensible people might not be down in a tunnel with strangers at this time of night, but they were committed to this now. He took a breath and then went in. Better him first than Vega. Not that he'd be much use if something went wrong, he kept thinking that. But needs must and people had expectations of the men in such outings. He'd do the necessary thing.

The room he found himself in was square, maybe eight feet on each side, and three of them made of brick. Frankie nodded once. "This'd be Miss Beaumont?" He didn't stick out a hand, largely because his were more or less coated in soot. Or possibly grease. "You've an idea where you want to be going, then?"

"That was her singing," Bill said, cheerfully. "Like a nightingale. This way, you said, miss?"

Vega nodded. "This way. A definite tug from..." She frowned. "It's easy to lose track of the curve, isn't it? Can I again, will it carry to be a problem?"

"Nah. Nothing near us, 'cept some cellars, thirty, forty feet up," Frankie said. "Please do."

Vega nodded, and without any fuss, took another of those half-steps, settling into what Farran assumed was the best posture for this sort of singing. It was the same chant, but this time, in a much smaller space, it sounded different. There were harmonics implied. He knew enough music to understand what they were doing. She sang it once through, the same words in a language she was confident about. And then she sang it again, as if chasing some thread of magic through a larger bit of weaving.

This time, the silence was a little longer when the last note trailed off. It lasted until Vega cleared her throat. "That way. Can we go that way?"

The two older men conferred, speaking in a dialect that was nearly as incomprehensible as the singing had been. This time, Farran was certain that they were, in fact, speaking English. But between what he assumed were a range of specialised terms, a smattering of station names, several combinations that he thought weren't actually stations, and more, it became increasingly baffling.

Finally, though, they nodded in unison. "There's a door, bit past. Tunnel goes a bit. There's some dunno. Spaces. Too deep to be proper cellars, but I suppose they might have been someone's once. We can go to the opening with you, don't wanna go further. Not our territory, right?"

"Will there be other people down here? Do you know?"

"Might. Might not. Some people get a mind to live down here. Don't think anyone right now. But you know, men who had a Bad War and want somewhere no one can sneak up on them, to sleep, or keep their things."

"The last was Johnny, though, three months ago. Just before the flood, anyway. You was worried, until it turned out he'd been put up in hospital for a bit."

"And then someone found a sister, and she took him in. No, you're right. Don't think there's been anyone since Johnny. Down here, needs someone who knows where things are. This way. None too much time. We'll need to be heading out prompt, before they turn on the trains."

"All right. Which way?" The thing of this was, it was like sorting things out at Thebes had been, when Vivian and Uncle Cadmus had needed to be brave and go forward. The way to change something was to move. Into the unknown, or at least the personally unknown. But other people had been down here, maybe recently. And it needed doing.

Frankie led the way, down a narrow passage, through another door, and then across something that could generously be described as another tunnel. It had a dirt floor, not cement or any sort of man-made brick, and the roof also looked suspiciously like dirt. The sides were held up with some wood supports, every eight or ten feet. And across from where they came out, just at the edge of the light, there was a dark opening on the other wall.

"There. Can give you..." Bill fumbled, then looked at a watch he pulled out of his pocket. "An hour. One of us will be by here, the other needs t'do some work."

"Sixty minutes." Farran pulled out his own watch. "Four." They'd been down here even longer than he'd realised, if it were already three. "Best get moving then."

"Yell if there's something, blow your whistle. That'll carry. We know which direction you're going, but if you make a turn, you leave a mark with chalk." Farran held up the stick he'd brought; there were three more in different places in his bag, and two more in the bag Vega was carrying. And he patted the bag, reassuring himself that the set of potions was still where it ought to be.

"Thank you." Vega made it like a regal blessing. "Come along, Farran." She took a step across the tunnel to the dark gap. Farran immediately followed her, holding the lantern up to get the best distance out of the light that they could.

The first room was long. It might well have been someone's cellar, ancient storage for food over the winter. Or wine, maybe. Farran saw shapes further back in the spaces to each side of the central walkway that might have been great urns for wine. "Still going the right way?"

Vega nodded. She hadn't reached to touch him, but both of them needed a hand free for the lantern. And if one of them slipped, better if both of them didn't tumble. "I'll try again, that end. Maybe something a little different. I can feel something, though. In my pocket, the talisman, as well as the singing."

That was, at least, a little reassuring. Farran kept wanting to crane his neck, to see what was tucked into the storage spaces— they must be storage spaces — along each side. "Do we think this was Roman?"

"Maybe. The arches look it, don't they? And the bits of pottery. Most of it long shattered, I suppose." They seemed to be coming up to the end of whatever storage they'd been in. Maybe it had been a stable, or for docks, when the land and water levels were vastly different. Farran knew people could figure that sort of thing out, but he had not nearly as much idea as he ought about how they did that.

Vega stopped, and he immediately halted. "One more time?" he asked.

"Yes. Can you hold both lights?" She sounded

almost distracted, handing the lantern to him.
Farran turned, so he was facing her at an angle, able
to see both where they'd come from, and then the
wall in front of them, with two darker hollows on
either side. "Something different, this time." Vega
definitely sounded as if she were focused on something else now.

This time, it definitely wasn't anything like any
language Farran had ever heard. It had a rill to it,
like Welsh did, an inherent musicality that suggested
harmonies and echoes and counterpoint. But it also
had the spareness and beauty of early monastic
chant, a mobility that wasn't like anything modern.

He'd heard something somewhat similar when
he'd visited Vivian's family estates, but nothing that
was quite like this. Those were all designed for many
people to sing, with harmonies and moving voice
parts. This was just Vega, her voice filling the room
with waves of sound that seemed like they couldn't
just come from one body.

It wasn't just the sound. As she went on, a
pattern of theme and variation, coming back to the
same line, then expanding, then returning, Farran
realised that the air had changed. Where it still had
the damp smell of ground— nothing dangerous, just
the eternal damp of England— it seemed warmer,
more like a spring day after a few hours of sun.
Then there was a far stronger scent on the air, night-
blooming flowers with a compelling fragrance, and
beyond where the light was strongest, what seemed
like a shimmering of stars.

CHAPTER 35

3AM, BELOW LONDON

As Vega let the last sounds die away, she could feel they were close. Close to something, anyway. The talisman in her pocket was warm enough to feel through the fabric of her trousers. She kept blinking to try to clear her vision before she realised it was stars. And not just stars, but particular stars.

Most people didn't notice that. They saw a pattern some artist had made of the night sky and didn't concern themselves with the accuracy of the placements. Now, she could see stars, constellations, laid out against the wall in front of them. Two sets, one on either side of where she now stood. There were flowers along with it, night-blooming ones, moonflowers and star jasmine, along with entirely unseasonal honeysuckle. The moonflower was a little unexpected, but it had been turning up in a whole host of moments across the various estates. That did not matter here. She was fairly sure of it, anyway.

"Can you put out the lights, please?" Her voice

didn't shake as she spoke. Farran didn't argue. He
didn't even ask the entirely reasonable question. He
just extinguished his own light. Granted, she knew
they could both produce charmlights, and he had an
electric torch and she had candles and matches and
a lighter in her own bag.

It left them in the dark, with just the stars. Vega
didn't move - there was too much rubble scattered
on the ground to make that safe. She needed her
eyes to adjust too, and that took a minute. Finally,
she blinked once more and the points of light were
clear. "The stars." She gestured. "Do you know your
constellations?" If he did not, he was just going to
have to learn, if they kept on with things. No, he'd
mentioned appreciating Aunt Ancha's paper about
the stars in art, that suggested he had at least some
knowledge.

"I took Astronomy all through Schola, and Time
and Place." Farran sounded amused beside her. "But
those aren't constellations. They're asterisms, aren't
they? The Little Dipper and—" He hesitated.

"Yes." Vega cut him off quickly. She didn't
entirely want to say the name out loud. The Pleiades,
the stars her Grandmothers were named for, seven
sisters dancing eternally in the sky. "Which would
you take?"

"Without the context, that one." She could just
barely see his gesture. Perhaps he felt as cautious as
she did. Then he took her hand in his and made it
plain by touch. "But."

She nodded, and then pulled his hand, like a tow
boat moving a much larger liner, toward the other.
"Yes. Can you make a light, please? Only one?"

"I can do something that shouldn't bother our

night vision as much." He did, producing a deep red
glow. He might, in fact, have sufficient astronomy
knowledge to satisfy her family. It was enough to let
them see the rubble on the floor without ruining
their vision in the dark. That done, they could move
carefully toward the wall with the Pleiades on it.
That wall, however, seemed to be utterly solid. She'd
expected some opening, or perhaps a door. Instead,
it was smooth stone, as if it had stood for centuries.
It likely had.

"Do you? Is there?" Her voice cracked. "We
don't have much time." Coming back here would be
complicated. There were so many more chances
Vandermeer might catch a scent or whatever one
called it. He was just the sort who'd figure out how to
bribe someone to come down here and spend the
day with equipment and men with strong arms. Or
maybe to bribe people with the right cellars to let
Vandermeer dig a hole.

"Give me a minute, all right?" Farran sounded
distracted. "Can you hold the lantern?" She
reached out and took it and then watched his
shadow move. He was feeling along the wall,
lightly, with his fingertips. One of his hands
twitched, or the shadow did, to the other side,
before he shook his head and focused back on the
wall in front of him. "Is it a problem if I do a
charm?"

"Not that I know of. But I don't know that it isn't
a problem." Vega swallowed. "Why do you ask?"

"I know a charm for stonework, and a charm for
jammed doors. Well, it works better on dresser draw-
ers, but it's adaptable." His tone of voice made her
laugh, despite the seriousness of the situation. He

took that for agreement, and said, "Right. Stand back a step or two, just in case."

It turned out to be three different charms in sequence. The first two didn't seem to do anything she could see or hear, but they made some sense to him. A muttering sort of sense, like he was talking to himself, talking to the stone, maybe talking to whoever had been here long before. She couldn't make it out.

Then he tried a third charm, and something made a sound. It wasn't like stone scraping on stone, or wood, but it was as if something took a breath after a long time. Then there was a movement of air, strong enough that it would have put out a candle if they'd had one lit.

Farran took a breath— she could see the shadowy shape of his shoulder move first— and then he put his hands against the gap. Something creaked then, and Vega stepped over to bring more light. She could see perhaps six inches of blackness. Clipping the lantern to her bag, she set her hands a bit below Farran's. "On one."

Of course, she counted it by habit, "Five, six, seven, eight." But Farran guessed how that worked, and after eight came one. It wasn't the only way to count in, of course, but they were used to working with the dancers, who often thought in eight counts. Whatever the reason, it worked, and she could feel the door begin to move. They got it about halfway across the likely opening.

Farran peered at it. "Is that enough space, do you think?"

"Give it a go." He wasn't a burly man, but he was taller and broader-shouldered than she was.

Though she had more of a bust, that squished down. He nodded, and took the lantern from her when she handed it over, then squeezed through. Nothing trapped him, and she heard a scattering of small stones, then a sound that was like awe and wonder. Like stepping into Jack Cade's caves, but more so.

Of course, she followed right away, pushing against the door to get her last foot through. The light wasn't strong, but even so, she could see why he'd been amazed. There were mosaics or something of the kind on the walls, niches for burial or worship or maybe both along both sides of the room. "More light, please?" Her voice shivered at the last word. "I want to see." Then, she realised what else she was feeling.

The talisman in her pocket was vibrating, strongly enough it was more like a tambourine than anything else. "The talisman," she said. "Can you hold up the light?"

Farran nodded. "Let me make it brighter, all right?" He extinguished it just for a second, then a warmer golden light was back, and much brighter this time. The space must have been some sort of temple or particularly valued place, because yes, those were decorations all over. Some were geometric, a few glittered with reflective stones. Others made patterns, bulls and horses and people, a fountain, a pond. And then, above them, a night sky, with constellations picked out.

"That way, I think." She could feel the pull more clearly now, to an area across the room, not quite the furthest niche. "Careful, there's a lot of fallen rock."

They picked their way through, moving slowly, a few feet apart, in case anything unexpected happened. Farran glanced around between steps. "A lot of the fall here looks recent. The ceiling there, some down the wall, there?" He gestured with his free hand. "Construction nearby, maybe?"

"Maybe." That was entirely beyond Vega's scope of knowledge. Then they were standing, looking at a small enclosed bay with a niche built into the end. It might have been an altar at some point, or a shrine, or something of the kind. It drew the eye to something on it, or maybe in it. Now, she stopped and looked at it more carefully. "What do we think this was?"

"Some sort of temple. Underground, maybe. A Mithraeum, I'd think, but there aren't nearly enough bulls." Farran gestured again at the ceiling. "Your Grandmothers, maybe?"

"Not the right number of niches for that." There were ten. Muses, maybe, Muses came in nines. "Do you think I should go forward?"

"I think your particular Grandmother might have had that idea. The stars. And we're short on time. We can't dither about it for hours." Vega realised with a start he was right, glancing at her watch. They really had very little time at all. She took a breath, then made her way forward, step by step. After each one, she waited to see if anything moved or shifted. There was more rubble here, from gravel-sized pieces to a couple as big around as her head. It brought her in front of a space about three feet wide, with about another foot beyond that on either side of the niche. The base looked like it had been painted at one point, perhaps brightly, but now it was a little dingy with damp and faded to hints of blues and greys.

The tug from the talisman was so strong she could feel it like her heartbeat. All Vega could say, when it came to it, was "Grandmother Alcyone, guide my hands." There was a burst of that scent of nighttime flowers again, then Vega was reaching to brush dust and gravel off the top of the flat surface. Her fingers found it first, a surge of magic against them.

She brushed more, frantic now, to reveal something like a torc. There it was, a circle of metal with an opening at one side, but small enough she thought it might be meant to be a bracelet instead. She picked it up, feeling the magic of it pulse, before it settled. As if it knew it was in the right sort of hands now, and could stop fussing. It made her think of the way the youngest cousins, still babies, reacted when one of their kin picked them up. Mama was best, or their favourite auntie, but any of the other people they knew as family were just fine. This was like that. She was not the person who would keep this, and she didn't need to be. Vega was simply the one bringing a treasure home to be properly tended.

"I have it." She turned, finally. Some part of her was afraid that Farran would change in that moment. Or that Vandermeer would appear out of the shadow and gloom. Vega hated that thread of fear. But the magic of the torc rose like a wave, washing away that fear. When she blinked again, Farran was smiling. "Good. Do you need a cloth to wrap it up in?"

He didn't take it. He didn't even try to touch it, or her, while she was holding it. When she didn't say anything, he just rummaged in his satchel, pulling out an absurdly large silk scarf, the sort women

would fold and tie over their hair. She carefully
wrapped up the torc, then settled it gently into her
own satchel, nestling it into an interior pocket and
fastening that as well as the outer buckle. Only then
did she turn back. "We should get back to Bill and
Frank."

"And promptly," Farran agreed. "Are you all
right, though?"

"Enough." There were dozens of things she had
questions about, but they could wait for later. Farran
went ahead of her this time, a few steps, so he was
already slipping through the door as she got there.
As soon as she did the same, they felt another
rumbling, the door closing, and the sound of more
falling rock.

Farran looked at her. "Maybe it should remain a
mystery? Later, for that." He pressed his hand once
against the stone, murmuring something that
sounded like a prayer or a thanks, and then he held
his hand out to hers. Going back was faster, at least.

CHAPTER 36
LONDON ON MONDAY MORNING

"There you are, then." Bill had just been looking at his watch. "Cutting things tight."

"Thanks for waiting. Made a difference." Farran was more than a little out of breath, but it also wasn't a good idea to explain exactly what they had with them. "How do we go about getting back up?"

That, of course, involved a rather gruelling bit of walking along the flat into a different tunnel, then climbing stairs, steep enough they had to stop three flights up. Farran felt something rumble, and he blinked.

"That's the trains." Frankie shrugged. "It's no bother here, but you can feel them better. Even if there's none down on that line now."

Farran nodded, focusing on taking a deep breath and then another. Another two flights, another two, and they were out at the street level. He cleared his throat, rummaging for the last bit of the payment, passing it over in a somewhat smudged envelope. "Is there a cafe nearby that wouldn't mind us taking a table for a bit until the office is open?" It had taken them a while to get to the surface. The city was waking up properly.

Frankie gave them directions to one up near the Monument Tube stop, the sort of place that didn't care much who turned up so long as they paid. Farran couldn't tell if it was actually open all night or if it opened early to give cabbies and delivery men and whoever else a place to get something. There was a small table open by one window. Farran sorted out strong tea and some slightly dubious toast and eggs. They tasted grand, though maybe that was the combination of their night's exertions. The jam was excellent as well, surprisingly so.

"What do we do now?"

"You've work." Vega hadn't said much in their retreat from the depths. He'd thought it was partly from the exertion, but looking at her now, Farran worried it wasn't just that.

"I took the day off, so not today. Though I was thinking more about sleep than anything else."

"Probably, I ought to go see my family. Now, soon. I mean, not at six in the morning. We are not morning people, most any of us. Unless it's the sort of morning that's about having stayed up all night first."

Farran tilted his head. "Astronomers."

"Exactly. How far does your knowledge go? No, wait, that's a question for later. You're not dressed to come with me, really." She looked him up and down. "I'm not either, but I've got clothes in my room there."

They were, honestly, both more than a bit

grubby. Soot got everywhere, of course, and there
was plenty of that from coal fires, even if the Tube
was electric. And there'd been plenty of dust in the
rooms they'd gone through, as well. "So, we could go
back to our respective places, wash up, and meet to
go out to your family. If you wanted me there. I'd
understand if you didn't, not right away, anyway."

Vega looked down at her hands. "I want you
there, and I'm not sure how it'd go, both." She didn't
look up, and Farran tried to decide what she meant
by it. First, he pushed the rest of the jam closer to
her. She still had some toast left.

Then he swallowed, before asking, "Do you think
they'll be difficult to me?"

"I think they won't pay attention to you. Not
properly. It's only because of you that we're— I
mean. I couldn't do it myself." Now she looked up,
and she was blinking away tears. Farran rummaged
in his jacket, pulling out a clean handkerchief and
handing it over.

"I couldn't have done it without you. We did it
together." Farran did his best to keep his voice firm
and clear. This was not actually what he'd been
taught, or why he'd been taught it. The kinds of
speaking he had to do working for an auction house
were entirely different, honestly. "I'd not have been
doing anything with it if you hadn't asked." He
shrugged. "I don't know how to tally that up or
appraise it. No tidy checklists of best practices."

The way he put the last of it made her giggle,
which was all to the good. She blew her nose on the
handkerchief. "All right. So we finish breakfast, we
go back to our own places, and we meet at the portal
at, what? Ten?"

"Is ten reasonable for your people? Would eleven be better, or does that look like we're hoping to get them to feed us lunch?" He got another little laugh out of her, and Farran was very pleased with that.

"Oh, if you come, we're not getting out of there without a meal. And also you talking to at least three aunts. Senior aunts. Maybe more." Vega leaned forward, considering him. "Treat them like you did Vivian when you started? Though she's younger than they are."

"One thing Ormulu teaches you early is how to be exceedingly polite to elderly women. Including the varieties I expect won't be a problem here. More money than sense, for example, or people who cling to the idea that a valuable thing stays the same kind of valuable, no matter how time passes." He shrugged one shoulder. "It's not like that. There are fashions in auctions, like everything else. Should I pick up some sort of hostess gift? Or whatever you call it here."

Vega shook her head. "If it were purely a social call, maybe. Though we go in for books for that, and that's not something you can just pick up anywhere. The right sort of book, obviously. Cut flowers are a bit, er."

"Implying things about your local gardens and greenhouses?" Farran offered. He'd seen that one often enough, too. "Or allergies?"

"Mostly the first. Wine goes over well, but you've got to hit the right mark with it. A small decorative object, attentive to our interests— that means astronomy— doesn't go badly. But again, I'm assuming you don't have one tucked away in a wardrobe waiting for the occasion."

"No." Farran leaned back. "Though there are a few things coming through on sale I'll keep an eye on. Or there's someone runs an antique shop in Trellech, and if I go in, he'll be wondering what I'm up to for days. That's always fun." He shrugged. "I've settled up the bill already. Shall we go find a cab or whatever?"

They were out on the street, at the corner near the Bank station entrance, when Vega saw something. She tugged on Farran's elbow, hard enough to almost pull him off balance. They both saw the shape they'd been worried about. Tall, long coat, hat. Then he turned, and Farran was sure it was Vandermeer. He was ten feet away, maybe.

"Tube?" Farran hissed it in Vega's ear. There were too many people between them and the stop, though. More than enough to slow them down.

She shook her head abruptly. Then, inexorably, as if drawn like a magnet, Vandermeer spotted them and started moving toward them. He held out his hand. "There you are!"

Farran felt it before he saw anything. Vega's hands had come up, spread out, a gesture of placation. Or at least, that was what it was supposed to look like. One of her hands flipped from palm up to palm down, as if she were smoothing something out or brushing something away, and she was humming. He couldn't hear words, just the pitches. It wasn't a song he knew, but it was like the singing she'd done with the well.

Vandermeer's chin came up, as if a wave had pushed against him. The people around him didn't react, other than the usual jostle and bustle of a city street. Vandermeer staggered back on one foot, then braced himself. "You, there!" His voice was clear and carried well.

Farran could at least play along in the right direction. He looked around, as if Vandermeer had to mean someone else, and he caught Vega doing the same. Both of them shrugged at each other, glanced at the people around them, joining in on the confusion. Then he felt Vega's hand rest on his wrist, squeeze, and disappear again. He didn't know how to read that.

"You can't fool me!" Vandermeer's voice was even more clear.

"What are you shouting about, mate?" A voice from elsewhere in the crowd, nearer the corner.

"Some madman." That was a woman, older and disapproving. Farran suspected he might not care to spend too much time with her in the ordinary course of things.

"I'm no madman! You can't fool Tom O'Bedlam." Vandermeer was trying to come closer to them, but the people between him and Vega and Farran weren't making that any too easy. Farran heard Vega's inhale, but she didn't say anything, just tugged his arm.

"Oh, go sleep it off." That had the gruff nononsense tone of someone who'd seen a lot of drunk men in the morning and had no patience for it.

"Tom O'Bedlam wants no drink!" There was more of a sharp pitch to it now, something urgent. He sang, then, the line from the song, Farran knew it well enough. He then started patting at his pockets, his trousers and his coat, both. "I don't need this either!"

Vandermeer started pulling things out, a leather

wallet, then a handful of coins. He flung them into the crowd, one landing on a ledge above a storefront, others clinking as they hit the ground. It just made things even more confused, some bending to grab a coin, others trying to sidle away from the increasing chaos.

Farran reached for Vega's elbow, pressing to suggest they retreat back into the Tube. Vandermeer kept shouting. "Am I not a bonny mad boy? Am I not bonny enough for you?" It sounded slightly ridiculous in an American accent, for all the words tumbled out of his mouth in rhythm like the song. "Come show me your treasure!"

Vega was gaping at him, as if caught in place, and Farran tugged. "We'd better leave. Look, there's a constable, coming along." A constable and two burly shopkeepers, moving steadily. "Now."

Finally, she moved with him. The crowd between them and the entrance to the Tube had melted away, wanting none of the chaos and cacophony. As Farran managed to nudge Vega back down into the depths, they could hear the last calls. "I live by the air! I shall go bare, as all bonny Bedlam Boys do!" Farran could just see a bit of cloth, his coat, go up into the air, then they were away, back down into the dark.

They had to stop to buy tickets, of course, but by that point there were people queueing up behind them. Then they were on the platform, nervously watching the people coming in from the entrance. "Where are we going?"

"I think in the circumstances, Bedford Square." Farran searched through what he knew of the Tube. "If we get separated, get off at, um." He tried to remember the station. There was a little sniff of some commentary behind him. Not in words, but Farran could tell by the sound he'd flubbed something, then glanced to find a map. "Tottenham Court Road." He usually came at the British Museum or the library from the portal, not the other way round. "No, wait. British Museum." The sniff that came from behind his shoulder sounded more approving this time, so that was probably right. "I'll look for you on the corner. It's only a block or two."

Vega nodded, but she had her arm tightly through his at the moment, as if being separated would be a problem. She'd mentioned hating the Tube, but it was only a few stops, and hopefully it'd be a help. There were people piling on after them, a few of whom had also been in the crowd above, but there was no sign of Vandermeer.

There were no seats, of course. People were a bit packed in, it was now past eight. They stood awkwardly, trying to keep other people between them and the windows on that side. Farran kept glancing out, worried that they'd be followed, but then the doors closed and the train pulled away without further delay. Farran let out a sigh of relief. A few moments later, so did Vega.

Of course, he couldn't say anything about here. Not with dozens of non-magical people within earshot, who were likely already wondering about the pair of rather dirty people wedged into the Tube. At best, it'd sound like madness. At worse, he'd be pressing up against his oaths to the Silence, and that was no good at all. Three stops later, they piled out of the train onto a platform, and Farran immediately tugged Vega's hand to lead her out of the Tube.

"All right?" He wanted to get on to the portal. "I'm thinking the sooner we get to your family, the better all round."

Vega had been leaning one hand on the bench where they'd come out, but that made her straighten. "Yes. I— yes." Then she squared her shoulders. "Where are we going from here?"

Farran at least knew where the portal was, and he tucked her hand into his and led the way.

CHAPTER 37
LATER THAT MORNING AT ASTRALIS

Vega stepped through the portal, onto familiar land, taking a breath and moving to the side. She needed a word with Farran before the family descended. There hadn't been time at the Bedford Square portal. It had been tricky enough to set the portal location here, or rather to slip a coin to the portal attendant so he wouldn't do it himself. She immediately turned to offer a brief formal greeting to Aeterna. It was important to do that first.

Farran came out just beside her, blinking a little. Vastly less smoke and soot in the air, for one thing. The light made it clear exactly how covered in dust both of them were. They'd need to deal with that first. Vega cleared her throat. "In approximately a minute, there'll be someone here to see who came through. Do you mind if I arrange clean clothes for you? Someone will escort you to a guest room and bath, but not let you leave or wander on your own."

She swallowed hard. "We'll have to talk about, about that. But maybe with my family." Her voice wavered.

"I would very much like clean clothes, actually. And you're right about the talking." Farran sucked in a breath. "I wish to be polite. Please tell me how to be polite?"

Vega turned to face him, to find him looking unsettled. He had every reason to, given the day they'd had already, never mind being about to face her family. "You have excellent manners. Use those, you'll be fine. It is safe to accept any gift offered without obligation. I am functionally the one offering them. And I am telling you that you are under no obligation by accepting." That was also important to state outright. She added the formal phrase in the family language for good measure, and felt the magic of the estate respond to it.

She went on. "But also, the senior aunts and uncles know you're helping. This is continuing to help. You got me— and the torc— here safely. That will count for a great deal. You'll be waiting an hour probably, but there will be someone who can bring you food or drink or the regular sorts of potions or a book. You should feel free to ask for any of those, or any other ordinary household thing of that sort."

His smile came back a little. "So, hospitable, then."

"We take our hospitality, our xenia, most seriously. You know xenia, you'll be fine. Here they come." Two of her cousins were coming out, Zenobia and Halicarnassus. Two of the better duellists from their generation, and that was almost certainly not an accident.

Vega's chin came up. She planted her feet, and as the two recognised her, she made a couple of gestures, indicating that she had things to say. "Halicarnassus, could you escort my guest, Farran, to one of the guest rooms, get a bath going, and ask someone to find him some clothes to change into? Zenobia, could you let Aunt Mera and whoever else she suggests know that we've some significant news? We'd like to present it together to whoever she thinks should hear it initially once we've changed."

Zenobia wrinkled her nose. "Rather." She shrugged. "As you wish. Do you need me to send anything up?"

Vega shook her head. "I've got things in my room." She certainly wasn't letting anyone take the bag with the torc in it. "Farran, I'll see you in a little, all right?" Then she continued, in the family's private dialect. That was a jumble of Greek, Latin, Old English, and a good few dozen pointedly chosen references, and she expected Farran wouldn't get most of it. She told Halicarnassus firmly that if he weren't kind to Farran, she'd do something about it. He snorted, but half-bowed at her, acknowledging her point. Vega let them go off first, before veering off to the shortest route to her room. That involved turning into one of the side wings as soon as they got closer to the house.

An hour later, Vega was standing outside the observatory when Halicarnassus brought Farran to join her. Vega felt vastly better. She'd gone through three changes of bathwater before all the dust and grime was out of her hair. Now, though, she had a clean dress on, in a clear sky blue, and comfortable shoes. Someone had gone to some effort to find

Farran clothing that fit well, or maybe they'd taken a
charm to it. It was country clothing, of course,
trousers and a tweed jacket. But the shirt was clean,
the tie was the tawny brown of Owl House rather
than grey, and made his eyes gleam a little more
blue, perhaps.

"You look grand." She turned to him, holding
out a hand. The other had her bag at her side.

"You look decidedly better." He'd recovered a
bit, good, because he was smiling far more naturally.
"Your family is very thorough. I'm not surprised,
really, given how you go about things. Where
are we?"

"The observatory. Not because we need the telescope right now, but because it's one of the larger
spaces with room for chairs. Also, it's nicely imposing. Woodwork and leaded glass on the ground level
and beautifully made shutters and so on." Then
someone opened the doors and gestured them inside.

Vega walked forward, and Farran matched her.
She was certain he must have wanted to stare, but he
didn't. The main telescope, massive as it was, rose
from the centre of the room. On this side of it, there
were a dozen of the family elders: Aunt Mera and
Aunt Helia at the centre of the semi-circle, Aunt
Ancha and Uncle Thuban right next to Aunt Mera,
and the others ranged out beside them.

"Aunts, Uncles, Cousins." Vega made a fully
formal curtsey, the sort she almost never used. She
bent down low enough her back knee was a bare
inch from the floor. It was perfect, of course. Her
profession made her aware of her body and what it
was doing, and she used that to her advantage. As
she straightened, she saw Farran had bowed politely,

keeping his eyes lowered, as he might over an older woman's hand. "I am pleased to present Farran Michaels to you, as he has been a great help with the task I was asked to undertake. Farran, these are my aunts, uncles, and cousins. At the centre are Aunt Mera and Aunt Helia."

She then worked her way through in order of seniority, keeping to the current argument about whether Aunt Melitta was senior to Aunt Iphigenia. It was a complicated matter, having to do with births some distance away from each other, the matter of time zones, and the imperfections of clocks in both locations. At the moment, however, Aunt Melitta was acknowledged as senior.

There was a silence, and then Farran spoke, his voice clear. She was certain he must be nervous. She could see hints of it. But only hints. "Kyries kai kyrioi, I am honoured to be a guest in your hall, and to have been able to lend my skills to Magistra Vega's search." It was polite, not only polite, but with exquisite attention to detail. He'd addressed the aunts first. He'd used the Greek. That avoided a number of tricky circumlocutions expected in English. And he'd leaned on the proper aspect of being someone she considered a guest-friend. Well, rather more than a guest-friend, but that was for later in the conversation or visit, or perhaps a future visit.

Aunt Mera inclined her head once, accepting that as her proper due, then focused on Vega. "Explain, please."

Vega reached into her bag and pulled out the torc, still wrapped in the handkerchief. She came forward, using the same sort of step she'd have used in one of the processionals, a ritual walk, slow and stately. Her head was up, her movements so even she could have balanced a book on top of her skull without a hint of a wobble. Vega came within two feet of Aunt Mera and Aunt Helia, then placed the torc on one hand while the other unfolded the silk. Presenting it with both hands, she bowed and waited.

Aunt Helia reached out a hand, her fingers hovering over it, but decidedly not touching it. "Where?"

"Underground, in an area that showed some signs of recent rubble. Perhaps from building or tunnelling nearby. About— how far down were we?"

"Quite deep, kyria." Farran's voice came from behind her, but then Aunt Helia crooked a finger at him and he came closer, a hair behind Vega's right shoulder. "We began about seventy-five feet below the surface and climbed ten feet in inclination from there. Perhaps as much as fifteen." He hesitated for just a second. "I don't believe we could return easily. The space sealed itself as we left. It looked as if it might have been some devotional space, perhaps a temple, though we did not get a good look at the whole."

"And you brought it here in some hurry." Aunt Mera did not make it a question.

"We ran into Mister Vandermeer, after." Vega flushed. "There was a problem there. It seemed best to come here as quickly as possible and ensure the piece was somewhere with substantial protection. We've not handled the piece directly beyond when I picked it up." More than anything she wanted this thing out of her hands and into better keeping. She nodded at it, and Aunt Helia's hands came up under Vega's. Her aunt eased the torc into her own hands, then onto her lap, like a delicately held infant. Vega added, "I set the portal location myself, and Farran kindly blocked any line of sight."

"Indeed." Aunt Mera considered. "Vandermeer?"

"Yes, Aunt Mera. Mister Vandermeer found us when we were about to go wash up and prepare to come here." She swallowed hard. "I tried a charm, to deflect his attention, and it went horribly awry."

Farran, just behind her, went still. She hadn't explained what she'd tried, they'd not had time or privacy for it. Now, Vega braced herself. "It's one I've done often, there's no reason it should—" Her voice caught. "Well, there is a reason."

Aunt Mera inclined her head. "The artefact."

"It amplifies." It was incredibly foolish for her to have done any magic with it near her. Even if it had been wrapped up in silk and whatever other protections Farran had organised. "I should make a report to the Guard." She didn't want to think about what it might do here, in the heart of the family's magics.

"What happened?" Aunt Helia's voice was even, deliberately neutral.

Vega explained what she'd done, the casting of the charm, meant just to make him go the other way or have his eyes slide over her. How instead Vandermeer had been snared up in that particular song. "It looked like he might have been stripping his clothes off, when we left. He certainly sounded— well, not himself. There was a constable coming, and a couple of bigger men."

Aunt Helia pursed her lips. "He's a man with

obvious money?" Vega nodded once. "They'll stick him in a cell and get a doctor to have a look at him. Nothing too miserable will happen to him right away, I suspect. Go take a minute, if you would, write to the Guard and to Vivian. That first, while we think about the rest of it."

Vega knew an order when she heard it. She stood, taking herself off to one of the tables in the back corner and writing a brief note. Wording it was a bit tricky, but she sent one note to the Guard explaining there had been something odd, possibly needing their attention. She could give the location and the time and Vandermeer's name.

The note to Vivian was much more detailed, including the fact Vega thought the artefact had messed with things. She made it clear Vivian could convey what she thought relevant to whomever else might need to know. That was entirely beyond her own personal remit. Vivian could be trusted.

When she came back, Farran was still standing where she'd left him. The aunts had been apparently conversing with him about his general background, his family, and one of his previous visits to Vivian's family estate.

Aunt Mera picked up as if there had been no interruption. "Now. Where was the artefact, in detail?"

Beside her, Farran cleared his throat. "May I speak, Kyria?" Aunt Mera nodded once.

"First, may Vega have a seat? It has been an exceedingly long day for her. She came straight from her performance last night, without any pause or rest." Vega had at least managed food and a restorative potion, but she was indeed tired and her feet

were complaining. Someone behind her brought
over a chair, one of the reasonably comfortable
wooden ones, and Vega thankfully sat down. Farran
took up a spot still behind her to the right. Now,
though, he stood with his hand resting on the wood
back by her shoulder. She could just feel his fingers.

Once that was sorted, he began speaking, carefully. "Anyone familiar with London's long history
understands that there are many spaces below the
modern streets. There are buried rivers, entire sets of
tunnels that safeguard silver and gems, archaeolog-
ical discoveries. Near to where we were, they discov-
ered forty-some skulls in the 1830s, not near any
bodies, all tumbled by the bank of the Walbrook,
buried for centuries now." He gestured with his other
hand. "We used a combination of techniques to see
if we could find an item that held the characteristics
that Vega had been told."

That was her part to tell. "In the end, I think
Grandmother Alcyone showed us the way. There
were certain signs, constellations. It was in something
that might have been a temple." Vega wasn't entirely
sure how to describe the space still. "The sort of
thing that someone of the line would know
unerringly, and someone outside it would not." She
gestured at Aunt Helia's lap. "I have done as I hoped
to do. May I leave it in your care?"

"You may." Aunt Mera glanced at the torc, then
back up. "What of Mister Vandermeer?"

Behind her, Farran spoke, "I am wondering if
the methods he is using are entirely, shall we say,
aboveboard in Albion. Vivian Porter has contacts
within a number of places, and could likely consult
appropriately."

"We're aware of the range of Vivian's contacts." Aunt Mera's voice now had a dry amusement to it, which certainly suggested they'd discussed it and recently. "But she might, yes, act even more swiftly at your request than ours. She's always had a clearly defined sense of precedence in certain matters."

Vega couldn't help smiling at that. Aunt Mera glanced over at her. "And you, Vega?"

"I'd like to follow up with Vivian, beyond the note I just sent. I've two days free— well, tomorrow — before I need to be back at the club. I admit I'd rather Mister Vandermeer not be able to appear to be a bother."

"There is that." Aunt Helia nodded. "We shall let you do that, then. We would appreciate a proper report— for provenance reasons, young man— with whatever you feel should be known about the process. The location it was found, properly described. Within the fortnight, if possible, though if you need more time, we will grant you more."

Farran shifted a little behind her, then he nodded. "Thank you, kyria. Vega, may I escort you home? Or..." He hesitated. "Vivian's likely at Thebes still. I can check."

"Thebes, if she's there, please," Vega said. She'd been wanting to see the house for ages. "Let me go pack up a few things, just in case I end up somewhere other than my flat tonight."

That, of course, brought a murmur of amusement from her aunts and uncles, and she didn't care. Aunt Mera waved a hand. "Off with you. We'll discuss and let you know if we have further questions."

Vega took the opportunity and stood, reaching

for Farran's hand. They made quick work of retrieving a package of his clothes. And she packed a case with another change and her overnight things for herself, and a book to read. Not that Thebes wouldn't have books, Farran had been very clear about that.

CHAPTER 38

MONDAY AFTERNOON, AT THEBES

Farran let out a deep breath as soon as he came out of the portal. He'd written ahead, and he could see Uncle Cadmus there with the pony cart as he moved to the side, to let Vega join him. He hadn't been sure if they'd need to walk, and honestly, he was also exhausted and his feet were definitely tender. A moment later, Vega had her hand on his. "Your uncle?"

"Yes. Here, let me introduce you." He took Vega's case in his other hand and walked the twenty feet to the cart. "Uncle Cadmus? This is Vega Beaumont. I'm sure Vivian's told you a certain amount. Vega, this is my Uncle Cadmus Michaels. The pony is Rex." Rex was a sturdy cob, well suited to the back and forth on mostly level ground.

Vega raised an eyebrow at that, but she didn't dwell on the name, more suited for a dog than a pony, honestly. "Magister Michaels, a pleasure to meet you. Farran has spoken so warmly about you." She added, glancing at Farran, "Also, his Greek is excellent and made a fine impression on my aunts and uncles."

"Ah, I wouldn't expect anything less on that count. A pleasure to meet you as well, after hearing about you. Glad to bring the cart out, I gather you've had a day of it. It's about two miles." Farran reached a hand to help Vega climb into the back, and then followed, and Uncle Cadmus set off at a comfortable trot. "Have you had lunch yet? Or rather, if you have, do you have enough room to avoid disappointing Lena?"

"Not lunch." Farran hadn't been sure about that part. Vega had, fairly obviously, wanted to leave her family to talk over things without her. And they'd had food before the meeting. He wasn't starving. "How, erm, extensive are Lena's plans?"

"Well, she's pulled out the jar of the best of last summer's jam she hasn't been letting us touch. And she was going to set up the small dining room. Soup and quiche, I believe, and something for pudding that involved the jam. Though she might be planning a trifle for supper instead, that takes more warning than you gave us for luncheon." He glanced over "If that's not a problem. We weren't sure if there's anything you don't eat."

It was a gently put way to ask. Vega laughed. "Oh, not so much on my part. And I'm eager to try her cooking, please. A lot of what I eat is takeaway or at the club, and it's well cooked but not homey." She glanced over at Farran, and then added, "I have a change of clothes. We weren't sure about our plans."

Farran immediately said, "Uncle, would it be a bother if we stayed tonight? For multiple reasons."

Uncle Cadmus chuckled. "Never a bother, and I was hoping you'd say you could, both of you." He drove on, pointing out a few places of local interest before turning up the drive to the house. Farran was waiting for Vega's reaction as the front came into view. She was delightful, as Farran had hoped she'd be.

Of course, now he'd seen Astralis, Thebes wasn't terribly impressive. Astralis had quite a lot more in the way of buildings, and also had been decidedly larger, even if he hadn't seen most of it. But Thebes was showing rather well right now, even if it were too early in the spring for much in the way of blooming flowers just yet.

Vega leaned against him, peering as the drive twisted and turned up to the doors. Uncle Cadmus let them out at the front. "If you're staying, why don't you go sort out where to leave your things? You know where everything is, Farran." Farran did, of course, and he was amused that Uncle Cadmus was not making a point of inquiring where Vega stayed.

Farran offered her a hand out of the cart. As Uncle Cadmus drove off to stable the pony, he said, "You're welcome to stay in my room, or there's a guest room free in my hall. The residents are in the other wing, so it's just me and Uncle Cadmus and Vivian there."

Vega narrowed her eyes for a moment. "Yours, then. I'd like to see what you're like at home, anyway."

Farran couldn't repress a grin, so he brought her upstairs, unlocking his room with a hand on the warding, and then letting her in. "Bath through there, water closet on the left off the hall. Please make free with anywhere sensible to put things." The room was entirely tidy. Of course, he'd learned from early on that making more work for Lena wasn't done. Not least because if she had to spend more time cleaning, there was less time for baking.

But the room was cosy, in all the ways Farran liked, and the sunlight coming through the window warmed it all. Vega set her case out on one of the low tables, then took her time wandering around to get a sense of it. "No desk?"

"I go down to the library, usually, or there's a room further down with a decent desk. Shall we?" He hesitated. "Lena signs. I'll translate. It may just take a minute."

"I know a little, but I'm not fluent," Vega said, promptly. "I'd appreciate that." They went back downstairs, into a small room in the same wing, on the ground floor, where a meal was laid out. Lena had, in fact, managed some baking. She was fussing about the last placement of a bit of decorative greenery on the plate. Then she straightened up, her hands moving rapidly as she came over to hug Farran.

He laughed, then made the introductions, signing and speaking at the same time. He was used to doing it, thankfully, because most of their residents didn't sign, or at least not at speed. "Lena, this is Vega Beaumont. She'll be staying tonight. Vega, this is Lena, our housekeeper, who keeps everything going." He added, then, "Vega is a singer."

That produced a flurry of questions about what kind of singing, or rather what the physical things that went with the singing were. Farran did his best to explain some of it. Vega snorted and positioned herself, gesturing with one hand at where the illusions would go, the moves of a nightclub. That was a lovely trick of making it real— Lena's eyes lit up with it— as Uncle Cadmus and Vivian came in.

Farran finished the sentence he was signing and then turned. "Vivian, we've had a busy morning."

"So I gather." Her voice was amused, rather than acerbic, that was good. He kept signing, but Vivian said amiably, "Let me take that over, so you can eat." She picked up, her fingers moving with the same slight slowness at the end of her fingers that flavoured her signing compared to the crispness of Lena's.

Vega tilted her head at it, not asking, but Farran said, "Vivian learned her signing underwater, mostly. I'm guessing that's not as relevant for your family."

"No. We do less than some lines between the stars needing darkness, and the fact you can't see them well underwater. Distortions." She managed to spell out the last word nimbly enough, and Lena beamed at her. Once everyone had food who wanted it, Farran settled into explaining how they'd spent their previous night, and Vega summarised the conversation with her family, touching briefly on the complexity with Vandermeer. She didn't highlight the artefact, just that the charm she'd used hadn't worked as expected.

Vivian was visibly relieved that the piece was in safe hands, but then she paused in her signing, as if she needed to think. Uncle Cadmus picked it up, so Farran could continue to enjoy the meal. When Vivian spoke, she began by saying, "As to Vandermeer, I've passed along what you told me to someone in the Guard who'll handle it delicately. I will follow

up on the other matters with a note to your family,
Vega, though it may be tomorrow. I'd like to confirm
a few details first." She tapped one finger on the
table. "I have some connections to those with an
intelligence service background, and one of those
sources finally suggested some interesting information about Mister Vandermeer."

Farran blinked. "International concerns?"

"Yes, and no. I can lay out the specifics. But the
summary comes out to the fact that it's possible he
was sent over here to get the piece— or something
like it— with an eye to amplification of magical
devices. You both know, I suspect, that there are
concerns about a buildup of munitions. The Americans are lagging us in several areas, or it's always
possible Vandermeer is working for some other
country. It's a tricky thing to confirm, obviously."

That was an understatement of the first order.
"And? What does that have to do with
Vandermeer?"

"We've some inklings of parties in the United
States who might be assisting with such research. Or
who might be interested in an item that allowed for,
shall we say, controlled magical amplification?"

Farran wondered if Vega would realise that the
signing was continuing fluidly, that Uncle Cadmus
knew the relevant language, and so did Lena. She
was following, however, so when Vivian paused,
Vega had a question. "So, rather than Vandermeer
being a relatively run-of-the-mill treasure seeker, he
might have been looking for this item in particular?
Or something that does what it does, at least?"

Vivian nodded. "It's possible he had a talisman
on his person that was leading him either towards it,

or towards someone who might be a lever. One theory I've heard, given one of the people who might be interested, suggests he might have taken a potion to enhance his own magic. And that you, being a Cousin, might be more sensitive to the effects. The person I'm wondering about wouldn't have taken that into consideration."

"You have someone specific in mind?" Vega ventured the question.

"Someone who left Albion several years ago, tried in absentia and exiled. This attempt was not to return, whatever it was, but to give the person leverage, I suspect. The problem is proving it. Or doing anything about it."

"Has Vandermeer done anything that has consequence? Mostly, from our point of view..." Vega glanced at Farran, "He's shown up and been creepy, as you say. Not just me, though, now I think about it. Or Farran, who might be biassed. But the owner of the club. Or your friend, Farran?"

"Maddie." Farran said promptly. "That's an interesting question, actually. She didn't care for him, of course, being a woman of taste. But she didn't describe him as creepy."

"In Maddie's case, though I will ask her, I should see her tomorrow, it may be that he did not stand out amongst other men of that general age and class in relation to her." Vivian said, a bit briskly. "There is a certain amount of background annoyance, sometimes."

Vega snorted at that, amused. "Yes. I don't think I would have noticed in Vandermeer's case if I'd met him at the club, initially. It was more audible, being out on the bridge, or at the Tower. Fewer magical people around, too, the other things stood out more. And he was directly focused on me, for whatever reason. That makes a difference."

"I'll think about whether there's any way to test that further. I can make some inquiries, but I think it's possible we might arrange for Mister Vander-meer to have just enough annoyances that he goes home. Especially when there is nothing he can find."

"My aunts and uncles have that part well in hand, yes," Vega said, promptly. "Though I believe if you wanted to examine it properly, they could arrange that."

Vivian nodded. "Let us see if we can encourage the man to find his way home across the ocean, then. I'll let you know if I learn anything further. You should let me know— and another person, I'll write in the journals— if he turns up again."

Vega nodded, then cleared her throat. "Not tonight. I'm off tonight."

"And I was going to show you Thebes," Farran said, firmly and warmly. Then he picked up the signing again as he went on. "Lena, supper tonight and breakfast tomorrow? I'll need to get back to work by mid-morning."

Vega hadn't even given much thought to that part of it, but she would not argue with Farran about his schedule in front of his family. He was a grown man and could presumably sort it out. That was the thing. He'd been reliable about managing himself from the start. He was like the performers she liked, the ones who hit their marks, who were ready on time, no dashing on stage last thing. Now, she said, "The food has been delicious. You might show me around more when we've finished the tea?"

CHAPTER 39
THAT AFTERNOON AT THEBES

Vega was not, initially, sure how to time their afternoon. They had lunch, of course, moving into chatting about lighter topics. She finished her tea. But Vega did not wish to be rude - not to Cadmus, not to Vivian, not to Lena. She was not sure when she and Farran might reasonably excuse themselves.

But Farran seemed to have that in hand as well. About the point at which everyone had finished their current cup of tea, he pushed his chair back slightly. It wasn't so much a movement as an inclination of his body, a change in state. "Supper at seven?" he asked, signing it to Lena, who nodded and added something as a question.

Farran signed something back, grinning, before he said added, "Come on, Vega, I'd like to show you the grounds." She nodded, making her own quiet farewell, and then found herself promptly shown outside, around the curve of the house.

The house was smaller than Astralis, but the

grounds were more extensive than she'd realised at first glance. Farran took her hand comfortably, not dragging her along anywhere, but wanting the close-ness, and showed her around. This was his uncle's blacksmithing forge, a mix of decorative items and practical ones. He had nails in progress, apparently. Farran glanced at what was out, and added, "Also, working on the repair for one of the gates at the back. That's the hinge."

"Do you keep track of the things that need doing in your head, then?"

"Oh. Yes. I have for ages." Farran turned to look at her, now a little shy. "Someone told me I'd make an excellent stage manager in a theatre, because of it. It's not just where things are, it's the sequencing, isn't it?"

"It is. Few people understand that. Cooks and chefs," Vega said. "Stage managers. Some perform-ers, not remotely all of them." She considered the list she'd just said. "Did you learn some of that from Lena?"

"I think so." They walked along a little, towards another outbuilding, before Farran went on. "I've always known Lena. The way she thinks about things. Signing. I don't remember not knowing."

"She's been here a long time, then." It wasn't a question.

"With my parents." He glanced away. "Uncle Cadmus has been a rock. I'm sure he hasn't known what to do with me, rather a lot. And he doesn't like fuss and bother, and there's been more of that than we like."

"Not you?" Then she remembered. "Your first apprenticeship." It wasn't really a question.

"That, mostly. And dealing with the residents. Mostly, Uncle Cadmus likes that? It's a big place, better to have people in it. And mostly, they've been academics who don't mind a modest walk to the portal or train. They like quiet for their evenings and days off. Some people stay a long while, some for a year. There's always interesting conversation at supper. Oh, you should think what you do and don't want to say. We've a folklorist at the moment, so decide if you want half an hour of theory about this ballad or that poem or not."

It made Vega laugh. "You think ahead, as I was saying. The structure of it. Most people wouldn't warn me like that." She hesitated. "Haven't warned me like that."

"Ah, well." They went past a long building. Farran identified it as being used for metalwork, the sort that could leave shavings and other bits that had more risk to the casual bystander. "I like to think I can offer you something specific."

Vega let the quiet continue as they curved along the side of the house, past a rose garden and greenhouse, then took a path toward the trees behind. "We should talk about what's on offer, then."

"I don't want to pin you down into anything. Your singing, you won't be in London all the time. Not forever. Besides the schedule."

"No." Vega agreed. "I should at least go do a few months somewhere else." She tilted her head, though she kept walking. "Would Ormulu find it useful for you to spend a few months in, oh, Paris or Berlin, or any other European city you'd like to name? I'd suggest to America, but I don't particularly want to make it easier for Vandermeer or whoever is behind him to notice me."

Farran turned to her. "I could ask. Especially if it's three months or so, and a particular collection or style of art or something. I haven't taken that kind of work; I'm only recently at the level where they'd suggest it? But I could."

"Well. That's one solution, then. You figure out a place you want to be that has work for you. I get myself hired at a club there. Easier that way round, I expect, especially if there's a bit of lead time. And then we come back, and with any luck Madam Helena will have me back. Good for her, too, a little variety without quite so much stress about whether every person will be easy to deal with. On my singing nights, you can do whatever amuses you. On my days off, we can explore whatever city we're in, around whatever you're doing." Vega rather liked the idea of diving into a new city in his company.

Farran took a breath. "We're doing this, then. Together. Whatever that looks like. I mean, I'm..." He gestured. "I'm committed here."

"And I have plenty of aunts, uncles, and cousins who can tend to things at Astralis. For a long time to come. Maybe in sixty years we'll have to do some more negotiation, but probably not. Not as long as I can get there when needed. The portal makes that easy enough."

Farran swallowed. "And your family won't mind me?"

"Oh, no. You made quite a good impression. Come on, show me the rest of the grounds? I should probably change before supper. Make a good impression on your residents." Vega had the sense that if she let him, Farran would dither about that piece until firmly stopped. Best not to do that now.

Supper was excellent, as a meal, but also as an occasion. Vega could certainly make pleasant conversation with strangers. She was even better at making conversation with people who were strangers to her, but whose opinions mattered in a particular setting.

She chatted with one of them about London, another about a bit of poetry, navigated the complex channels of folklore, inquired about a piece of Cadmus's translation. That last she was rather proud of. She'd remembered something about how the Greek looked at colour-words, the quality of colour rather than the shade sometimes. That got the folk-lorist off onto a delightful tangent about lucky and unlucky shades.

After supper, Cadmus firmly invited just the two of them up for drinks with Vivian, and none of the residents argued. Vega got the impression that he rarely exerted himself like that, but that when he did, it was usually about Farran.

Vivian began, in private, with only the brief comment that she gathered Mister Vandermeer had been released to one of the Guard, and that he was being told to go home to America once they were sure he was all right the next day. "None of it was against the Pact, which made it easy, but making that sort of public fuss isn't exactly a help. My contact thinks he'll go without a fuss. It was clear to her that as he'd come back to himself, he'd realised whatever he'd been chasing was out of his reach."

Vega would be thinking about that for a bit, honestly. And how, if the artefact was that powerful, why her family had thought she was the one to take it on. There had been the public reasons, her familiarity with London. But she rather thought it might be a larger test of her skill and what she was good for. It was another reason she wanted to be out of Albion for a few months, the better to figure out how to talk about it when she returned.

She kept thinking about that, through the conversation, until Farran said they'd had an extremely long day, and they were going to stop making sense soon.

Once they were in his rooms, Vega held out her hand to him. "Sleep? I feel like I'm on my fifth wind, but I'm also used to late nights."

Farran shrugged one shoulder. "You're different. Did you want something in particular?"

"I think." Vega took a breath, let it out, as measured as if she were about to sing. "I want to share a bed with you and see what comes of that. Not tonight, if you think you're too tired to properly appreciate it. But soon."

"Soon." Farran was about to say something else. Then he yawned. "But perhaps better in the morning? I need to get back to London, but not too terribly early."

It made her laugh. "Morning, then. Wake me up, though, I can sleep the afternoon away after. If you wait for me, you'll be late."

Farran made a slight bow, then tugged her into the bedroom. Both of them undressed, though he was still more shy of his body than she was. Once they were in bed, curled up companionably with the lights off, she checked he wasn't asleep yet. "I very much like how you are with your uncle. How he is with you."

"Different from yours?" Farran's voice in the dark was warm.

"Warmer. Focused on you in specific, in a way my uncles and aunts aren't. I just, I like that he's so firmly there, wanting good things for you."

"Good model." Then Farran's voice went even fuzzier, and there was another yawn, right in her ear. Vega just nestled against him, feeling him against her back, and liking that particular and novel closeness as well.

When she woke, there was light filtering through the curtains, though she thought it was not terribly late. Immediately after, she realised why she'd woken. Farran's hand had slipped up to cup one of her breasts, and she could feel him against her, rocking gently.

She moved, deliberately, back against him, and was rewarded with a delightful grunt. "Waking up this way makes up for the time of day."

Farran's hand explored a bit more deliberately. "Is that you saying yes?"

"Oh, rather." She drew it out, teasing, then wriggled a little to find just the right angle and get a grunt of his pleasure into the back of her neck. The thing about this position was that she couldn't do much, except respond to what he did.

That, however, suggested that he was just as thoughtful about bedding a woman as he was about assessing a piece of art. His touch was not ticklish, but he had a precision and attention to the details that had her whimpering several times.

Also, he did not rush. Vega arched back against

him, after a deft shift of his fingers between her legs, and he kissed her shoulder. "Shall I do that again?"

"The thing I like about you, one thing, still a thing." She sucked in a breath. "You don't rush. You do the thing in the proper time, the buildup."

"Why would I rush? Mmm." Vega was, however, satisfied to realise that he was getting quite worked up, by all the evidence she had. He was hard as anything against her, but his breathing had changed, the little shallow breaths and higher pitches that suggested his eagerness.

"Do you want me to move?" she asked. "Either's good for me."

His hand paused, thumb a moment away from teasing her nipple. "Like this." She had only barely nodded when he moved his hand briefly to rearrange the angle, arched to check it, and then pushed inside her. It brought out music. Certainly, she could not have stopped herself moaning for all the magic in the world.

It was wrong to say he didn't rush. Farran had an exquisite sense of pacing, and now was not the time for languid movements and slow desire. Almost as soon as he'd seated himself, he was moving like ripples on a river or the flap of a bird's wings. Steady, but then speeding up, bringing her along with him every step of the way.

Vega had not, in all her other experiences, given much thought to what it would be like to have a proper partner. She'd had plenty of pleasure with other lovers, but nothing that made space for her like this. That assumed space for her. It would need more thinking about, more duets, but then she was not thinking of anything at all. Her body was carried away by the urgency and the delight and Farran's utterly unfeigned pleasure at everything.

Her climax took her in a rush, the sort of glorious crescendo where everything came together perfectly. She could hear the percussion of his huffs of breath and grunts of determination in her ear. He held on just long enough for her to begin to come back to herself. Then she felt him explode inside her.

It left them both panting softly, not wanting to move apart. They lay like that, relaxed and entirely comfortable, for some minutes, before his hand moved against her arm. "More to look forward to, I hope?"

"Oh, yes." It came out breathy, just as she wanted. "When we've leisure, and when we don't, and in the morning and in the evening, and I rather hope at all the points between." Vega reached for his hand, bringing his clever fingers to her lips and kissing them. "I suppose we should get up and wash and all that."

"Mmmm." Farran did not move for a good thirty seconds. "Should. I'll run the bath for you?"

He finally pulled away from her, and she let herself fall onto her back. The future was going to be excellent.

CHAPTER 40
JUNE 18TH AT THE CRYSTAL CAVE

Farran set his shoulder against the wall from what had become his usual seat on Friday nights. Saturday, too, most of the time. He'd enjoyed the evening tremendously already, but tonight was a little special. This was Vega's last performance for the summer, and that was why he was here, unusually, on a Sunday.

Tomorrow, they'd sleep in. Then they'd finish the last of their packing and spend several days at Astralis for the summer solstice gathering. Once that was done— or rather, once they'd recovered from it — he and Vega would set off for three months in Paris.

He had an arrangement to work with an appraiser there, and to become familiar with one of the key magical collections. Vega had been snapped up by one of the better magical clubs in the city. They'd gone over at the beginning of June, and found a flat that overlooked the Seine, entirely magical. And far enough above the streets they could keep the air sweet and quieter with charms, too.

He looked forward to a lot of things to come. The food, the art, the architecture, the different approaches to how magic twined with all those things. But mostly, he looked forward to exploring them with Vega. She was only singing three nights a week, giving them four days to see a bit of the city in the evenings.

And if Farran was a trifle nervous about the solstice gathering, well, it wasn't his first time at one. Vega would be right with him the entire time, and he was still in extremely good favour with her older aunts and uncles. Politeness, a certain amount of competence in Greek, and Vega's visible fierceness about him all worked to his advantage.

Vega came out for the last set. As she'd told him, this one was all songs of magic, taken from folklore, from myth, and two modern compositions, both set to words from some of the War poets. They were haunting, enchanting, a tangle of emotions, with Vega's voice like a light on the path, showing the way forward.

He was always torn about whether to watch her or close his eyes and focus on listening to her. This time he watched, because Pasco was outdoing himself with the illusion work.

After the last song, the encore, the second encore, Vega finally kissed her fingers to the crowd. "Darlings, I'll be back in the autumn, I promise. And I expect with some new songs to delight you with. Do keep coming by. I know Madam Helena has several surprises in store!" Then she blew a kiss into the crowd, turned to thank the band, and walked off the stage.

That was Farran's cue to slip out, go down the other stairs, and through the staff door into the dressing rooms. By the time he opened her door, Vega had her shoes off, her fingers undoing her hair. "Can you get the zipper, my love?"

He did, letting his fingers flow down her back. He did not touch beyond that, not now. They'd have time when they got home, and more privacy. It wasn't kind to the other staff of the club to walk in on that. Vega had set that quite sensible limit. Besides, both of them liked the anticipation.

Once she'd wriggled out of the dress and packed it properly, she slipped on her more comfortable frock, and turned around to kiss him on the nose. "Did the roses come out right?"

"Excellently. The shadows were perfect." Pasco had been fussing over that for the last three days. "How do you feel about it?"

"Like taking off my shoes at the end of the night. Comfortable. Glad I'll be coming back, that this isn't goodbye forever. But looking forward to, to having a new face, somewhere different."

Farran nodded, feeling he wanted to talk more about that, but moving out of the way. She circled the dressing room, packing up the last few bits and bobs. There were only the things she'd needed at this stage left. Once she had them all in her case, he offered his arm. "Home?"

"Home." That, of course, involved a certain amount of fuss. The rest of the performers were done for the night, she'd been the last soloist. They worked their way along the lines of doors, ending with Madam Helena by the stage door.

"Do write, darling. And let me know where to send notes, so you know all the gossip when you come back." Vega promised, and Farran knew she'd do that. A relationship with a club owner like that was precious.

Finally, they were in the cab, the last ride for a while, with Fred wishing them both well. It wasn't until they were back up in Farran's flat that Vega closed her eyes. "You were thinking?"

"I am often thinking," Farran pointed out. "Tonight, that I think it's good for you to have a space to show a different face now and again."

Vega blinked at him. "Explain?"

"Bedroom." Farran said it comfortably. They'd been together long enough for that to feel easy to say, though still always a thrill.

She snorted and went to wash off the last of her cosmetics while he made his last evening preparations. Once they were both in bed, his arm curled around her, she said, "Explain now?"

Farran kissed her nose. "I was thinking about how each song is a face. Each set of songs, a different lens. Your family looks at stars through them, you shape them to look at other things, or be seen in certain ways. But that also has to be limiting with an audience who expects certain things from you."

"And in Paris, there's more space." Vega let out a breath. "And you? What's it like for you?"

Farran shrugged. "Different eyes. Or eyes looking for different things, I suppose. Goes well with your faces. I can appreciate each one, and the ways the foundation is the same. All these paintings, done on wood, in oils, they have things in common, but they are not the same."

"Huh." Vega shifted to put one leg over one of his. "Will you draw me sometime? Show me some of the faces you see?"

"Might take some time," Farran said. "And I'm not near as talented an artist as you are, with your voice."

"Let me judge, don't you assume ahead of the art. Art comes in its own time, and its own form, and yours will be interesting because it's yours."

Farran let out a slow breath, letting himself relax on his back. He felt that, securely, for the first time in a long while. That things were good, that they had strong roots, that other people saw him as competent. An excellent start to the summer, to Paris, and to whatever he and Vega did together next.

If you enjoyed *Harmonic Pleasure* and would like to read more of this series, please sign up for my mailing list to get all the latest news and fun extras.

Your reviews (on whatever review site you use) are much appreciated, too!

Read on for some notes about a name, a lot more about the lore of London, and some other authorial details!

AUTHOR NOTES

Hello, and thank you for joining me on this trip through London with Vega and Farran. My deepest thanks as always to my editor, Kiya Nicoll, and to my early readers. In particular, Elise Matthesen had an excellent suggestion that improved the end of the book.

A note on naming: Kevin Stafford is named thanks to his wife supporting my Kickstarter in 2024 to create my first audiobook. One of the options I offered was the chance to name a minor character. Kevin chose both the name and — as a musician himself — what role that character had in the band.

Cadmus and Vivian have their romance in *Seven Sisters,* where Farran also appears as a secondary character. I couldn't resist spending a little more time at Thebes or with a different line of the Cousins.

Robin (who Vega spots at the club) has his romance in *Fool's Gold*. He's from a different line of the Cousins, as Vega notes.

London is, in many ways, the city of my heart. It's not a city I've ever lived in (though I've visited multiple times), but my father's family lived and worked in London, including someone active in the Chartist movement in the 1830s. Getting a chance to explore London in a book is, of course, a delight - but I also wanted to do it justice.

London is notoriously a city of many layers and so many odd eddies of history. There are a number of great books that dive into the topic. For a general overview of London as a city, I loved *London* by Peter Ackroyd. It not only explores the history, but wanders into topics like what the city sounded like at various points - and where it was known to be unusually quiet. *London Under* (also by Peter Ackroyd) and *Underground London* by Stephen Smith are different takes on underground London.

I'm indebted to Elise Matthesen for reminding me about the various closed and abandoned Tube stations. And also for sending me a copy of *London's Disused Underground Stations* by J.E. Connor. It's excellent to have friends who can pinpoint that kind of resource! The book talks through all the Tube stations no longer in use with all sorts of dates, ticket stubs, and other details.

Finally, *The Secret Lore of London* (edited by Nigel

Pennick) and *London Lore* by Steve Roud both have extremely useful gazetteer sections. These allowed me to build a map of potential locations and figure out which ones I wanted to explore through the plot.

I do hope to come back to London in a book in the not too distant future. The mention of the Keeper of London had all my early readers noting they wanted more about that! I'm currently looking to see how it might fit in the Mysterious Societies series, the next 1920s Albion series. Keep an eye on my newsletter and blog for more!

On to the specifics:

Chapter 6 : My inspiration for Vega's approach here is thanks to my hearing Nadine Dubois sing a 1920s style version of "Bedlam Boys" at Lili's Burlesque in Minneapolis in 2005. As you can guess by that date, it made a tremendous impression, even though I've been unable to track down a recording in the two decades since. The song has a number of verses and variations, but there's also something compelling about the determination of the protagonist.

Chapter 9: The Guild Hall has so much history it's tricky to get into it. Once I started digging into the figures, however, I was fascinated. Some version of Gog and Magog have stood in the Guild Hall for many centuries, and they were paraded through the streets in the reign of Henry V. Exactly who they represent is a good question, but some version of giants or mythical figures dating back to the arrival

of Brutus and the last remnants of the survivors of
Troy is a common story.

The current Magog's shield has a phoenix rather
than the eagle present when Vega and Farran see it
in 1928. Some people think the phoenix was put on
the shield after the Great Fire of London, but no! It
turns out that the shield was changed after Gog and
Magog were destroyed in the Blitz. They've been
remade due to fire and disaster several times, but
these current figures date from 1950.

Chapter 13: The London Stone has been
somewhere near that spot (with brief intermissions)
since 1100. No one is entirely sure why it's important, but it keeps mattering. The Wikipedia page in
this case covers the details well. When I was last in
London in 2015, you could peek around the counter
in a W.H. Smith's bookshop to see it, but it is now on
protected display on the street, much easier to visit.

Chapter 14: When I went looking for a particular
kind of art that Farran might have thoughts about, I
stumbled into the Huguenot silversmiths. A number
of the Huguenots came to London (many of them
were known for fine weaving), but others ended up in
North America. The references here are based on
summaries of collectible silver.

The changes in treasure and hoard law in the
United Kingdom are complex! These days, they're
made even more complex by advances in metal
detectors and other technology. This has been a
boon for archaeologists when the finds are properly
reported and can be studied in situ first. Farran and

Philemon are discussing the standards as of the 1920s, of course.

Chapter 15 : Ceadda is known as a patron saint strongly associated with wells, and thus his saint's day on March 2nd is a day to clean them out. And as I've been known to say, it's hard to go terribly far in England or Wales (or a fair bit of Scotland) without coming across a holy well.

Chapter 18 : The story of St Alfege is historically a bit tricky to document, but he was in fact thought to have been killed on the site and the church was a key location for a number of Tudor events.

The cemetery in Greenwich Park was excavated in the 1780s. Some of the mounds were destroyed due to planned construction in the 1840s, but outcry from a number of people prevented that from happen. Other smaller excavations have taken place, finding items from the 5th or 6th century CE - just about the right time period for my plot!

Chapter 20: Jack Cade's caves have a rich history. Fortunately for my purposes, they're also surprisingly well described. During the 1920s they were not accessible to the public, particularly for safety reasons. But in the Victorian period, they'd been used for parties, drinking, and other activities, including some well-documented graffiti. All the comments about the appearance here are taken from period sources or later descriptions.

There was major flooding in London in January of 1928 along the Thames, and so I have made the reasonable assumption that the water table in the well is still quite high.

Chapter 22: The clock mentioned here was removed in 1828 but finally returned in 1935. As Farran notes, the statue of Queen Elizabeth (then the first and only) went back up on display at St Dunstan's in June 1928, a few months after the scene takes place.

Chapter 26: If you're familiar with the Tower of London, some aspects of this description might seem out of place. I had a lot of fun consulting the guide to the Tower published in 1927, and have drawn all the specifics from that guide. The Crown Jewels were in the Wakefield tower in the 1920s, and not moved to their current location until the 1960s. Visiting involved a number of stairs, and a number of areas (like the church) could only be seen by touring with one of the yeoman warders.

Chapter 33: As Farran mentions, the London Tube at this point was in fact several different companies, with whatever connections occurred being a matter of negotiation, chance, and other details. Wikipedia has an excellent history of the London Under-ground, which includes the stations. The connection between Monument and Bank stations doesn't happen until 1933. Depths for the relevant stations were taken from various sources. My hearty thanks to people who have a passion for transportation!

Chapter 37 : If you know your underground London history, you might be aware that there's a surviving Roman temple right near where Farran and Vega find the missing artefact. The extant temple was a Mithraeum (sacred to Mithras). I used its location as a reasonably proximity for where other underground spaces might have survived. (I also checked for plague pits and Tube lines.) Of course, those open spaces may not have survived long past Vega and Farran's discovery.

Thank you again for joining me for this journey. The best way to get all my news is by signing up for my mailing list. Check out the contact page on my website at celialake.com for other places to find me and more about my Patreon and Discord.

ALSO BY CELIA LAKE

VICTORIAN

Mysterious Fields trilogy

Enchanted Net

Silent Circuit

Elemental Truth

Charms of Albion - standalone

Pastiche

Sailor's Jewel

Four Walls and a Heart

1920S

Mysterious Charm

Outcrossing

Goblin Fruit

Magician's Hoard

Wards of the Roses

In The Cards

On The Bias

Seven Sisters

Mysterious Powers

Carry On

The Fossil Door

Winter's Charms

Forged in Combat

Learn more about the world of Albion and future books at my website, celialake.com. Additional information linking characters, places, and timelines is available at my authorial wiki at bit.ly/celia-lake-wiki (or get there from my website under the menu that says "more information").

Sign up for my newsletter to be the first to hear about future books and learn about fascinating bits of research. Happy reading!